Skyriders

Skyriders

Vimbai Gore-Strachan

AuthorHouse™
1663 Liberty Drive
Bloomington, IN 47403
www.authorhouse.com
Phone: 1-800-839-8640

© 2012 by Vimbai Gore-Strachan. All rights reserved.

No part of this book may be reproduced, stored in a retrieval system, or transmitted by any means without the written permission of the author.

Published by AuthorHouse   04/18/2012

ISBN: 978-1-4685-0493-4 (sc)

Any people depicted in stock imagery provided by Thinkstock are models, and such images are being used for illustrative purposes only. Certain stock imagery © Thinkstock.

This book is printed on acid-free paper.

Because of the dynamic nature of the Internet, any web addresses or links contained in this book may have changed since publication and may no longer be valid. The views expressed in this work are solely those of the author and do not necessarily reflect the views of the publisher, and the publisher hereby disclaims any responsibility for them.

To my parents, for their constant encouragement and enthusiasm, and to my sisters, for their support and ideas. Without you, this book would never have happened.

I love you all.

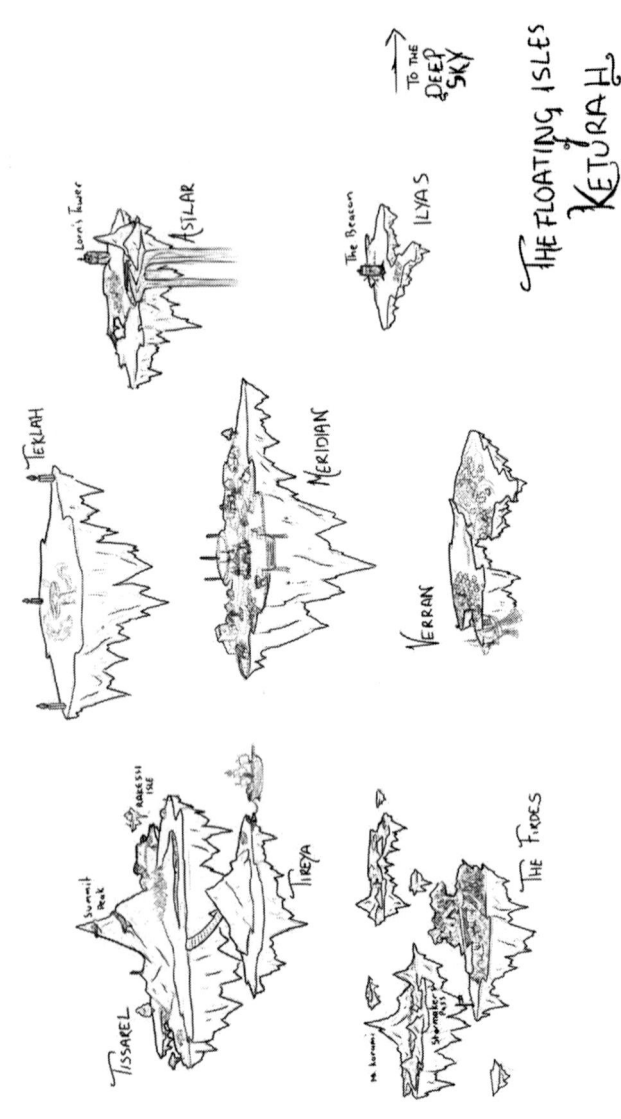

ONE

If Kai had to find a root cause to blame it all on, he'd have said in a heartbeat that it was moving to America. Everything was fine with his life until his mother was offered the job in Florida: he liked his school; his home, a comfortable apartment in Bracknell; and even the little things, like the bus he took and the rain. He liked the unpredictable weather; he liked the cat that sometimes turned up outside the front door, hoping for a meal. He liked everything familiar about life.

She'd accepted the job, of course. They'd packed up and moved, leaving behind the comforting familiarity of their old existence, and started up elsewhere. It was all right for her; she was a social person, adaptable and good with people, and soon settled in to her new life as an accountant in Orlando. He wasn't much like her. He took after his father, whom he had never met. Florida, for him, was a living nightmare. He'd only been there three months and hated it. He didn't fit in well at school, he was struggling to adjust to a new environment, and now . . . this.

Kai stared bleakly at the coffin in front of him, trying not to let the tears overwhelm him. His mother had been with him all his life, until the news arrived that she'd died in a car accident on her way home from work. Now he could vaguely hear the priest quoting some Psalms from the Bible in grave, solemn tones that echoed throughout the small church, but the bleary sadness of Kai's mind obscured most of his voice.

Farrell, his aunt, sat beside him, one arm comfortingly around him, the other occasionally reaching up to wipe away the tears that ran down her face. His mother's older sister, she lived a few minutes away from them and had a cheerful, kind disposition and a lot of cats. He didn't know most of the other people in the church; they were mostly his mother's colleagues, family friends, and people who didn't really know her much at all—there more out of respect than anything else. There were no familiar faces, no friendly smiles.

He felt truly alone in the world.

The service ended with a brief prayer from the priest, wishing bravery and good fortune onto her offspring and forgiveness to all gathered there. At first, Kai remained in his seat as the church slowly emptied, seeing but not really acknowledging the people streaming past him, murmured condolences passing from their lips as they left. Kai soon got up and wandered around, pausing occasionally to stare blankly at the light filtering in listlessly through the stained glass windows. The church was empty now, save a few people who lingered in the hall. Even so, Kai didn't notice the man weaving his way over to him until he heard someone clearing his throat politely beside him.

Kai looked up sharply. The man was tall and appeared to be in his early thirties, although on second glance, he looked much older, with warm blue eyes and a crop of blond hair flicking causally into his face.

"Good morning."

"Morning," Kai replied, his voice flat. He didn't know this man any more than he knew the priest, and he always felt awkward around people he didn't know.

"The name's John. I assume you must be Kai Hunter?" He waited for Kai's affirmative nod before continuing: "I knew your mother." He paused. "She was a great person. I'm dreadfully sorry for your loss."

Kai nodded politely.

"How're you doing?"

"Fine," he replied. The response was automatic. He wasn't used to opening up his feelings to people, let alone strangers.

"That's good," John said. "Anyway, Kai, I'm here to ask you something. You see, I'm a teacher at the school your mother went to in Keturah."

The name didn't ring a bell, but his mother hadn't spoken very often about her school life. When he'd asked her, she mentioned a small school in Wokingham she went to, and occasionally she'd pop in little anecdotes about her school life, how she'd once sneaked out of her dormitory and had a midnight feast with her friends up a tree in the schoolyard and things like that.

Farrell, having composed herself, wandered over to the two of them, a pleasant but curious smile on her face.

"Kai, are you okay, honey? And, hello, Mr . . . ?"

"Call me John," the man said, extending a warm hand for Farrell to shake. "I knew Faye quite well. I taught her in her last year of school."

As their eyes met, something passed between them, a flicker of silent, mutual understanding.

"Ah," Farrell said, nodding. "Can I talk to you for a second? Are you busy or anything?"

"No, no. I've got plenty of time. Excuse me, Kai..."

The two of them trailed off, talking in low, hushed voices. Kai watched them. Farrell seemed accepting yet concerned, and despite his casual demeanour, John looked slightly drained. With the church emptying rapidly around him, Kai sidled closer, trying to catch what they were saying.

"You want to take him to Keturah?" Farrell was saying. "But... he can't even ride. He doesn't know anything about it..."

"He doesn't?" John asked, his voice rising slightly with surprise. "Faye didn't tell him?"

Didn't tell me what? Kai wondered.

"She told me when she moved to Orlando... not to tell him about it. She said she didn't want to cloud his opinion of her."

There was a hesitant, contemplative pause. Then he heard John's voice: "Farrell, I think you should consider it. You said he's not enjoying school, and he seems lonely here. Perhaps there he'll make new friends and enjoy it a bit better."

"Perhaps. He's been through a lot lately; I won't ask him now. Come over in a couple of days. We'll all talk about it then."

She came over to Kai. "Kai, honey, are you ready to leave?"

"Yeah," he replied. "You two know each other?"

"He's an old... colleague of your mum's," she said evasively. "I wasn't expecting him to come all the way down here; it's such a long trip."

"From where? Bracknell?"

She gave him an odd look. "Something like that."

Something must have shown on his face, because she smoothed back his fringe and kissed him lightly on the forehead. "It'll be fine, hon. I promise. Let's go."

Farrell drove them home in silence, the whirr of the little blue car the only sound between them. Her house was a cosy little house on a road that contained many other equally cosy-looking abodes. Short trees lined the road, fringed by neatly cropped grass and the array of potted plants in front of her door. One of her cats, a ginger tabby that had taken a liking to sunning itself on the front steps, meowed at them as they entered. Kai tried desperately not to think about it too much, harbouring some sort of remote hope that if he distanced himself from anything that related itself to his mother's death, he might just wake up tomorrow morning and find it was all some terrible nightmare.

But his ever-present killjoy sense of logic assured him that this was no dream. You couldn't run from reality. You had to suck up and face it, but that was the last thing Kai really wanted. What he *did* want was to hide under a rock somewhere and forget about everything. You couldn't miss what you didn't know. And the knowledge that his mother—his beautiful, caring mother, his closest relative—was no longer with him was killing him.

He couldn't eat much. He managed a few mouthfuls at dinner, but the desolate atmosphere just reminded him of what he'd lost. Farrell's face was strained. He knew that she was putting on a brave face for his sake, and it hurt to see the troubled anguish that shadowed her expression when the mask slipped. He remembered previous visits to his aunt's house, with the three of them engaged in light-hearted, avid conversation across the table. After a while, he gave up and excused himself, going upstairs.

His life had been slowly delving into a downwards spiral of self-depression ever since he'd arrived, but now it was hurtling into a pit of all-consuming grief. The sadness clouded his mind, lurking behind every thought, like the cats that you couldn't seem to avoid in the house.

He sat down lightly on his bed, thinking about what he'd overheard John and Farrell talking about. It sounded as if they were planning to send him to his mother's old school. He didn't know whether he wanted to go. The middle of Year Ten was a terrible time to start a new school, especially one on a new continent. People would have already formed strong friendship groups, and Kai was too quiet to introduce himself.

It was getting late, but Kai didn't want to go to sleep just yet, so he padded across the hall to the study. The room was small, with bookshelves with all manner of literature ranging the walls, a window overlooking the gloomy street below, and a desk nestled with a swivel chair comfortably in a corner. He switched on the laptop and logged in, then typed "Keturah" in the Google search bar. After leafing through several pages of Bible texts, Jewish etymology, and an Australian spa site, Kai saw nothing that vaguely resembled a school or even a country or city of any kind. He felt doubts setting in.

He sat back in the chair, feeling uneasy. If Keturah *was* a place, then surely he would have been able to find something about it on the Internet. But if John was lying, then how did Farrell know about it too? It seemed too unlikely to be a coincidence, but how could he believe someone who claimed his mother came from a non-existent place?

The more he thought about it, the less sense it made. Hoping he'd be able to think clearer after some sleep, Kai returned to the spare room and climbed into bed. Night was drawing in; he could see the sky outside the room's window. It was marbled with streaks of deep red and soft purple, early-rising stars already flecking the heavens like drops of paint on a canvas. The world looked so beautiful in the half-light: the houses framed by the vibrant backdrop, the street lamps carving holes of light in the approaching dark, the trees swaying listlessly in the lazy breeze. The atmosphere seemed to be holding its breath, waiting in anticipation for something to happen.

Kai lay on his back in the darkness and tried to coax himself into sleeping, but the hours dragged on slowly. He'd heard his aunt moving around the house earlier, checking the doors and closing the blinds before going to bed herself. He doubted she'd be able to sleep either. He tossed and turned in his bed, watching the hours creep by in an achingly slow fashion, questions without answers spinning around in his head until he couldn't decipher them anymore, let alone try to solve them.

Kai managed to eat the breakfast that Farrell had made, and he wasted the rest of the morning doing sudoku in the living room. His mother had given him his love of sudoku. To organize her mind, she'd loved to do little puzzles like that after a long day of work, but Kai sought them out for the exact opposite reason: to distract himself from life, to distance himself and his thoughts.

The sudoku book was an old one of hers. She'd worked steadily through them, but she'd left some unfinished and others hadn't yet been started, and he was more than content to fill in the gaps she'd left. He was turning the pages, flicking through a couple of completed ones, when he found a wedge of folded paper stuck between two of the pages like a bookmark. Kai was about to unfurl it when the doorbell suddenly rang. Farrell went over to answer it. He could hear John talking with his aunt for a bit before the two of them came into the living room and sat down, John moving a cat that had been sleeping on the patterned armchair.

"Afternoon, Kai," John said cordially.

Kai put down his sudoku and regarded the two of them in turn. The air was charged with expectancy, as if they were about to spring something big at him.

"Hi," he said finally.

"Kai," Farrell said, leaning forwards. "John and I are here to ask you something. I've noticed for some time that you don't seem to be getting on well with life here . . . and after what's happened recently . . . well, it's literally going to be us two here. Now, I love you very much, and I'd be so happy if you stayed here, but on the other hand . . ."

"You want me to go back," Kai said bluntly. "To her old school."

Farrell looked surprised. "Well, perhaps. That is also an option."

John spoke up. "You don't have to come, of course. I'm not forcing you. Just say, 'No, thanks. I'm happy here', or any words resembling those, and I'll be gone. It's entirely your choice. But we would like to see you there. I'm sure you'll enjoy it."

Kai hesitated. "Yeah, well, I kinda overheard you guys talking earlier about it . . . ," he began uncertainly, rushing over his words. "So . . . I looked up Keturah on the Internet, and I didn't find anything about schools or anything on it . . ."

"Yes, well, naturally . . . I wouldn't expect there to be any information about the school in the first place. The very prospect in itself would be quite alarming . . ." John's voice trailed off, and then he coughed and began again. "What I'm about to tell you, you must understand, will be very difficult to believe at first, mainly because it defies most laws of gravitational physics and everything else you've come to accept as real.

"The reason you didn't find a place named Keturah on the Internet is because few people have ever heard of it. Strictly speaking, it's not even on Earth but above it, consisting of a group of floating islands that hover somewhere over the Atlantic Ocean."

Kai blinked. "Uh, right. Okay. You're joking, aren't you?"

Farrell smiled slightly. "Nope. It'll take a while to accept it, I guess . . . but it's true, honey. I promise."

For a moment, he was stunned by the unlikelihood of the statement, but more so by the force of his mother's betrayal, how she'd apparently lied to him about her childhood.

"But . . ." he said, arguments against this immediately surfacing. "Why haven't people heard about it? Surely you'd be able to see them if they were over the ocean, like in a boat or something? How've you managed to keep it a secret?"

"They exist over a very small part of the Atlantic, an area between the edge of Florida and a small island a ways from here, Bermuda. No doubt you've heard of it. They are surrounded by a barrier of energy that won't

9

allow you to see them from outside Keturah's borders. It also has a rather . . . detrimental effect on electronics and machinery of sorts, which is a tad hazardous for any unsuspecting aircraft flying too close to the border."

Kai shook his spinning head. He couldn't quite lead himself to accept what he'd just heard, especially considering he'd known John for about a day or so. Part of him *wanted* to trust John—after all, why would he spin such an elaborate tale when there were stories that were a lot easier to believe—but it was a lot to stake on just a feeling.

"But . . . what?"

"I understand how you feel," John said. "It's quite a lot to take in right now. And I'm afraid this is one of those things you'll have to simply trust me on. Your aunt and I are probably the only people here who know about this."

Kai stared at her, incredulous. "Why didn't she tell me? Either of you?" he demanded, trying to keep the frustration out of his voice.

"I . . . *we* . . . were born there," Farrell said to him. "On Tissarel. Your mother and I went to school and everything together, although I left the island a few years after I completed school. She still had three years left of her education when I decided to move here."

"Why did you decide to move?" Kai asked her. "What about jobs and stuff? Surely you wouldn't have any qualifications or a passport or anything?"

"Well, we learn English and maths, same as you do, up on Keturah. The sciences are roughly the same, although biology tends to be more about the world as it relates to the species that live up there than down here. If you're thinking about moving, the school can allow you to take exams similar to the ones you take down here. I took English, maths, and physics, and they can get you your passport and birth certificates and things."

Kai considered this. "So if I were to go to this school, what next? What about my life and stuff here?"

John spoke up. "Well, after you graduate school at eighteen, you can become a permanent resident of Keturah and live there, or you can come back here. We teach you the core subjects—English, maths, and science, as your aunt mentioned—and that is the end of the similarity between the curriculums, so you wouldn't have the qualifications that you would have if you'd stayed at school here. But that's the path your mother chose, and I understand that she made quite a successful life for herself here. Then again, she always had a talent for excelling in everything she put her mind to. She had a truly prosperous life on Keturah."

"And . . . the school? What's that like?"

"It's quite different from here, but I expect you'll have no trouble settling in. You'll be put into the apprentice stream at first, to familiarize yourself with the way we do things, but I expect we'll move you up very soon, seeing as you're already old enough. Most people make the transition at around the age of thirteen, and you're already . . . fourteen or fifteen, I'd say."

Kai nodded. "Fifteen."

"There you are, then. And afterwards, if you show sufficient talent, you are moved up into the elite stream, which is the highest standard achievable. And you only get three hours of school, which is an added bonus. Most elites already have a lot more training than you'll get, I'm afraid. The only thing you'll have to worry about now is the riding, if you want to move out of apprentice, but that's not too difficult."

"*Riding?*"

"It's a long story, but basically, a while ago, a scientist called Richard Fall managed to mix the DNA of a few species, including an avian sample, creating three new completely different animals, all capable of flight and, more importantly, carrying people for substantial lengths of time. He did this quite by accident, and he spent the rest of his life trying to recreate the process, but to no avail. He died, taking any sort of revelation with him.

"Two of his Fallite—that's the name we give them now—species proved to be difficult to tame and eventually escaped, but the final set were docile enough, and then the system of riding came about: breeding these and teaching people to ride them. We mainly use them now for transport, and they can be trained for martial use, amongst other things. The Fallites he created inhabit most Keturahn islands, although the wild ones aren't seen much anymore. Anything else?"

Kai shrugged, nothing coming to mind. "What was my mum like? At school?"

John smiled. "She was a great person. I only taught her for a year, but she stayed around for a while afterwards, doing supply teaching occasionally. She was very good with kids, and they loved her. She got on with nearly everyone, really. An excellent rider, needless to say—she graduated to elite long before she left. So . . . are you in?"

Kai paused for a minute. He thought about his current life now: him and his aunt and her cats, with the lingering grief of the death of his mother, the school where he'd never really fit in and doubted he ever would . . .

His mind was reeling with the suddenness of it all. "I . . . It's a hard choice to make just now."

"Oh, yes, of course. I'll give you a few days. Here's a number where you can contact me . . ." He scrambled in his pocket for a pen and scribbled a phone number on the back of a piece of paper. "Here. Take it. Call me when you've made up your mind. I'm here for several more days; I've got some errands to run right now. You can ask Farrell anything you want if it occurs to you."

He stood up to leave. "Well, it's been nice talking to you, Kai. I'll see you soon. Enjoy your sudoku."

Kai looked down at his hands, listening to the sound of John closing the door gently behind him on his way out. Farrell moved closer to him and placed a hand softly on his shoulder.

"Kai? You okay?"

"Farrell, if I go . . . you'll be okay, won't you? I don't want to leave you on your own . . ."

She gave a wry smile. "I was alone for a while before your mother came to live here," she said. "And besides, I've got my lovely kitties for company. I'll be fine. Don't let me get in the way of whatever you think is best."

So over the next few days, Kai thought about it. The very idea of abandoning life as he knew it scared him. He hadn't finished getting used to his new surroundings, and already the foundations were being pulled out from underneath him. But change was looming on the horizon; the fact was inevitable.

John's words lingered in his mind: *"Just say, 'No, thanks. I'm happy here . . .'"* Kai didn't know much about his life anymore, but if there was one thing he could say with conviction, it was that he was definitely not happy. That was part of the reason he hadn't just denied John

13

at the first opportunity. He wanted to get out of the looming cycle of depression that was overwhelming him. He wanted to escape, and to do that he had to trust *somebody*.

It was the evening of the third day when he managed to persuade himself to act on his decision. After dinner, he walked over to the phone on the desk in the hall and punched in John's number. He held the receiver up to his ear, waiting with baited breath for a response.

"Hello?"

"Hi, John? This is Kai. I've been thinking about what you said to me earlier and . . . I think I'd like to give it a try."

"Excellent," John said, sounding satisfied and almost slightly relieved. "I had hoped you would."

"So what happens now? How do we get there?"

"I've got a few things to sort out while I'm still here—shouldn't take more than a few days. As for getting there, that's easy: we'll fly, using the Fallite I told you about earlier, the type we managed to tame. That's how I got down here. Once you see it, it should be easy enough to convince you of the rest. Well, thanks very much for the call. I'll see you soon, okay?"

John called two days later, in the evening, just after dinner.

"It's done," he said triumphantly. "I've got it all sorted and everything, so all that's left is for you to pack your stuff and we can go. It's best that we leave very early tomorrow morning; saves the trouble of having to worry about people noticing. Let me talk to Farrell, please."

Skyriders

He handed the phone to his aunt, who was midway through feeding her cats. "Finish this up for me," she said, taking the phone. "There're only a few bowls left."

Kai absentmindedly poured cat food into a plastic dish on the floor. He felt a bit as if he were playing chess in the dark. He had no idea whether the move he was making was a good move, one that could help him, or if it would ultimately hinder him. The future spread out in front of him like a path extending into a deep fog, with no way of knowing where his steps were leading him.

He realised that he'd over-poured the food. It had quickly spilled over the bowl and was spreading over the floor, a few cats already nosing through the food. Hastily, he distributed the spilt food between the few remaining bowls, reassuring himself that it had been less than five seconds and the cats probably didn't mind anyway. He heard Farrell saying goodbye to John, and then she turned to Kai, hanging up the phone.

"Well," she said finally. "It looks like you'll be leaving."

"Yeah," Kai replied awkwardly.

"It's been nice having you here. I'm sure I'll miss you. And the cats will too."

Kai would miss Farrell too, that he knew. He looked down at the floor. "Thank you for having me," he said. "You've been very kind."

Farrell smiled. "Thank *you*, honey. I wish you the best of luck in your new place."

Kai could only see the situation ending in tears or a hug, neither of which he really wanted at that stage. He excused himself, saying that he needed to go pack. He left quickly, feeling uncomfortable and sad and guilty and happy, all at the same time.

TWO

John arrived ridiculously early the next morning to pick up Kai. It was still dark outside. Kai hadn't thought it was worth his time trying to sleep, so he'd spent the night packing all his things, which fit into a backpack and travel bag, and talking to Farrell about the islands.

"Are you ready to go, Kai?" John asked, taking one of his bags for him.

Kai nodded. "Ready as I'll ever be."

The three of them left the house in a quiet procession. Around them, all the lights of the neighbouring houses were off, their inhabitants likely sleeping soundly. The stillness of the dark morning conferred an awed silence amongst the three of them. They finally stopped outside a secluded field five minutes away from the house.

"This'll do," John said decisively, sticking two fingers in his mouth and giving a shrill, high-pitched whistle. The wind seemed to pick up suddenly, and Kai heard the powerful beating of wings as a large furry creature descended into the field in a flurry of cream and white.

"What the—what *is* that?" Kai said, taking a few steps back as the animal landed, stretching out its large pure white wings before regarding Kai with curious interest. Its face was open and friendly, despite the small sharp teeth showing in its open mouth. It had soft whiskers extending from a wet nose, bright eyes, and pointed ears flicking interestedly whenever something rustled in the background.

"*Terexile Fallite,*" John said with a flourish of pride. "Although we usually just call them 'Talites' for short. These were the ones we managed to tame and, as you will soon see, learned to ride."

His aunt looked at the Talite, a quiet awe reflected in her eyes. "I haven't seen one of these in ten years now. It's beautiful."

She reached up a hand to stroke it, running her hand down the back of his head in smooth, even strokes, much like Kai had seen her do to her cats. It closed its eyes and gave a sound like a purr, a whirring clicking in the back of its throat.

It looked like something clean out of a fantasy novel: around the same height as him and a couple of metres long, its fur a sleek creamy white colour that rippled along right to the end of its long tail, which flicked casually back and forth, sweeping discarded crops out of its reach. Pride of place, though, went to the large wings that extended out of its back. It displayed itself with a kind of grace, a unique sort of dignity that gave it an air of magnificence as it moved, its wing feathers ruffling slightly in the whispering zephyrs that threaded through the air.

"Come on, Kai," John said cheerfully, straddling it with ease. He loaded Kai's bag onto its back in front of him, then gestured for Kai to follow. "We'd better get going. It's a bit hard to balance at first, but you'll get the hang of it soon enough. Hop on."

Farrell looked at him sadly. "I'm really going to miss you, Kai."

"I'll miss you too," Kai said. Then, a thought occurring to him, he added, "What will you tell people if they ask where I've gone?"

"It's okay. I don't think many people will be asking for you. I can tell your school you've transferred to a boarding school somewhere. But don't worry about that. Have fun, all right, honey? And don't forget to visit me if you've got time!"

"I will," he replied.

Farrell gave him a brief, tight hug, a lingering cat smell hanging between them. "Have a safe journey. Good luck!"

Kai lifted his backpack and deftly slipped it onto the leather saddle-like seat secured onto the Talite, tightening the straps for extra security, before shakily climbing onto the Talite's back. John gave him a pair of leather loops to slip over his hands, which connected to a band around the Talite's neck, before giving him a few instructions from his position in front of him.

"Just tighten your legs around its body. Lean forwards a bit and grab on to a bit of the fur . . . *loosely*. We don't want to pinch the skin . . . Okay, that's good. I'll go slowly for the first bit. Yell if you think you're going to fall off."

"W-what?" Kai said in alarm, but the Talite had already stood up and was flexing its wings, ready to take off. It took a few steps forwards and launched itself athletically into the air, its wings beating around him as it slowly gained altitude. Kai watched the ground beneath him decrease in size as they flew farther away, until the figure of his aunt beneath him was too small to distinguish any features. The Talite's body beneath him fluttered with its shallow breaths, smelling of straw and a stale, dusky scent. Its fur was warm with the exertion, a stark contrast to the gathering cold outside, and Kai could feel the faint throbbing pulse underneath his fingers.

"There you go. Not too difficult, is it?" John said. "How're you doing?"

"Good," Kai said, and he meant it too. After the original shock wore off and he started to realize just what he was doing, he'd felt a thrill of exhilaration run through him, a sort of inane rush of adrenaline that removed all apprehension.

"It's quite a long journey," John informed him. "At least it's a lovely clear night, great for flying, so you'll be able to see the stars, and I expect the sun rising later on. Riding in bad weather is . . . difficult, to say the least."

"So if the islands are invisible, how will you know how to find them?"

"Most of it is just knowing where to look. The rest is down to your navigation and map skills. It's happened that people have accidentally got lost trying to relocate the islands on a trip back, and we've had to send teams out to find them again."

It was like an aeroplane flight, but there was no place to sleep without fear of falling, and there were no inbuilt TV sets. Kai hardly noticed this; the simple exhilaration of flying provided all the entertainment he needed. He watched with growing fascination as they passed over Florida, seeing the dense, sprawling fields of light below and the occasional moving car's headlights. He saw some illuminated swimming pools, glowing an eerie azure from the pool lights under the water. Soon even the coastline disappeared, replaced by the deep black void of the rippling ocean underneath them as they sped onwards.

19

John didn't say much during the journey, presumably concentrating on flying the Talite. Over the journey, the sky lightened, tendrils of light against the bleak darkness. The clouds were highlighted pink and white as they skimmed through them. The sun rose, slow and majestic in its magnificence, and the sky morphed from a pinkish hue to a deep, clear blue. The odd bird fluttered by with a fleeting call, the figures of ships small in the ocean below them. A few hours later, John paused in mid-air and turned to face Kai.

"We're here."

Kai looked around. The sky looked no more impressive than it had at any other point during the journey, and there was a clear lack of any island presence, floating or otherwise. The only thing out of the ordinary was a slight flickering pain in the back of his head, like a dull headache. "We are?"

"You feel anything?"

"Yeah, like a . . ." He paused, struggling to explain. "It hurts a bit . . . kind of . . ."

John nodded. "That's the energy field I was talking about; it forms the barrier. It also has a somewhat detrimental effect on most electrical devices that you bring through it. But don't worry—that only happens when you get close to it. Watch this." John smiled and eased the Talite forwards gently.

Kai felt a shiver of anticipation run down his spine in excitement of what was to come. There was a flicker around them, the air seeming to shimmer slightly, and the pain sharpened slightly before easing off. In the next moment, there were a group of islands hovering below him, stretching out into the distance.

Skyriders

There were seven islands in all, arranged in a rough circle, with one island in the middle of the ring. They hung in a silent, majestic equilibrium in the sky. On the surface, they were peppered with small buildings, some more densely populated than others, with a strong metal fence circling the edges. From one of the islands, a waterfall plunged off the edge, the water catching in the wind, the droplets scattering a thin rainbow across the sky; others had green plains that gave way to gently sloping hills and steep, jagged mountains—or dense forest and marshy swamps where the rivers seeped into the ground. Underneath the islands, the ground spiked downwards, occasional green plants protruding from the rock.

"Woah," Kai breathed, unable to take it all in. He couldn't imagine how either Farrell or his mother could think about leaving such an extraordinary place. "It's amazing."

"Quite a marvel, isn't it?" John agreed. "We're nearly there now. Shouldn't be more than ten minutes, and then you can get off and stretch your legs."

It was just after midday when they reached the island of Tissarel, where the school was based. John slowed down, guiding them low over the island so Kai could see everything clearly. The buildings held a vague resemblance to the mock—Tudor houses he'd seen sometimes in England, but with more simplicity; they weren't more than two or three storeys high at the most, constructed mainly of wood, although some of the taller buildings were fashioned from stone blocks. The town was fringed by rolling green plains and, farther back, a huge looming mountain that overshadowed the whole place. The air was pleasant and cloudless, the sun's rays bathing the atmosphere with a warm light.

John brought the Talite to a smooth landing outside a large building on the far side of the island, about fifty metres from the edge. The brick exterior was crumbling in places, with a slanting black-tiled roof and trailing plants growing up the sides of the building. Smaller buildings around it varied in size and stature, ranging from a small ancient-looking building to a fairly new dormitory annexe.

Vaulting off the Talite with practised ease, John gestured for Kai to follow. He swung his legs over the side and shakily jumped down after him, stumbling a bit as he found his bearings.

John grinned at him. "What do you think?"

Kai shook his head. "It's pretty *insane*," he said breathlessly, looking around him in amazement. "It's so unreal. I'd never imagined in my life that I'd ever do this."

"Come on, let's get inside. I'll take your stuff."

The school was constructed of crumbling red brick, with a black slate roof and large windows. The building was arranged in a vague L shape, with a tall three-storey bell tower on the other side of the grounds. To the side was a small wooden shack-like building hidden within an orchard, and another similarly constructed shelter to house the Talites.

Inside, the walls were painted white, although the colour had faded over time to a creamy grey, and the floor was covered with rough brown carpeting. Inside reception was a curved desk in one corner, a row of chairs just by the front door, a few potted plants, and a notice board detailing the upcoming events and school clubs.

The receptionist looked up sharply from her work at the front desk as they came in. She was a small woman with mousy brown hair and glasses that lent her a look of constant disapproval.

"Good afternoon, John. And who's this?"

"This is Kai," John replied.

"Kai? Faye's son?" she asked sceptically, leaning slightly over the desk to get a better look.

"You knew my mother?" Kai asked.

"Everyone knew your mother, kid. She was the greatest rider I've ever seen in all my life."

"She was?"

"C'mon, you must know. She's your *mother*, after all."

"Quit hassling him, Meg," John said. "I've got to sort out some stuff for him. What's the time?"

"Ten past one," she replied, and then, with a sort of condescending smirk, added, "You're late."

"Late?" John asked, mystified. "Late for what?"

"You've got a geography class at one, remember? I've had three pupils come and ask where you are."

"What? That's today?"

Meg nodded, clearly enjoying this. "You're not very good at this, are you?"

"Here, look," John said, flustered, running a hand through his hair. "There's that room on the third floor with a spare bed, isn't there? Who stays there?"

"Ah, yes, I know that one. It's . . ." She opened a large folder on her desk and flicked through the pages, finally stopping with a triumphant noise. "Valcor and Rafael, room eighty-seven. And so you don't have to ask, Rafael left for Meridian about half an hour ago."

"And Valcor?"

"He's doing advanced riding theory. Room seven."

"Excellent. Kai, let's go."

He led Kai down the corridor at a brisk pace. "Sorry about that. I quite forgot I had a class. But don't worry. I'll get Valcor to show you around the place. He shouldn't be too worried about missing his lessons."

John paused outside a door marked ROOM 7, knocking loudly before pushing it open and peering inside. A small class full of pupils looked back at him, interest flickering over their faces. Any interruption was welcome in the class—sought after, even. Their teacher stood at the front: a lithe woman who glared at John as he poked his head round the door.

"I should have guessed it was you," she remarked. "I can't teach a decent lesson anymore without some passer-by coming and disturbing it, can I? What do you want? And make it snappy; I've got work to do."

"Is Valcor in here?"

One of the boys sitting near the front looked up and answered lazily, "Yeah?"

"Come here, you. Pack your stuff quickly."

Valcor grinned, started to stuff his books in his schoolbag, and got up to leave.

"Excuse me—you can't just pick students from my class like that," the teacher retorted indignantly.

"It's important!" John assured her. "He needs to show Kai here to his room; the poor soul's just arrived here. Forty-five minutes away from class won't kill either of you."

"This doesn't mean you don't have to do your homework!" the teacher shouted after him as he left the room.

"Thanks for that," he said, slinging his bag over his shoulder. "I hate theory lessons."

He was tall, with a pale complexion and sharp blue eyes, his deep brown hair hanging over his forehead as he studied Kai with a cursory glance.

"You look familiar," he said. "I'm Val."

"Kai."

Valcor turned to John. "So I just show him to his room, right?"

John nodded. "Help him unpack, show him around, that kind of stuff. Now if you'll excuse me, I really must be going." He departed quickly down the corridor.

Valcor nodded at Kai. "Let's get a move on. No point hanging around when I'm missing class."

He led Kai down the corridor, coming to a decisive halt at a small red-carpeted rectangular room at the end of it. The walls were made of a dark brown antique wood. The sun's rays shone through the large stained-glass window that made up most of the far wall, dappling the carpet in front of them with glimmers of multicoloured light. The room held an air of opulence that was hard to ignore.

"This is the visitors' entrance," Valcor said. "This is the way we enter the school if we want to impress someone. The way *you* came in, through reception, that's the main entrance, where everyone else comes in. You're not supposed to come through here unless you're instructed to. That way, Meg at the front can keep track of who's here and who's not.

"The guy in the stained glass is the founder of the school, Sir Tenil Lennhan. Next to him is the person who bred the first Talite—you know what that is, right?"

Valcor talked fast, and Kai was struggling to keep up with what he was saying. It took a few seconds for him to realize what he'd asked.

"Yeah. We rode here on one of them."

"Oh? You're not from Tissarel, then, I take it?"

Kai shook his head. "From, uh . . . Earth."

Valcor whistled. "You've come a long way. Was it your first time riding?"

"Yeah. So . . . what's there to do up here?" Kai asked him as they backed out of the room and ascended a flight of stairs on their left.

"What's there to do?" Valcor replied, only hesitating a fraction of a second before continuing. "Awesome stuff. There's schoolwork too, but that's kind of boring. Riding's probably the coolest thing you'll ever get to do in your life. It's like flying, sort of. Well, not really, because we can't *actually* fly, but you get what I mean . . . Seeing as the islands are floating, the best way to travel between islands is by Talite. Once you've learned how to fly them, you can pretty much visit anywhere."

The staircase led to a corridor that overlooked the dining hall, which Valcor pointed out with a dismissive wave of his hand before moving on to a different room. It was a kind of central hall: larger and even more luxurious than the first, with a huge sweeping staircase that held pride of place in the centre of the room. Aside from stone statues of the Talites on either side of the stairs and a few potted plants and framed portraits along the back wall, the room was practically empty.

Skyriders

"This is the main hall, first floor," Valcor said. "Although everyone calls it the hall of fame. The pictures at the back are the greatest riders of all time. There's Tenil again—gosh, he's popular, considering he's been dead for nearly fifty years now. Then there's Casana Gilforde, Jessi White, Taneel Peres, and Yel Drew. And this is the most recent, Faye Hunter."

Kai felt himself flinch as Valcor said his mother's name. The picture looked exactly like her as he'd known her before she'd died, stirring up memories that threatened to bring tears to his eyes. He blinked once to steady himself; crying now would only prompt awkward questions that he didn't want to bring up.

"They say she was the greatest rider ever, but she left Keturah a while after she graduated. Apparently she died, quite recently, which is a terrible shame. I know a lot of people who'd have liked to meet her, myself included."

Luckily Valcor didn't dwell much longer on the subject, instead leading Kai up the next flight of stairs. "The dormitories are up from here." Valcor's voice drifted down the stairs as he walked ahead. Kai was having a harder time because he was carrying both his travel bag and his backpack, and by the time they reached the second floor, he was getting tired.

"The girls sleep on this floor. We're on the third. You look a bit tired, Kai. You want some help?"

Gratefully, Kai accepted the assistance, and they reached the third floor with no trouble. Valcor pushed open the door of room 87 and slung his bag casually onto one of the beds. He put Kai's bag next to the bed right by the window.

The room was small but cosy, the three beds fitting snugly against the walls. The ceiling sloped downwards at the end, by the window, which overlooked the edge of Tissarel, set against the expanse of the pure blue sky.

"Well, this is our room," Valcor said, sitting on his bed. "Raf's not here yet, but he has the other bed. He's cool. There's some space in the drawers over there, although I think we've been using some of them for random stuff. That bed's been spare for nearly a year now."

Valcor talked about miscellaneous things while Kai unpacked, which suited him fine. He was relieved, in fact. He could never carry a conversation well with people he didn't know, and the awkward silences that inevitably followed meant that he tended to shy away from unwarranted company altogether. But Valcor seemed to have no such inhibitions and effortlessly filled the silence with a range of loosely related questions that kept the conversation going.

"So what happens now?" Kai asked when he finished unpacking.

Valcor shrugged. "Well, I don't have school again until this evening, so I don't really know."

"You go to school in the evening?"

"Yeah. Everyone goes to school from eleven thirty in the morning until two in the afternoon. Then the apprentices have their lessons until half four. Riders go to school from half seven until nine, and then the elites get the last hour, from nine till ten. Lights out at eleven and you wake up at nine. Hey, we should see if we can get your timetable and stuff. They should have come up with something by now."

"What subjects do you they teach here?"

"Well, English and maths, which is pretty much the same wherever you go," Valcor explained as they made the short journey back to reception. "Then there's natural science, which is studying plants and animals and stuff. There's chemistry and physics and motion. And there's navigational science, which is how you navigate around the sky using different methods; practical technology, which is making stuff, like woodwork, textiles, and other crafting; and cultural studies, which is studying ancient cultures and languages."

The clock at reception showed five to two as the two entered.

"Kai, I've got some things for you," Meg said. "Oh, you've got Val with you. Is he showing you around, then?"

"Working on it," Valcor replied cheerfully.

"Here's your timetable, Kai. I've just finished writing it up. And a map of the school, one of Keturah, and your rider's gear." She tapped the parcel containing the gear. "Take that to every practical you have," she warned. "Otherwise, Ms Greeve will eat you alive. Anyway, ask Valcor if you need any help with anything, or Rafael, when he gets back from Meridian."

"What's a practical?" Kai asked, unfolding his timetable.

Valcor tapped the box marked APPRENTICE RIDING on his timetable. "It's your riding lesson," he explained. "Where you learn the basics of riding and stuff. It's all on Talites and usually outside, so it's much more interesting than the theory lessons, which suck. Ms Greeve teaches all the apprentice lessons, so you'll be seeing a lot of her. She's not exactly . . . *friendly*."

Meg gave him a stern look. "You're not supposed to give opinions of your teachers to new students, Val," she said. "We don't want him forming negative images before he's even met her."

 29

"Aw, but *everyone* hates her," Valcor said. "That's probably why she's not even married yet . . ."

"Don't listen to him, Kai," Meg said, exasperated.

Kai unfolded the map Meg had given him of Keturah. Meridian was the easiest island to spot; it was dead in the middle of the page, streets arranged in a strict grid fashion, with small patches of space for parks and fields. "Raf's always at Meridian when he gets the chance," Valcor said. "Although, strictly speaking, he went there this time for an errand. Otherwise, he'd be in lessons."

"What's there to do down there?"

"It's the biggest trade centre in Keturah. They've got shopping, and there's always stuff worth watching at the arena at the back. He goes there for the fishing, though."

Kai immediately pictured some sort of winged fish, which, given what he'd seen today was not entirely unfeasible. Cautiously, he asked, "Fishing?"

"Yeah. You bait the line and catch birds. He sells them to the shopkeepers sometimes. The term 'fishing' originated where you come from, which you might find confusing. It's good fun, though. You should try it."

"You have the day off today to get used to everything," Meg said. "So I'd familiarize myself with the layout of the school if I were you. Lessons start tomorrow."

"And besides, lunch is in a few minutes," Valcor added, glancing at the clock. "We should go drop off your stuff and then get something to eat. You hungry?"

Kai hadn't eaten since the breakfast Farrell had given him that morning, and he suddenly realised he was starving. He nodded quickly, but he couldn't help feeling strange as he followed Valcor back upstairs. It was hard to believe that a few hours ago was the last time he saw his aunt; it seemed so much longer ago than that. His home life seemed very far away all of a sudden. It was as if he'd been dreaming for a long, long time, and he'd suddenly woken up.

THREE

Valcor resumed the tour after lunch, showing Kai the school at such an alarming rate that he was having difficulty remembering it all. They finished off outside in the late afternoon, at what was commonly known as the stables, where they kept the Talites while they were not in use. They were large wooden constructions, built with rudimentary individual stalls for the animals. Beyond that, on the very edge of the island, was a fenced field of grass in which their offspring could frolic around freely.

They hadn't been there for long when Rafael walked in, just back from Meridian. He had a dark complexion and black hair, his eyes placid, in stark contrast to Valcor's, which flicked deftly from one place to another almost all the time.

The Talite he'd been riding padded after him, its eyes bright with interest, constantly surveying the scene around him. Eventually, it noticed Kai and began to nudge him gently with its nose, cream fur tickling his skin as it moved, a sort of high-pitched whirring, clicking noise emanating from its throat.

This caught Rafael's attention. "Oh, Val, hey. I didn't see you there. Who've you got with you?"

"This is Kai. He just arrived today—he's sharing our room, so I'm showing him around."

Skyriders

"Kai, hmm?" Rafael asked, his gaze transferring to Kai, studying him slowly with a sort of calm awareness. Then, finally: "You're Hunter's son, aren't you?"

This took both Kai and Valcor by surprise.

"No! What, really?" Valcor said, glancing rapidly between Rafael and Kai. "I knew I recognized you! Are you, Kai?"

Kai nodded slowly, wondering, like Valcor, how on earth Rafael had managed to pull that fact out of nowhere within seconds of meeting him. "How'd you tell?"

He shrugged. "You look really similar. You've got the same eyes and stuff. And..." His gaze slipped downwards, towards the Talite, who was lying on its back at Kai's feet, rubbing its head against his legs. "It doesn't take to strangers that quickly," Rafael continued. "Talites are usually quite hesitant when they first meet new people, especially this one. I ride it often, so we've gotten used to each other."

"It ran away from you the first time, if I remember correctly," Valcor put in.

"That just proves my point," he responded with a wry smile.

"But how'd you connect that with the two of them being related?"

"Faye had that sort of quality. They trusted her almost immediately." He turned to Kai. "Like he does you."

"It's actually somewhat disturbing," Kai said, inching away from the animal.

"That's a shame. It really likes you."

"That's really awesome, having her for your mother," Valcor said enthusiastically. Then, coming to his senses, he added awkwardly, "I'm sorry, you know, that she..."

33

Kai said quickly, "It's fine. She . . . didn't really tell me anything about this place."

"She didn't?" Rafael asked, his expression tinged with puzzlement. "She never mentioned it, not even once?"

"Nobody knows why she left Keturah in the first place," Valcor mused. "She wouldn't tell anyone."

"So can you ride one of these?" Rafael asked, motioning to the Talite.

"No. I mean, I've ridden on one on my way here with John, but I don't know how to control them or anything."

"That'll take some learning. It helps, you know? Then you can go out and stuff." He glanced out the window. The sky was starting to darken; dusk was setting in. "It's getting late. We'd better go inside."

They were greeted with a rush of warm air as they pushed open the door to reception, accentuating the bitter cold that had suddenly descended outside. "Shut the door," Meg said tersely as they entered, and Valcor quickly obliged. "It's freezing out there."

Kai hadn't noticed the cold until he entered the warm room, but now the bitter draughts that had been let in when they opened the door made him shiver slightly.

"Look at that—just in time for dinner," Valcor remarked, glancing at the clock. "And it smells good."

"It always smells the same, no matter what it is," Rafael said. "They just use the same spices and stuff to trick you into thinking it's good. Like the time they served up that hideous soup?"

Valcor grimaced. "Not that again. I think that's given me a permanent fear of soup. There should so be a word for that. Soupophobia or something."

"Really, Val," Rafael said. "Was that the best you could come up with?"

"It was just a suggestion," Valcor replied defensively. "I mean, what else is there?"

"You'd never have to use the word more than once or twice in your life," Kai remarked.

They'd reached the dining hall by now. It was a large, long room, imitating the manner of a medieval-style hall, with stone flooring, chandeliers hanging from the ceiling, and electric light bulbs in place where typically there would be candles. Already the room was filled with the chatter of students as they took their places at the distressed wooden tables, filling up the hall slowly. Valcor and Rafael sat on the table at the far side of the room, near to the front. There were a few people at the table already, including two girls, one of whom waved at them as soon as she spotted them.

"Kai's right," Rafael was saying as they sat down next to her. "People don't talk about fear of soup on a day-to-day basis. No point inventing a word if you don't need it."

"Who's Kai?" she asked, turning to face them. She had a pleasant, open face peppered with freckles and blatantly orange hair that fell down her back in rippling waves. "And what was this about soup?"

"This is Kai," Valcor said, gesturing to him. "He's new here. Kai, this is Sacha. She's a friend of mine. As for the soup..."

"Valcor just invented a word," Rafael said.

"Oh, this'll be good," Sacha said with a grin. "Go on, Val. Impress me."

"Soupophobia. Fear of soup," Valcor replied. "And before you start with the criticism, it has a logical purpose."

"I just *can't* see how we could've survived without it," the other girl remarked drily. She had a hat on, pulled low over her face, which made her expression almost completely unreadable. "Those poor souls around the world who're scared of soup will thank you for this."

"You see, *that's* the problem," Sacha said. "*Normal* people aren't scared of soup. I don't think *anyone's* scared of soup."

"You've probably just deeply offended someone," Valcor said. "Not only do you not admit it's real, but you've called them mad too."

"I'd be mad enough already with a label like *soupophobic*." As she grinned in response, a loud ringing cut the rest of the conversation short. The conversations dwindled slowly into low murmurs as the kitchen staff wheeled in a long tray with serving dishes of steaming food, cutlery, and plates.

They called the students up table by table, starting with the teachers, rhythmically spooning out servings of the meal onto their plates. Kai was relieved that the dinner tasted fine, and the meal flew by as he listened to Valcor, Rafael, and Sacha talk about pointless things—until Rafael looked over at the clock and pointed out what time it was.

"We'd better hurry up," he said, getting to his feet. "We'll be late for school."

"School?" Kai asked. Then he remembered what Valcor had told him earlier. "Oh yeah."

"You'll be all right, Kai?" Valcor asked, also getting up.

"I'll be fine. I think I can at least remember my way up to our room."

Valcor nodded. "See you soon."

He left with Sacha, and the other girl had left at some point without anyone really noticing, leaving Kai alone to finish his dinner. Once he cleared his plate, he managed to get back to the dormitory without too much difficulty.

The stuff Meg had given him wasn't on the bed where he'd left it. Someone had come in and made the bed up while he was out—a fresh duvet and pillows laid out already—subsequently moving the papers. He managed to locate his things in the bedside table drawer and unfolded them all, reading them over, familiarizing himself with what was going to be his new life from now on.

He did a few sudoku puzzles that he'd brought with him, but they brought back poignant memories of his home life and his mother. Eventually, he left the room again, exploring the school once more with the help of his map. The corridors were still and empty; when he happened to see anyone in them, the person was much younger than he was, around eleven or twelve, or older, which made him feel out of place and awkward. Every now and then, he'd pass a classroom where a lesson was taking place.

He ended up outside in the bitterly cold air. The sky was marbled with deep purples and blues, rogue streaks of yellow and orange occasionally flashing into view. A few early stars were out; they seemed to be inexplicably close, larger than he'd seen them before. It wasn't light, but it wasn't dark either—the perfect bridge between day and night. He typically liked the quiet stillness of the world around him during that time, but now an occasional voice punctuated the darkness at unpredictable moments.

By tracking the sound, he rounded a corner of the school and ended up facing a large brightly lit flat field at the edge of the island, looking down onto the dying light of the day. It was a class of about ten or twelve students, all of them sitting astride their own Talites. John was teaching the class, and as Kai drew closer, he could hear what he was saying:

"Stability and agility are the two key aspects of this. Keep your weight centred until you make the turn, and then we want one swift move, like this." He did a little demonstration on his own Talite, flying in a straight line until suddenly the animal tilted slightly before skilfully pivoting around the farthest tip of its wing, spinning around 180 degrees in a move so fast that Kai could have blinked and missed it. Then he centred again. "There you are, see? Clipped, precise."

"Oh, Kai. Nice of you to join us," John said, catching sight of him. "This is advanced rider practical, which is a bit above your level, but you're more than welcome to watch. You may even pick up a few tricks."

Kai hadn't much else to do, and he was more than content to sit and observe the lesson, watching the class with barely suppressed awe as they expertly imitated the technique John had taught them in mid-air, with all the grace and finesse of a dancer.

"Excellent for a first try. Remember to centre your weight immediately after you perform it; otherwise, when you start combining this with other moves, you'll lose your balance. Now, we can use this in two ways—mainly it is used defensively, for instance, to dodge, or to get out of the way quickly, or to change direction quickly when being chased. If you use it offensively, you can use it to gain the element of surprise before you deliver a swift counter-attack; used well this way, it can prove to be very effective. Okay, let's move on to—what the . . . ?"

Everyone turned to look at what had disturbed their teacher mid-sentence, and judging by their response, it was evidently something worthy of causing alarm. Confused, Kai peered at the dark sky, struggling to pinpoint what was going on, but he couldn't see anything except the twinkling of distant stars.

Whoosh!

Something flashed past him so fast that he had no idea what had happened until he felt a sharp tear into his cheek, leaving a thin crimson line across his face. He yelped in pain and stumbled backwards, instinctively raising a hand to his wound. Around him were screams, shouts of terror, and general chaos, making him feel disjointed and confused. Logic and panic blurred into each other as blood trickled down his face, and he watched the commotion ensue before him, not entirely sure what to do.

Kai could just about make out a sleek matt black animal at least the size of three Talites, with large leathery bat-like wings that beat furiously to keep it in flight and a thin writhing body that rippled down to a long tail lined with lethal-looking spikes. It had two forelegs but no back legs to speak of, which he figured made it slow and awkward on the ground, but it was lithe and nimble in the air.

"Calm down!" John was yelling. "Quit panicking! Kai, get over here!"

A voice of authority worked wonders on the students, dispersing the blind panic and reinstating order instead. The students started to mobilize, quickly getting onto their Talites. Kai scrambled forwards, reaching John breathless and still bleeding, but at least he was in one piece. Above them, the creature let out a hissing, grating screech and lunged forwards with the same breakneck speed as before. Kai managed to jump out of the way before it streamed violently past him, feeling the air rush past as it missed him by inches. Its lashing tail smashed into one of the pupils, sending her flying off her Talite; she hit the ground with a dull thud.

"Everyone, get off the ground! Try to remember what we covered last week on attack formations! You have to get it away from the school! But, Wave, wait here," John instructed, quickly making his way over to the fallen pupil. The other pupils immediately obliged, launching off the ground in a flurry of white wings and shouted commands.

One of the students paused abruptly before taking off, twisting round to look at him. She was a bit on the short side, with scruffy royal blue hair and sharp, dark eyes. "What?"

"This is Kai. Kai, you're riding with Wave."

She scowled. "Why me? He can stay here, right? He'll be safer on the ground . . . or inside."

"Because you're the most experienced rider in this class, and I don't want what happened to Jaz to happen to him."

"I can't ride with him on the back. He'll mess it up."

"Wave, I don't have time to argue. Kai, get on there. Quickly."

Grudgingly, Kai obeyed, but under the circumstances, he rather would have taken Wave's course of action and gotten out of there as fast as possible.

John took a few more steps towards Jaz and then paused for a second to look at Kai. "Hold on tight, okay?"

Before Kai had any time to ask what John meant by that, Wave took off, launching into the air like a missile in order to catch up with the others who had already fallen into an orderly pattern, three at the front, directly in front of the animal, and five just behind them to back them up, with the remaining two students hovering a little beneath them. At a shouted command, they launched into action, the three at the front driving forwards and tackling it head-on while the ones underneath it arced swiftly over it and attacked the rear.

Wave immediately joined in as soon as she reached them, her Talite powering upwards and slamming into the creature's underside. Her Talite lunged at its body, sinking its teeth into its skin. As it howled in pain, it dove down towards them, slashing at them with fast dark claws, and Wave jumped backwards, narrowly avoiding the attack.

The ride was as far away as possible from the gentle, sedate ride he'd been on with John earlier that day. It was a living nightmare—a jerking, high-speed series of unpredictable twists and turns that shook him to the very fabric of his being. The wind rushed in his ears, the unearthly shrieks of the animal scraping against his hearing like nails down a blackboard. Frightened, he clutched on to the Talite for dear life, muttering, "I'm going to die" under his breath repeatedly, until he could literally think of nothing else. He was certain he was going to fall off and die.

"Can't you slow down a bit?" he finally worked up the courage to say.

"What, can't take it?" Kai could detect the smirk in her voice. "Tough, kid."

She swerved violently to the side before shooting back in the opposite direction. Kai closed his eyes and tried to focus on not falling off or getting killed, but with the unpredictable, spontaneous moves Wave was making, he was having a hard time sustaining his grip on the Talite.

"Quit moving around," Wave said tersely from in front of him. "And watch out!"

She dodged again as it made another lunge at them. Then she powered upwards, slamming the Talite headlong into the bottom of its jaw. There was a sickening crack as it connected, the impact jerking Kai off balance.

He felt a sudden lurching fear but quickly managed to right himself before he slipped off. The animal gave another rasping screech and made a wild lunge at another student, who swiftly dodged and dealt a brutal lash across the creature's face with the tail of his Talite, drawing a long howl of pain. Another Talite jumped forward, sinking its pointed teeth into its forepaw. It hissed and twisted round, trying to break free, clawing at it until the Talite let go and jerked backwards with an angry snarl.

One of the lead students shouted, "Regroup!" The Talites immediately responded, swarming together before quickly branching off again into groups of three with perfect precision in less than a couple of seconds.

They launched forwards again, each group relentlessly attacking a different part of the animal.

Surrounded and only able to attack one group at a time, the creature was slowly weakening, and after a few more attacks, it fled with a final shriek, melting into the darkness. A ragged cheer erupted from the students as they acknowledged the victory, slowly circling back to the ground. Wave touched down smoothly and leaped off, Kai following shakily after her, swaying around slightly as he acclimated from sky to land. His mind was still reeling from the dizzying flight, his pulse marching out a livid beat as his fear started to slowly subside.

The other students had formed a loose circle around John, who was crouching by the girl who'd been knocked off by the animal earlier. He edged over to them to get a better look; she was unconscious, her face deathly pale, marked with little scratches and a red welt across her cheek, but her steady breathing showed that she was alive.

"How's Jaz?" one of the girls in the crowd asked, her voice laced with tension.

"Well," John said, "I think it's nothing more than a few bruises and sprains at the most, although the leg seems serious. What about the Dracaen?"

"It flew away," one of the boys replied.

John nodded, satisfied. "Good job, guys. Excellent work. Can I get someone to take her to the medical room?"

Some of the pupils looked concerned as Jaz was carried away by a couple of the class members. "I hope she's gonna be okay," someone said. "It could have been a lot worse. It's a good thing nobody was seriously hurt."

"That's not the point," Wave said brusquely. "It's getting worse, isn't it? The attacks. They're getting more frequent now. What's going on?"

There were a few murmurs of agreement.

"She's right. They're getting braver, attacking such a populated area. Usually they just go for people who are on their own."

John raised his hands. "I've no idea what caused this either," he said. "Like Kari said, it's good nobody was seriously hurt. I'm sure that under different circumstances, the outcome could have been much different. But this *is* very serious, and I think I'm going to have to speak with somebody about this. In the meantime, since you all performed so well, you can have the last fifteen minutes of the lesson off. Don't disturb the other classes, though."

There were several exuberant yeses hissed throughout the crowd as they quickly dispersed with their Talites, presumably back to the stables to put them to rest for the night before spending their well-deserved free time.

"Kai," John said. "How are you feeling?"

He shook his head. "Not the best."

John gave a little laugh at that. "I'm impressed you're alive, actually," he said. "Wave's a very talented rider, but I must confess that I find her methods a bit ... unorthodox. Where'd you get that cut?"

"When it first attacked, I think."

He studied it for a second. "It seems pretty harmless. I've got a first-aid kit here; I'll just clean it up a bit. It should heal pretty quickly, in a few days at the most."

"What was that thing?" Kai asked as John retrieved a small box from inside the equipment he'd brought out for the lesson. He deftly opened it and produced a small bottle.

"One of the rogue Fallite species Fall created, *Dracens Fallite*. We call them Dracaens. They're meant to have a nest in the Deep Sky, an area far to the east of here, way outside Keturah. But lately . . ." His voice trailed off, and he focused on dabbing antiseptic onto the cut.

"You said it was serious earlier. And what did Wave mean, 'It's getting worse'?"

John looked away. "This . . . this isn't an isolated incident. There've been quite a lot of attacks like this recently, and Wave's right about them getting worse. Generally, they won't attack heavily populated places like schools or villages unless something happens to provoke them. Most times they attack people who are alone, but lately they've been going up against bigger groups, and if they do succeed, it just gives them more courage."

"So basically there are deadly animals on the loose and they're getting *more* violent?" Kai answered caustically. "You somehow failed to mention this earlier."

He sighed deeply. "It's not all that bad, Kai. We've got defensive measures against them: patrol ships and emergency teams at the ready. And seeing as it ran away this time, they shouldn't attack like that again. There you go—that's done." With a flourish, he removed the cotton wad and packed up the medical supplies. "So . . . how're you finding it here so far?"

"It's not bad," Kai replied absently, still dwelling on what he'd just been told. "Lessons start tomorrow."

"So I've heard. Rest assured that any riding practicals you have will be much easier than this one. Well, I guess I'll be going now. Have a good night—and good luck tomorrow."

Kai hadn't been in his room for more than ten minutes or so when Valcor and Rafael entered from their lessons, dumping their bags on the floor by the entrance.

"Hey, Kai," Valcor said as he closed the door behind him. "How'd you get on?"

"What happened to your face?" Rafael asked gravely, catching sight of the livid cut across his cheek. "Were you outside?"

"Yeah?"

"With the Dracaen?"

This got Valcor's interest. "What Dracaen?" he asked, surprise outlining his voice.

Rafael shrugged. "There's this rumour going round that a Dracaen attacked the school earlier. Some kid got hurt, but they managed to chase it off."

Kai wasn't sure whether to be surprised or impressed at the efficiency of the school's rumour mill. At least it was good to see *some* similarity to his old school.

"You're kidding, right?" Valcor asked, jumping backwards onto the bed. "They're not supposed to come this far in. I thought they were scared of us."

"Like I said, it's just a rumour, but I don't think Kai picked that scratch up from around here."

"You saw it?" Valcor asked eagerly, turning to Kai. "That's pretty impressive for your first day. What was it like?"

"*Insane.* I'd rather not have been there, really."

"Who got hurt?"

"This girl," Kai said. "I think she was called Jaz."

"I know Jaz," Valcor said slowly, after a moment of quiet deliberation.

"You know *everyone,* Val," Rafael pointed out.

"Yeah, but I know her quite well. She's cool. She used to be in my riding class, but they moved her up to Wave's group."

Kai nodded. "Yeah, Wave. I rode with her."

Rafael whistled. "Talk about throwing you in at the deep end."

"I *thought* I was going to die," Kai said sincerely. "It was an absolute nightmare form start to finish."

Rafael shrugged. "It's a bit harsh, though. Wave may be a good rider, but they way she flies, it's a wonder she hasn't fallen to her doom by now. That said, she never rides double with anyone."

"I can see why," Kai said. "John made her do it. I was more content to sit back and watch from a safe distance."

"Aw, but that's so *boring,*" Valcor said. "I'd have traded fighting off a Dracaen for being stuck inside a history class any day."

"Boring but non-life-threatening," Rafael said pointedly.

Valcor said, "That's where all the fun is."

"Only till you die."

They talked like that for a while, about topics that held little relevance to anything. Kai listened, but his mind was elsewhere. It seemed as if he'd been there much longer than half a day. He cast a brief look down the road that he'd come, back through Farrell and her many cats, before meeting John, before his mother's death, when they'd lived together in Bracknell, back until his life was just a smudge of blurry half memories that he couldn't quite bring into focus.

A single ear-piercing call resounded throughout the corridors, shattering the easy quiet that had settled over the room, ringing in Kai's ears even after it had stopped. He blinked a few times in startled bewilderment, trying to clear his mind.

Valcor laughed at Kai's expression. "That's the lights out bell. You'll get used to it."

Kai looked over at the clock hanging above the door and saw that it was indeed eleven at night. Time had gone by quickly once he'd stopped being aware of it.

"You're doing lights tonight, Val," Rafael said. "Goodnight."

"'Night," Valcor replied cheerfully, leaning over and flicking off the lights, plunging the room into a quiet darkness.

FOUR

Kai had his first lesson in room 5, but the vague directions Valcor had offered over breakfast meant it took him ten minutes to find the room for his first lesson: riding theory. By the time he pushed open the door, most of the class had arrived, including the teacher, a tall ageing woman whose cheerful nature reminded him of Farrell. As he entered, she gave him a warm smile and beckoned him over.

"Kai, isn't it?" she said. "Good to meet you. I'm Mrs Rawthon. We're in the middle of a topic so feel free to ask if you don't understand anything, but I'm sure you'll dive right in, so to speak." She dropped her voice before continuing. "I'm sorry about your mother; we'll all miss her terribly."

Flinching inwardly, Kai felt a stab of sadness as she mentioned his mother. He gave her a weak smile in response.

"There, there's a seat next to Becky," Mrs Rawthon said, pointing to a seat two rows back in the middle of the room. "Why don't you sit there?"

Kai nodded gratefully and slid into his seat, aware of the mildly curious looks he was getting from the other students. He was feeling incredibly self-conscious.

Becky was tall and slender, with pale skin and eyes that shone with countless shades of brown in the rays of the morning sun. Most of her hair was gathered up into a long ponytail, but a few errant strands hung loose, interlacing in a complex chestnut-coloured web, falling down her back in untamed feathery long wisps.

She smiled shyly at him. "I haven't seen you here before," she said, her voice quiet. "Are you new?"

"Yeah." Kai nodded. "I just got here yesterday."

"I'm Becky," she said, tucking a strand of her hair behind her ear.

"Kai."

"All right, class, let's begin." Mrs Rawthon clapped her hands loudly together, silencing, with some difficulty, the class of fifteen. "First let's welcome our new student, Kai. I hope you'll help him settle in."

Kai felt a rush of self-consciousness pass over him again as the class's attention focused on him. Thankfully, Mrs Rawthon continued quickly. "Now, hurry and get out your work on weather conditions, please. We have a lot to cover.

"We did visibility for our last lesson. Let's quickly review the points we covered on that. Becky, start us off."

"Talites are adaptive, so they don't always rely on sight to navigate. They instinctively switch to their prominent sense if there's a problem with the one they were using, so low visibility doesn't bother them too much. In lower visibility, they're reliant on sound to navigate, so you have to be careful not to make too much noise; otherwise, they'll get confused."

"Yes. Very good." Mrs Rawthon scribbled down what she'd said in note form on the board behind her. "And . . . you, Zach?"

"Try to keep the sun to your side and behind you when it's a clear day, because Talites instinctively shield their eyes with their wings when they fly towards bright sunlight, which compromises their flying ability."

"Excellent. And I think one more . . . Renan?"

"There was something about . . . flying at night?"

"Good. There's a start. Anyone want to expand on that?"

Hands were raised, answers offered: "They're naturally diurnal, so they prefer flying in the day. You have to make sure they've had enough sleep before they fly at night-time."

"They're a bit restless at night, so they often don't respond to commands the first time."

"They view anything out of place as a threat and may act strangely or charge towards it or run away, depending on how dangerous they judge it to be."

"There you go. Excellent." She quickly wrote the points made and drew a large heading, WIND SPEED, before she put the cap back on the pen and turned away from the board. "Now, today's lesson is on wind speed. Talites naturally adjust their flight patterns based on the air around them, which means it is important to take note of the weather before you set off for anything and alter your position accordingly. For example, in a moderate wind speed, your basic position would be fine, but in very little or no wind, then basic is too restricting. So you shift to second, or maybe defensive. Who knows what the difference is between the two and how it'll alter your riding?"

Becky put her hand up. "Second allows for more movement leverage and greater control," she said. "But defence gives you more speed and agility because the

Talite will respond as if it really is under threat. But it means it is more likely to act instinctively than obey commands. And defence third—"

"That's a bit too deep," Mrs Rawthon said, smiling. "That's elite theory, which I suspect is a bit above the level we're covering at the moment."

This got the interest of a few others in the class.

"Elite theory?"

"Aw, you can tell us. Please, Mrs Rawthon?"

"C'mon, what's the worst that could happen?"

"Well . . . ," she said, hesitating slightly. "I suppose it won't hurt. Defence third is a variation on the defence position, which is similar to a pursuit stance, but you pull back a little and your grip is heavier. The aim is to make you more streamlined but with the ability to switch faster between basic, second, or standard defence, as opposed to the pursuit stance, which will help you switch to any of the attack stances quickly."

Kai had been struggling to understand the past five minutes of the lesson, but the last explanation had him absolutely baffled. He didn't want to draw attention to himself by asking Mrs Rawthon, so instead he leaned towards Becky and whispered, "What is she talking about? I don't understand it."

"It's riding positions," she replied. "Don't worry if you don't get it now; this is elite theory. You'll cover the main areas of it in your riding practical, which is usually in the evening. Do you know what stream you're in?"

Kai shrugged. "John said I was apprentice, and the rest of my lessons are in the afternoon."

She nodded. "Apprentice, then. You'll probably have a practical this afternoon."

"Anyway," Mrs Rawthon continued. "You don't need to know that until you qualify for the elite stream. Let's get on with our relevant information, shall we . . . ? Goodness, look at the time! So in high wind speeds, basic is too loose, and inexperienced riders often find themselves slipping and even falling. You need to switch to first, third, or attack position. To make sure you've understood this properly, here's a quick worksheet on this. Ronan, hand these out to the class, would you?"

Most of the words Mrs Rawthon had said passed clean through Kai's head without his understanding a thing. He stared blankly down at the sheet, the words in front of him making little sense to him, if any. Around him, everyone was scribbling away, so he picked up his pencil and managed to recall enough to answer the first question, but the rest of the answers eluded him. He absently doodled on the margin, trying to look as if he were writing.

Becky had finished well ahead of the class, and Kai could feel her watching him.

"Can you help me with this?" he asked finally.

"Sure." She leaned over and looked at the sheet. "Well, your first answer is right. And then . . ."

She worked methodically through the sheet, explaining the answers in a low, hushed voice, coiling a loose strand of hair around her finger as she spoke. They had just finished the sheet when the teacher clapped her hands together and started to check their answers.

"And, Xana, last question. Quickly now; the bell will ring any minute now. Wind speed five knots—what did you put for that?"

"Uh . . . attack position?"

"That's right. Anybody get a different answer?"

"Third?" one of the students on the other side of the room offered.

"That's good. I must stress that the problem with attack position is that you effectively reduce your weight load on the Talite, which means you're still likely to fall unless you keep a strong grip. First or third is safest, and there's no difference between the two in terms of effect on your riding. Just choose the ones that you find most comfortable."

The long, resounding bell drowned out her last few words. Immediately, the class launched into excited chatter, meaning their teacher had to shout to make herself heard over their words: "Homework for tonight is to start writing up some notes on this subject! Bring them to the next lesson so we can continue them! I don't want to have to go over it again!"

The next few lessons were applied maths, history, and double geography, which were much easier for Kai to understand, especially because his maths lesson seemed to follow roughly the same curriculum as the one he'd been learning at his old school. The topic they were on was the one he'd just completed, and he felt at an equal standard to the other students in his class.

Kai had geography with Valcor and Sacha in room 3, which was a large room on the second floor, overlooking the school grounds. They spent the first half reviewing a test the class had taken earlier that day and the rest of the lesson doing a field practical on recording atmospheric pressure. Just before the end of the lesson, they returned to the classroom, where they were instructed to write up their findings and a conclusion.

With three minutes of the class left, Valcor decided it wasn't worth it and spent his time less constructively, making paper aeroplanes out of spare paper and crashing them dramatically into Sacha's hair while their white-haired hard-of-hearing geography teacher had his back turned. Eventually, she retaliated and a full-out paper aeroplane war commenced, although Kai wasn't entirely sure who was winning by the time the bell rang.

Sacha grinned. "Freedom!" she said jubilantly, piling her books into her bag. "Three hours of no school. I really hate geography."

Kai hadn't even that much to look forward to; he faced another two and a half hours in apprentice classes after their twenty-minute lunch break. The lessons were housed in what was rather predictably called the apprentice block, which he discovered to be at the other end of the school grounds, in an ageing one-storey building that had seen better days.

He pushed the door open, the rusting hinges creaking loudly in protest, leading into a dimly lit reception area that resembled a wide corridor more than anything else. The large timetable on the notice board next to him revealed that he had physics and motion, navigational science, and then an hour of apprentice riding, which presumably was the practical Becky had told him about.

Registration was in room A1, at the far end of the corridor. The room was small and square, occupied only by the teacher and a couple of pupils. The teacher was a small middle-aged woman who insisted on carrying a long metre ruler around with her at all times, banging it on the table or any suitable surface when she liked to make a point.

"I don't know you," she said sharply as he entered the room, the ruler in her hand connecting with a desk with a loud *thwack* that made him jump. She pointed it menacingly at him. "What are you doing here?"

"I . . . I'm here for the . . . lessons," Kai said, very much alarmed. "It's my first day here . . ."

"Ah." Her face cleared and her mouth set in a fierce, satisfied smile. "You're Hunter's son, aren't you? I remember John telling me about you the other day."

This got the attention of the two kids in the room. One couldn't have been more than ten years old. The other was around Kai's age and lanky, with longish sandy-coloured hair and glasses. His face was open and honest, and his eyes were a bluish grey in the stale light of the classroom. The two of them looked at him as if he'd just dropped into the room riding on a unicorn; their faces wore a mixture of shock, disbelief, and awe.

"This isn't the whole class, in case you were wondering. Our full class is about eight in total. You'll be one of the oldest, though, along with Felix here." The teacher gestured to the sandy-haired boy. "And everyone else is late."

She said that last sentence with a particular relish, snapping her head back triumphantly and tapping her ruler against the ground. Kai hastily sat down next to Felix.

"Is it true?" he asked eagerly. "You're Hunter's son?"

Kai shrugged, not really wanting to dwell on it. "Yeah."

"That's so cool. You must be amazing at this stuff." He paused and peered suspiciously at him. "What are you doing here, then?"

"Hmm? Where?"

"Here," Felix repeated, waving a hand at the classroom. "Apprentice school. With a bunch of ten-year-olds."

"I didn't know anything about this place until around a week ago," Kai explained. "I had no idea my mum went to school here. I probably know less than the ten-year-olds here."

"No way," Felix breathed. "She never told you? Not once? That's really strange."

"Apparently so. What about you? You're a bit old for this as well, aren't you?"

"My dad used to go to school here. He wasn't legendary or anything. He moved to Earth soon after he left school, but then he got a job miles overseas, in Nepal or something. I guess he thought it'd be too much of a hassle to bring me along, so he sent me here instead."

"Do you like it here?"

Felix said, "It's not bad. I mean, Ms Greeve's kinda scary, but everything else is cool. Except riding . . . and the fact that I'm the oldest here, which is a bit depressing, to be honest."

"What's wrong with riding?" Kai asked.

"Nothing much. It's fun and all, but I happen to have the most insane fear of heights. Not good."

He looked as if he were about to continue, but three more kids had suddenly arrived, and realizing that they were late by furtively glancing at the clock, they attempted to sneak over to their desks without the teacher noticing.

It was a futile attempt, and they knew it. Almost immediately, Ms Greeve leaped forward, brandishing her ruler menacingly. "You're *late!*" she yelled triumphantly.

The kids obviously knew what to do in the situation, simultaneously producing a well-rehearsed apology: "We're very sorry, Ms Greeve. It won't happen again."

She snorted derisively. "We'll see about that," she said, but she looked satisfied. "Where're your friends? They're late, too."

The kids shifted awkwardly, and one said, "I don't know. I think Lucas went to look for his gear. He left it in room 9. I don't know about Sammy."

She *tsked* disapprovingly. "Sit down," she said. "You'd better hope they get here soon."

Kai leaned over to Felix, feeling the need to whisper all of a sudden. "Is she always like this?"

Felix nodded. "You get used to it. My theory is that they put her in charge of the apprentices to scare them into submission for the rest of their lives. She *loves* it when people are late. I think it's just so she can shout 'You're late!' at them as they come in, but who knows? Besides—"

"You're *late*!"

One of the pupils had appeared in the doorway, looking justifiably nervous. "I-I'm sorry," he stammered. "I was looking—"

"I know exactly where you were," Ms Greeve replied sharply. "Negligence is not an excuse for lateness. That goes for you three too." She waved her ruler at the kids who'd come in earlier and then turned back to the boy. "I hope there'll be no repeats of this in the future."

"N-no . . . not at all."

"Just sit down; you're wasting time. And where's Samantha?"

"She's ill," Lucas replied. "She wasn't in lessons this morning."

Ms Greeve didn't look impressed. "Fine. Well, everyone else is here, so we'll commence with our lessons, shall we?"

Physics and motion proceeded well, but then, Kai had always been good at physics. It held a simplistic charm that made everything look easy and uncomplicated. Kai hadn't the slightest idea about what to expect from a navigational science lesson, though. To his surprise, he found that he could actually understand and keep up with what the lesson entailed, despite the fact that the class was halfway through a topic. Better still, he was rather enjoying the lesson. He felt a rush of satisfaction as the bell rang, signalling the end of the half-hour period.

"How long have you been here?" Kai asked Felix as they walked over to what was referred to as "the field" for their final lesson of the day.

He shrugged. "A bit longer than half a year. I've probably still got a while to go before I take the test."

"The test?"

"Yeah, the rider's test. Once you pass it, you get moved up to the next stream. Usually you take the test at thirteen, but I'm fifteen already, so they might let me take it at the end of the term. That's in the middle of spring, though. Still a long time."

Considering it was referred to as a field, the area held disappointingly little resemblance to a field of any kind. It wasn't even a field but a cliff edge, platform like ledges jutting out from the rock beneath them, linked by a system of tunnels that were concealed within the cliff face. Their Talites were waiting for them at the edge of the cliff, some play fighting with each other, some hovering in midair, others dozing lightly.

The apprentice students mechanically lined up in front of Ms Greeve, betraying how often they had performed the action. Kai quickly fell into place beside Felix, narrowing his eyes against the glaring afternoon sunlight behind their teacher.

"I was going to do this lesson on flight patterns," Ms Greeve said to the assembled pupils. "But for the purpose of our new pupil—" she gestured at Kai "—we're going to do a quick revision of the basic principles of flying. That means that for homework, I want you to read the section on flight patterns in your textbook, and there *will* be a test on it tomorrow. If you fail, you can expect to stay after class and revise the subject one on one. Clear?"

Each member of the class nodded meekly.

"Good. It's time for basic principles. We'll start with your gear and mounting. Felix, why don't you get up and demonstrate for us?"

"What?" Felix asked, clearly distraught. "But . . ."

She tapped her foot impatiently. "Come on, Felix. We're waiting."

Seeming to realize he had no choice, Felix reluctantly mounted one of the Talites.

"That too high for you?" Ms Greeve sneered mockingly at him before turning to the class. "Okay. Which order do you assemble your gear, Trey?"

One of the younger boys, the same one who'd been in the classroom early, began reciting the order anxiously, stammering over each word. "Seat first. Then, uh . . . band, then . . . loops and gloves. And then . . . feathers?"

She snapped her head back triumphantly. "Hmm. Wrong. Anyone else?"

One of the girls stuck her hand up. "Feathers go first," she said.

"Good. At least one of you knows what you're talking about. And *why* do feathers go first, Trey?"

"Because you do them before you get on," he replied, eager to redeem himself from the first mistake. "Otherwise, you'd have to get off and repeat everything again."

"Exactly. So there *is* a brain in that head of yours. Feathers go on the tail, and they fit quite nicely around the tip." She held up a small cone-shaped wire cage, moulded to fit snugly around a Talite's tail. Large black fletching flared out from the sides. When fitted, they lent the Talite's tail the appearance of a handsomely furry arrow.

"What are feathers for, Felix?"

"They help the Talite angle itself and change direction quickly," Felix replied, shifting nervously from his position on top of the Talite. "And they increase the speed that they ascend at."

"Good." She held up a large leather saddle that fit over the Talite's back. "Your seat is very important—without it, you'd likely fall off whenever you want to turn. Next is the band." She held up a large collar-like strip of tough material that looped loosely around the Talite's neck.

"What's the band for, Lucas?"

"Grip," he replied immediately. "And stability. You attach the loops onto them as well. It helps to wear gloves with them, because they tend to chafe."

The loops were small circles made of the same tough material as the band, which fitted around the hands. They were attached to a length of thin rope that could be fastened onto the band.

"Indeed. Tie it *loosely*, remember. We don't want any dead Talites on our hands. For extra stability, you can grip the sides of the Talite's body with your legs. Loops clip onto the band, as Lucas said. Sometimes it's easier to ride without them; as they advance, some people stop using them. And that's all for gear. Now, let's see our volunteer over here do something. Come on, Felix, up we go."

Felix looked decidedly pale as he lifted the Talite slowly into the air, the band clenched securely in his unyielding grasp.

"Riding is all about cooperation with your Talite," Ms Greeve said. "They respond directly to your movements, so it's important that you know what you're doing. Right now we're in basic position, which you use for most things. That's taking off, landing, and flying normally. It's also the base for other movements such as speeding up, slowing down, and turning.

"What you can see here is a rather *poor* display at the basic position," she told the class, a sort of jubilant scorn in her voice. She seemed to be enjoying this. "Tess, if you were the teacher of this class, what would you tell our volunteer to do to improve his posture?"

She shook her head. "I don't know," she mumbled, looking at the floor.

"Well, you'd better think of something, and quickly now," Ms Greeve snapped, her voice already tinged with impatience.

Tess chewed on a strand of chestnut hair. "He's facing the wrong way?"

Their teacher sighed heavily. "For one thing, he's pulling the band too hard, his weight is shifting all the time and he's *still* leaning forward, even though I've told him a hundred times not to do that." She tutted contemptuously. "*You* should've seen that."

"Oh yeah," Tess muttered under her breath. She looked around thirteen or fourteen, which, if what Felix said was true, meant she should be taking the test soon. "I knew that."

"This is sending at least *five* different conflicting messages to his Talite," Mrs Greeve continued. "No wonder the poor thing's looking so confused. There are three rules of basic position—rules that Felix is breaking *considerably* well, I might add. Keep your weight centred, your lean evenly balanced, and grip the band loosely with your hands. It's the most effortless thing you'll ever need to learn about riding. Would you like to have a go at doing a correct basic position for us, for Kai's sake?"

Felix, with great endeavour, managed to adjust his position, although he didn't look any less alarmed. "Can I get down now?" he asked shakily.

"Nope. We've still got five more positions to cover. Do them right and we'll think about giving you a rest. Start moving forwards for us, would you?"

As the Talite started to fly slowly forwards, Ms Greeve turned back to the class. "To turn, we simply lean in the direction we want to move. To speed up, we lean forwards; to slow down, we lean backwards. Any questions so far? Good.

"Now, on to the numbered positions. Felix will demonstrate. These are easy, but you have to know which one is which or your riding will go to pieces. First position is the slowest, which makes it the easiest. Second position has a looser grip, still leaning backwards, and a centred weighting. This is good for dodging quickly, and you fly faster than first position. Third position has a loose grip, and you lean forwards. Hayley, what do we use third for?"

"For flying straight. It's best if you're flying in one direction because you're fast, but you can't change direction easily."

"Exactly. If you try to lean while you're in third, you're more likely to fall off than anything else. That's how most apprentices die: they forget to switch to second or first before they turn. Let this be a lesson to you."

The class nodded sombrely.

"And finally, attack and defence. Attack is simple; you lift your body up and lean forward. This will reduce your weight and give you better speed and agility while still providing enough grip to keep your balance. For defence, you crouch down instead but still lean forward, which offers good handling and grip. Got all that?"

Trey's hand went up. "What do we *use* attack and defence for? I mean, usually when we're riding, you tell us not to use them..."

"They serve little purpose in normal riding," she replied with a touch of irritation, as if the answer were obvious. "If you're fighting on Talite, then they're essential. They give the Talite more freedom to act instinctively as opposed to your guiding them. Any other questions?"

None were offered. Ms Greeve clapped her hands loudly. "Okay, so let's practise what we've learned so far. Get on your Talites, everyone. Felix, you may as well get down here."

Looking immeasurably grateful, Felix landed heavily in front of them, scrambling off his Talite as quickly as the laws of nature would allow. His face was still pale, his eyes clouded with fear and his hands shaking.

The rest of the students mounted their Talites, assembling their gear as they'd been told. Between what he remembered from the lesson and watching the other kids, Kai managed to get on his Talite without much difficulty.

He'd never ridden one on his own and had no idea what he was meant to do. The other kids had already taken off by now. They made it look effortless, as if it were no easier than blinking or breathing. Kai had no idea how to take off.

"What are you waiting for?" Ms Greeve snapped at him. "Get up!"

Kai didn't know if saying he had no idea how to get up would provoke her further. Luckily, Felix had appeared beside him.

"Pull back on the band and lean backwards," he whispered. Kai quickly obeyed and found he was indeed rising off the ground, feeling a rush of exhilaration as he saw the ground moving slowly away from him. However, instead of just staying still, the Talite suddenly jerked forwards, slamming into one of the other students.

"Sorry," Kai apologized, but the Talite was off again, dashing forwards in manic spirals through the air, despite Kai's best efforts to stop it. The world around him blurred as they darted around at a breakneck speed in mad, unpredictable patterns.

"*Basic position!*" Ms Greeve shouted from the ground. "Get into basic!"

Basic position, Kai thought frantically, trying to recall what she had told him earlier while simultaneously attempting to stay on the Talite and not crash into anyone. *Weight centred ... balance ... loose grip ...*

Miraculously, the Talite stopped jerking around, instead flying forwards at the sedate pace Kai had been hoping for. He breathed a sigh of relief, but the movement made the Talite tilt dangerously to the left.

"Weight *centred*!" He could hear Ms Greeve yelling. "Always centred, unless you want to turn!"

This was harder than he'd thought it would be. He managed to right himself again, this time paying more attention to his balance and position.

"Now try first position!" Ms Greeve instructed.

First position. Right. I know this...

The Talite started to speed up again, and Kai instinctively panicked. He grabbed the band hard, trying to secure himself in case it launched into another mad dash.

"That's *third!*" Ms Greeve shouted. "I said get into first!"

"Which one's first?" he asked desperately.

Tess was closest to him. She leaned over and explained: "Tighten your grip. Lean backwards and centre your weight."

The Talite started to slow down again, but just as Kai let down his guard, it suddenly flipped upside down instead.

"What the—"

Kai lost his grip completely and fell, dangling precariously in the air by his hand loops. He could see the rest of the class gaping at him atop their Talites, their faces reflecting a kind of startled admiration.

"What did I do *this* time?" he yelled, half at Ms Greeve and half at the Talite. His arms were already tiring, straining against his weight and tightening the band against the Talite's neck. It started to struggle, thrashing furiously, shaking its head in an attempt to loosen the band, sending Kai jerking wildly from side to side.

"What in heaven's name do you think you're doing?" his teacher screeched. "Get down here *now*!"

"How am I meant to do that?"

Fortunately, Tess managed to coax the Talite into its full and upright position. Kai quickly scrambled back onto its back, breathing heavily, his pulse racing.

"Thanks," he said gratefully.

"You're welcome," she replied shortly.

"Uh . . . how do I land?"

Tess raised an eyebrow. "You pull off a flip like that and tell me you don't know how to land?" she asked sceptically. "Is that your idea of a joke?"

"That was a fluke. I had no idea what I was doing."

"Lean forwards. Press your thumbs gently into the back of its neck. Pull back just before you reach the bottom."

Landing was probably the only thing he managed to do right in that lesson, and even then, it was a bit shaky. He jumped off just as Ms Greeve marched over to him, furious.

"We'll have no messing about in my lesson," she said. "What was that you were doing up there?"

"I don't know," Kai said. "I was trying to go into first, like you said, and—"

"You decided it would be more worth your time to flip over like that, did you? Too easy for you, is that it?"

"What? No! It was an accident, really."

"Riiiight." She didn't look convinced. "You may as well stay here now that the lesson's over. No more 'accidents' like that in my lesson again, please. *Ever.*"

Considerably shaken, Kai backed away to where Felix was sitting, looking somewhat depressed. The

Talite followed him, head bent low and ears flattened, a mournful clicking emanating from its throat.

"You okay?" Kai asked, taking a seat beside him.

"Been better. Ms Greeve knows I'm scared of heights. I think she sees it as a weakness, which is probably why she doesn't like me. How about you? That stunt you pulled up there was impressive. I thought you said you didn't know any of this stuff."

"I don't. That was an accident."

"Really? Because that's probably advanced riding, at least. Probably elite."

"You're probably meant to stay on the thing while it's upside down," Kai muttered. The Talite pushed its nose against his cheek, still making the same mournful sounds.

"Oh, so *now* you're sorry," Kai said, turning away. "What were you doing up there?"

Felix smiled. "No point rejecting it now. You'll probably have to stay with that one forever now."

"What? Why?"

"It'll take a bit of time, but they recognize you by the way you ride. If you keep switching, you'll have to go through that adjusting phase every time. The second time you ride it, it'll be easier."

"Hmm. It'd better. I'd rather not die next time I go out."

The Talite sat down next to him, looking up at him expectantly. "Fine. Whatever," Kai said to it, stroking it affectionately. "No more crazy stuff next time."

Ten minutes after the lesson ended, Kai had realised that he'd forgotten to ask Ms Greeve for a textbook for revising. Felix had agreed to share his, which meant

Skyriders

that the two of them had spent the better part of the afternoon revising in the school's library.

The library was at the top of a part of the building commonly referred to as "the tower". Four floors up, the huge wall-length windows that ranged around the walls overlooked the island, letting in gaping streams of light that pooled in squares on the red carpeting.

"I think I'll call it a day," Felix said finally with a sigh, shutting his textbook. "Kai, you've written *loads*. I don't think the *textbook* had that much in it. Do you always take that many notes?"

"I won't have the textbook if I want to look over this later," Kai said. "It's best to be prepared."

"Yeah, but . . . I think there's such thing as *too* prepared."

Kai looked down at his papers scattered over the desk and sighed. "I want to do well, you know?" he said finally. "Everyone seems to think I'm going to do amazingly well at this school."

"And you don't want to let them down," Felix finished for him.

"Yeah."

"Here's some advice: take it easy for a bit. I'll lend you my textbook tonight if it's really bugging you. But I think you'd better do something else for now."

Kai nodded slowly. "Like what?"

"I don't know," Felix replied after a moment of deliberation. "You got anything you want to do?"

In the end, they simply went up to their rooms to put away their school things. Felix's room was located in a one-storey annexe on the southern side of the school. It had been constructed fairly recently to house the growing number of students, which meant that instead of crumbling brickwork and ivy growing up the walls, it had a fresh coat of white paint and a rather impressive-looking statue in front of it. His room was about the same size as Kai's, the only difference being that Kai shared his room with two people, whereas Felix had his all to himself.

"It gets kinda lonely here sometimes," Felix said, sitting on the bed. "Because I'm in apprentice school still, most of the people I know well are two years younger than me. Most people go riding in their spare time too, but I've never really got the hang of it yet. You're the only person my age I've talked to for more than ten minutes."

"What do you do, then?" Kai asked. "After school and stuff?"

Felix shrugged. "I get by. Do homework. There's a tech club on Fridays that I go to sometimes. I used to do sudoku puzzles, but I've long since finished all the ones I brought up here with me. They don't do them up here. I tried making my own ones, but it doesn't work as well."

Felix and I have more in common than he knows, Kai speculated thoughtfully. "I like sudoku," he said. "I've got some in my room."

"Really?" Felix asked, looking interested. "Can I see?"

It was getting late now; the air held a sharp edge to it, and the sky was rimmed with a pale glow at the horizon. They went back up to Kai's room. It was empty when they got in. Kai wondered what Valcor and Rafael were doing.

He reached into his drawer and pulled out one of his half-completed sudoku books. "Here."

Felix looked overjoyed. "This is so cool. Can I borrow this for a couple of days? I won't write in the book; I'll just copy some out or whatever."

"Sure, go ahead."

They talked for the next half hour, until Felix looked at his watch and saw that it was nearly time for dinner. Kai met up with his roommates again in the canteen. Rafael was doing his homework. Valcor and Sacha were having an argument about whether it was possible to fly a Talite backwards, which lasted most of the meal and involved a lot of arm waving and accusatory pointing and not enough eating.

After dinner, Kai borrowed Felix's textbook and revised alone in his room for an hour, until he felt vaguely certain that he knew the topic. He had nearly finished the chapter when Valcor burst into the room.

"Hey, Kai, what're you up to?" he asked energetically, dropping his bag onto the floor and peering inquisitively over Kai's shoulder. Rafael trailed in after him, looking tired.

"Revising," Kai replied, massaging his temples. He didn't think he could take in much more information; his mind was reeling from the revision. "We've got a test tomorrow."

"You got a test on your first day? That's harsh."

"Ms Greeve's like that," Rafael said. "You remember her, don't you?"

"I blocked out all memory of her as soon as I moved up to rider," Valcor said. "She's still in charge of the apprentices? I thought they sacked her years ago."

"Chance would be a fine thing," Kai said.

"More like you *wished* they sacked her," Rafael added. "Fortunately, she's still alive and well, should you wish to pop down to the apprentice block and say hello."

"I think I'd be better off believing she was sacked," Valcor replied with a wry smile. "Anyway, why are we talking about *school* when it's finished? I'd rather do something interesting."

FIVE

Life started to blur around the edges as it did whenever Kai found himself settling into a routine: get up, get ready for school, eat breakfast, go to school. Although he shared a lot of his lessons with Valcor and Rafael, he still didn't see much of them during school time. Valcor had an insane number of extracurricular activities, which meant that he was busy most, if not all, of his afternoons. Rafael had a less hectic lifestyle—riding off to Meridian when the weather was good or hanging around school otherwise.

Most of Kai's afternoons were spent with Felix, doing sudoku, doing homework, wandering aimlessly, or working on their veritable lack of riding skills. He met up with his roommates again at dinner, and Valcor and Sacha spent more time than not arguing over something. Kai spent most of his evenings on his own, watching the advanced riding practicals outside or in his room, doing whatever he deemed to be suitably entertaining for the hour and a half until Valcor and Rafael returned.

He was managing to keep up in most of his lessons, although barely in some cases. He found that he had a natural flair for navigational science and practical technology, especially considering he had never done those subjects before. He could just about get by in theory lessons, where he sat with Becky, but apprentice theory seemed to sail right over his head. It didn't help him much that Ms Greeve seemed to expect him to know automatically everything there was to know about riding.

In fact, nearly everything about apprentice school was a nightmare. His teacher seemed to expect him to perform miracles on a daily basis, the other kids were all considerably better at riding than he was, despite being at least three years younger than he was, and although his Talite wasn't trying to kill him anymore, he still couldn't get the hang of riding. He spent more time overbalancing, falling off, and crashing dramatically into things than he did riding properly. He was sure that someone somewhere was laughing at him.

At the end of a similarly nightmarish session, he'd hardly been at school for a month. They'd just had an hour of cultural studies, which Kai felt was one of the most tedious lessons ever formulated. It was one of those drowsy sunny days that instantly conferred a sluggish lethargy on everything, making the world seem as if it were in slow motion. He'd been struggling to keep his eyes open for the majority of the lesson, the only thing stopping him dropping off being the prospect of incurring the legendary wrath of Ms Greeve. The faint resonance of the bell jolted him out of his sleepiness.

"And while Ilyasi is still considered a dead language, its etymology can still be used to show how people lived while the language was actually in use," Ms Greeve concluded as the students started to pack away their books in their haste to leave. "Felix, Kai, Tess, I'd like a word with you three before you leave."

Kai looked over at Felix, who shrugged his shoulders. Ms Greeve typically only talked to people after class if they were in for a detention, and as far as Kai knew, he'd done nothing wrong, except that time when he'd crashed rather spectacularly into a nearby tree on his Talite, but he'd already paid the price for that.

He felt rather nervous as he approached his teacher's desk. The other kids gave the three of them curious, sympathetic looks as they slunk out of the classroom. Felix looked justifiably anxious too. Tess was staring at her feet.

Tess and Ms Greeve didn't really see eye to eye. Most of her attention seemed to be focused on her socks. If asked a question, she'd reply with a shrug or, on rare occasion, a muttered "I don't know". Ms Greeve's solution to this was to wait for prolonged periods of time for an answer, yell at her more often than not, and hand out detentions on a regular basis.

"So," Ms Greeve said ceremoniously. "Mr Shorren spoke to me about you the other day."

Mr Shorren was the headmaster of the school. Kai had only seen him once, briefly, when he'd wished him good luck at the school and deep regrets for the passing of his mother. His talking about them could only mean that this was important.

"As you know, we are always hoping that our pupils will eventually graduate from the apprentice stream. This is usually done at thirteen. Tess, you are turning fourteen, I understand, and Kai and Felix are already fifteen. So he has decided you are therefore eligible to take the upcoming test."

"But . . . I've haven't even been here for a couple of months yet," Kai said. "Why now?"

"*Because*," Ms Greeve said, as if the answer were stupidly obvious, "if you'd been remotely up to date with recent events, you'll know that there's been a *marked* increase in the number of Dracaen attacks lately. You three are all above the age where most students take the rider's test, and right now you're not learning enough dithering around in the apprentice stream."

Out of the three of them, Felix was the only one who looked relatively excited. Kai felt nothing but shock and a kind of sinking dread, as if he'd swallowed a lead weight. Tess just looked bitter.

"The test is in three weeks, and it will take three hours. It consists of a two-hour written paper, which will test you on your theory and applied knowledge of what you've been learning at school. Your one-hour practical exam will test your practical riding skills. Any questions?"

The following silence seemed to last forever.

"Good," she said, a sly smile on her face. "Off you go, then."

Felix had chess on Tuesdays, so Kai had gone back up to his room after class. Rafael was in, which was unusual. Valcor wasn't, but that was no surprise. He went to Hunters' Guild on Tuesdays.

"What's up, Kai? You look depressed."

Kai sighed heavily as he sat down at the desk.

"I'm taking the rider's test."

"Isn't that a good thing?"

"No. It's terrible."

"Why?"

"I suck at pretty much everything here: I suck at theory, I suck at riding, and the only reason I'm taking the test is probably because the head teacher doesn't like the idea of me being an apprentice. I'm so going to fail this." Everything he'd been worried about came out in one breathless, desperate sentence.

Rafael said, "You're already jumping to the worst option before you've even taken the test. I'm sure you'll pass it. Me and Val can help you if you need it, and I'm sure Sacha would be willing to help too."

Kai took a deep breath in and tried to calm down. "You're right," he said, although he was having trouble believing it himself. "I was probably overreacting. Thanks."

"No problem. I expect Felix is taking it too; he's been here long enough," Rafael said thoughtfully.

Kai nodded. "You know him?"

"Vaguely. He comes to tech club. Who else is taking it?"

"Just this other kid, Tess."

"Tess is still an apprentice?" Rafael asked, surprised. "I thought she moved up years ago."

"What? No, she's still an apprentice. She's in my class. You know her too?"

"Most people know her," Rafael said. "She has a sister in the elite stream—Becky."

"Yeah, Becky. She helps me with my theory. She's really good at it."

"She's pretty much amazing at everything. Becky qualified for rider when she was eleven, elite when she was fourteen. Tess took the test when she was twelve. Everyone thought that she'd pass, considering her sister did so well."

Kai nodded, Tess's behaviour making a bit more sense now, like how she seemed so bitter about taking the test.

Rafael got to his feet. "I think I'll be going now," he said decisively.

"Off to Meridian again?" Kai asked.

"Where else?" Rafael replied. "Do you want to come?"

Kai considered for a moment and then said, "I'll have to pass. I still can't ride. I'd probably fall off and die."

Rafael nodded. "Next time, then, huh? Work on it."

"I'll have to," Kai replied glumly as he left the room, closing the door behind him.

The next morning, in Kai's riding theory lesson, Becky spoke to him before Mrs Rawthon came in.

"I heard you're taking the rider's test," she said softly.

"Yeah," Kai replied.

She smiled at him. "That's good. I bet you'll do great."

Kai sighed. "Becky, can I ask you a favour? The test is in, like, three weeks . . . a-and I really can't ride, and you're awesome at this stuff. I . . . I mean, if you've got some spare time or anything, could you help me out?"

"Sure," Becky replied, almost immediately. "When're you free?"

"In the afternoons and evenings all week," Kai said. "I don't really do much."

"I have school in the evening. I'm free most afternoons, though. Maybe Wednesdays and Fridays?"

Kai shrugged. "That's fine."

She nodded. "Okay. I'll meet you at the field at five 'o clock."

SIX

Becky was waiting for him. Ms Greeve had kept them in late as punishment for Trey and Lucas mucking about in class, and by the time Kai went up to his room and back again, he was wildly late.

He'd recently become paranoid of being late. He rarely sought conflict—was more likely to be shying away from it—and he wasn't keen on being pounced on as soon as he entered the class, especially since Ms Greeve seemed to take great delight in dropping comments about his mother's achievements into her speech. She preyed on lateness like a predator, often stalling lesson time until the unfortunate pupil arrived and dishing out detentions more often than not. She'd then add the time they'd been waiting to the end of the day's last lesson, which punished the whole class and guaranteed frosty glares from the other pupils for the rest of the day.

Luckily, Becky didn't say anything about his lateness. She was already on her Talite, her hair floating lazily about in the breeze. Kai hurriedly mounted his own Talite (whom he'd named Farrell, in honour of his aunt) and went over to where she was standing.

"Hi," she said with a shy smile. "So . . . uh . . . what do you want to go over?"

"I don't know. I don't get what's wrong with what I'm doing. It just never seems to work."

"Well, let's see you ride. Just fly for a bit and I'll see if I can help you."

Kai guided his Talite into the air cautiously, trying to remember what he'd been told so far. He still felt apprehensive about riding, especially when getting far away from the island. All he had to do was look down at the straight drop of sky below him and the faint blue of the sea, mostly obscured by clouds beneath him, and everything seemed a whole lot harder.

Farrell wouldn't keep straight. He'd veer dangerously to the left and right, and he once stopped flying in mid-air to chase spontaneously after something small that flitted across his vision. By the time Kai landed, he was visibly shaken.

Becky looked at him curiously for a few minutes as he hopped off his Talite. "What?" Kai asked awkwardly, feeling self-conscious again.

She paused for a minute before answering. "You're good at this," she said finally.

"I think you missed me flying," Kai said. "I suck at this. I can't even get him to fly in a straight line, let alone stop him from running off whenever the feeling takes him."

She smiled. "Talites don't have genders," she said.

Kai felt embarrassed. "He feels like a boy," Kai said. "I guess I just assumed, seeing as I didn't know . . ."

"No. That's good. It shows that you've already bonded with it; you can feel its personality. Talites are like people in that respect: they have different quirks and characters that make them unique. Riding is about the bond between the Talite and the rider. Your Talite has to know you—and you, in return, have to know about your Talite."

Kai nodded. "But that doesn't explain why he doesn't listen to me. Like, he turns when I'm pretty sure I'm not telling him to."

Becky nodded. "I picked that up too. It's difficult to master the positions at first because they all seem the same, but there are subtle differences between them that you have to distinguish."

"It sounds so hard."

"It's just a matter of getting used to it. For instance, when you were trying to turn, which is a flat rotation, you were actually slanting, which is a tilted movement. Then, because you weren't expecting it, your balance shifted, which told your Talite something different—and everything repeats itself again."

"Oh," Kai said miserably.

"Don't worry; it's easy to correct this. All you need to do is revise the positions."

"How do I keep it from chasing after stuff?" Kai asked.

Becky frowned. "That I don't know. Do you spend time with it outside of school?"

Kai shook his head. "No."

"Well, maybe you should. If you let it play now, then when it comes to riding, it'll probably be more focused on riding. If you're trying to pressure it into working all the time, it'll get frustrated and won't listen so readily."

It sounded suspiciously like what Felix had said to him earlier in the library, Kai thought.

"Might as well try it now. It's our first lesson, after all, so we don't need to do anything too heavy."

Kai wasn't about to complain. They spent an hour or so just messing around in the field with his Talite, and Kai had to admit that he felt a lot less worried about everything once they finished. It seemed to be helping more than just Farrell.

Becky gave a satisfied nod. "I think we'll call that a day," she said finally. "So . . . next Wednesday, then?"

"See you then."

The three weeks seemed to whip by like lightning and crawl sluggishly along at the same time. There was so much to learn: three years of theory and practise crammed into three weeks. He learned about Keturah's history and geography, about the islands and the Deep Sky to the east, and what little there was to know about the far north. He learned about Talites and the other two Fallite species: Dracaens, which he'd already seen more of than he ever wanted to, and a less deadly species, *Redanses Fallite*, which were more often referred to as Rayeds.

Riding was the tricky part. Becky was a great teacher, easily trumping Ms Greeve. Their lessons were the only thing that kept him from veering off into complete panic. They had six lessons in total, excluding their first. Her theory was to take each position one lesson at a time instead of all at once in twenty minutes, as his apprentice teacher had deemed sufficient.

She had a way of teaching that was so easy to understand, probably because she lacked the condescending superiority and general aura of menace that Ms Greeve wielded on a regular basis. She taught him different things too, little bits of advanced theory when she thought it was relevant and half a lesson on slanting because he still couldn't distinguish a clear difference between slanting and turning.

Their first lesson was about basic and first positions. Because it was the easiest lesson, he quickly grasped the concept of it. Just before the end of their lesson on second position, Becky had stopped, pointing to a distant figure in the sky, shooting vertically upwards on a Talite. Kai wouldn't have been able to tell who it was, but her distinctive deep blue hair gave her away. It was Wave, the girl he'd ridden with on his first day, subsequently giving him the encounter which still made him feel sick thinking about it.

Wave was something of a legend at the school. Pretty much everyone had something or other to say about her, ranging from urban myths like the fact that she'd graduated to rider when she was eight, to random observances such as that blue really was her natural hair colour. Kai wondered what Becky thought of her.

"Something to aim for," Becky said with a shy grin as Wave levelled off before expertly performing a loop in mid-air.

"Are you kidding? I'll never be that good."

"I think you will. You're a fast learner, and you and your Talite are already close. Those are signs of a great rider."

Kai didn't say anything for a while, instead focusing his attention on Wave with silent awe. To be able to fly like that without fear that something was going to go terribly wrong seemed so far out of reach, yet part of him desperately wished he *could* do that. He wondered what it felt like dipping and looping freely through the air, each movement revealing years of flawless skill.

The next lesson was on third position.

"Third's probably the hardest of all the positions," Becky told him. "So don't worry if you don't get it immediately. Let's just start flying in a straight line for now."

Farrell wasn't concentrating; he'd been restless all day and was prowling around the field, sniffing at flowers growing amongst the grass and rolling around on his back. Becky's Talite was curled up beside her, watching him play with apparent disdain.

"Come on," Kai said softly to him, rubbing his head to get him to focus. Farrell flipped back over onto all fours and nudged Kai with his warm, wet nose before springing backwards and chirruping eagerly. Kai hurriedly assembled his gear and hopped onto his back.

Flying in straight lines was easier now. Kai was getting the hang of riding, and he completed the first task easily. The sharp breeze flowed into his face as he picked up speed, Farrell's fur flicking out behind him.

"Good," Becky said with a nod as he landed beside her. "Your riding's definitely improved. Now let's get some turns in. Remember, you can't turn in third, so switch to one of the other positions. Second is easiest."

Kai started with rather wide turns, tracing an invisible oval in the air as he flew. Feeling more confident, he tried some narrower turns, flying low around the side of the apprentice block, but for some reason, Farrell wouldn't turn as he tilted. He wobbled precariously and then lost his grip completely, falling with a lurching jolt of fear that snapped into a dull pain as he hit the ground a few seconds earlier.

Farrell gave an apologetic chirp as Kai stood up, his arm throbbing where he'd landed on it.

"You were still in third," Becky said. "Try again."

The second time, he managed it three-quarters of the way around before he tumbled off for the second time.

"Why is this so difficult?" Kai complained, brushing a couple of leaves out of his hair.

"Your movements are too subtle right now," Becky told him. "The key thing here is to get the position right. The movement falls into place later. Exaggerate the change from third to second if you must. Try again."

Kai started to settle into a rhythm. *Switch, turn, change back . . .* kept repeating like a mantra in his head, and he shakily curved around the corners of the apprentice block, so focused on the task that it was only when he saw Becky standing in the grass below him that he realised what had happened.

"You did it, Kai! See, I told you it was all right."

Farrell was getting bored now, winding up Becky's Talite by snuffling in its ear. Becky looked thoughtfully at him.

"Okay, let's really test your skills. How about a race?"

Kai looked doubtfully at her. "A race? Where?"

"Just in the orchard." Becky gestured to the dense coppice of apple trees just behind the apprentice block. Most of the fruit had fallen to the ground by now in the face of winter, rotting gently into the ground. "Keep low so if you do fall, it won't hurt. Don't go higher than the treetops."

"But there are trees everywhere," Kai said.

Becky grinned, jumping back onto her Talite. "That's the point. First one to make it to the other side wins. And the trees are school property, so try not to crash into them."

Kai hastily mounted Farrell.

"Ready . . . and . . . go!"

Farrell jumped forwards in a burst of speed, flicking eagerly into the orchard with Becky just behind him, swiftly nipping between the slender trunks of the trees. After the first few seconds, Kai realised what a challenge this really was. The trees popped up in front of him with startling speed, Kai just barely missing some of them, and all the time Becky was inching farther and farther into the lead. Kai's pulse was racing with adrenaline, fear of crashing headfirst into something mingling with excitement as the orchard blurred around them.

A shout in the distance broke his concentration, and despite himself, he turned to look. Farrell gave a cry of alarm as a tree loomed in front of them, right in their way. Snapping back into focus, Kai tried to swerve. Farrell wouldn't move.

Kai thought desperately, trying to remember the position for second, but panic obscured his mind and he couldn't remember. Desperately, he threw everything he knew into oblivion and flung himself to the side, still gripping onto the band around Farrell's neck, and he spun sideways in a tight corkscrew, tucking his wings in close to his body to avoid clipping the tree, before unfurling again, wings flashing.

Kai's mind reeled, spinning with dizziness and exhilaration, and he slowed down to try to clear his mind. The looming crisis had taken the edge off his speed, and there was no way he could catch up with Becky when he was that far behind, but he'd never really expected to beat her anyway. He burst out of the orchard, nearly barrelling into her as they left.

"How'd it go?" she asked. "You did that pretty quickly. No falling over?"

"Nearly hit a tree," Kai said breathlessly, his arm throbbing slightly with a dull pain from where he'd fallen earlier. "I'm getting the hang of it, though."

She nodded. "Good. I guess that concludes our lesson for today. See you next week."

But the apprentice exam was just round the corner, and Kai was getting a familiar sinking feeling as the test loomed over him like a thundercloud. By the time they'd reached their last lesson, he was feeling the familiar fronds of uncertainty set in.

He didn't want to fail. He couldn't fail. Everyone seemed to be counting in him to pass the test: Ms Greeve, Mr Shorren, even his mother. He didn't want to ruin her esteemed reputation by screwing up his test. This must have been pretty evident on his face because as they met for their final lesson, Becky picked up on it almost immediately.

"What's up, Kai?" she asked.

He shrugged. "Nothing."

"Well, it's our last lesson. What do you want to do?"

Kai shrugged again. "I don't know. You're the teacher."

In the end, they went on a ride across the island together to brush up on their skills. Normally, Kai would have been excited, but nervousness still got the better of him.

"I don't think I can do this, Becky," he said finally as they landed back at the school. It was getting late; the sun had set and the light was withdrawing, the darkness spilling in to replace it. It would be night soon.

"Of course you can. You're the best pupil I've ever had."

"I'm the only pupil you've ever had," Kai said, forcing a smile.

"That makes you the best by default, then, doesn't it?" she said with a grin. "Come on, Kai. You'll do great. You've picked everything up so quickly."

"I don't feel like that. Ask me a question."

"Fine." She paused, considering this. "You're flying flat out, low over the school. What position?"

"Second."

She smiled. "Why?"

"You'll need the extra agility if you're flying low, especially over the school. And it's fast too."

"There you are, see? Perfect answer."

"That was easy, though. Ask me something harder."

"Harder? Fine, let's see. Vertical drop from the edge of this cliff. Providing you want to survive, what would you do? That's considering you're still an apprentice so stick to basic theory."

Kai paused for a while. "Attack."

Becky considered this. "I was going to say defence or first. You need the grip if you're going to pull up sharply."

"But if you slant to the left slightly, then you'll do it in a curve, like this." He demonstrated with his hand, adding a fluid curve out to the side as he neared the bottom. "It'll take the edge off your pull so you won't need as much grip."

There was a long, contemplative silence. Then finally Becky spoke. "Show me."

Kai hesitated for a minute. He then got to his feet, patted Farrell lightly on the head to arouse him from his half doze he'd settled in since they'd arrived, and mounted him quickly. They padded to the edge of the cliff. Kai looked down at the edge of the grass, into the gloomy depths of the sky below. He could see the inky blackness of the dark sea beneath him, an empty dark void in the night.

It seemed so much easier when he'd mentioned it earlier.

At Kai's command, Farrell leaped into the air, then twisted and shot downwards like an arrow. *At least I don't have to worry about hitting the ground*, Kai thought wryly as air whooshed past his ears, almost deafening him. Sensing he'd covered enough distance, Kai braced himself mentally for what could either get extremely interesting or rather messy.

On the grass above him, Becky peered over the edge, half anxiously, half curiously. She'd never heard a suggestion like that before, like the one he gave. It was so outlandish, so unexpected, just plain crazy. But if it worked, it would definitely be something worth watching.

"Who's that?"

Becky jumped and looked around. Standing next to her was Wave, watching Kai dive with an unreadable expression on her face. Becky vaguely remembered seeing her riding earlier that afternoon. She must have passed them on her way to the stables.

"Kai. I'm teaching him how to ride."

She snorted. "More like how best to commit suicide."

Wave had never spoken to her before of her own free will. Becky didn't know what to think about her. She admired her deep down, but she was so cold and unforgiving on the outside that Becky always felt a bit uneasy around her.

"This is different. He's showing me something. I asked him what to do in a vertical drop situation, and he said attack position."

Wave raised an eyebrow, her voice incredulous. "That definitely sounds like suicide to me. Why'd you let him do it?"

Becky said, "He seemed pretty confident about this. His theory was to slant it at the bottom, instead of pulling up."

Wave tilted her head slightly, considering this. "Hmm."

"And if it didn't work, he'd probably just switch into defence and pull up like most people would do." Becky was feeling slightly more confident for both her and Kai.

Wave was clearly unconvinced. "Now this I have to see."

Kai inhaled sharply, his fingers tightening against the band around Farrell's neck. Now that he was actually doing it, his suggestion seemed a lot more dangerous. Attack had little grip; all you had to do was lean too much to ruin your balance, and falling off and dying dramatically was probably the most likely option from there.

You could just back out. You're still an apprentice anyway. Nobody really expects you to do this.

For some reason, Kai couldn't quite get himself to agree with his logic. Something—some insane, reckless urging—drove him onwards. He raised his body slightly, leaning forwards over the Talite's head before tilting slightly to the left, the wind and the approaching evening screaming in his ears. The Talite slowed before swinging in a wide curve to the left, picking up speed again as it looped upwards. The lights of the school and Meridian and Tireya in the distance flickered above like millions of sharp fireflies set out against the sky. Clearer than ever, he could see the moon, a sliver of silver in the sky, and stars flecking the horizon. He let out a whoop of joy as exhilaration overtook him, making the deep colours of the night seem brighter, more vivid. He was feeling more alive than he ever had before.

This was *amazing.*

Farrell made some joyful clicking noises as they hurtled back upwards in wide loops through the sky, clearly enjoying it as much as Kai was. Below him, Becky gave a little yell of excitement, of relief, her eyes riveted on him. Beside her, Wave watched just as intently. A flicker of something, of awe, of admiration, passed over her face as he shot upwards before dropping back onto the island and landing rather shakily.

"See?" Kai said happily and somewhat breathlessly as he slid off his Talite, his eyes alight with exhilaration. "Oh, hi . . . Uh . . . ?"

He'd caught sight of Wave standing by Becky. Not quite sure what to make of this unexpected visit, he let his voice trail off instead. He only remembered her because she'd seemingly tried to kill him that first time they'd met.

"Kai, that was incredible!" Becky breathed, hardly able to control her excitement.

Wave tilted her head to one side, never taking her eyes off him. "Kai? Hunter, right? Faye's son? When's the test, then?"

"Tomorrow."

"Well, at least you've got the festival to look forward to afterwards," Becky told him. "As a reward for all the work you've put in."

"What festival?" Kai asked.

"The spring festival. It's in a couple of weeks," Becky said. "To celebrate the beginning of spring—or, you know, something like that."

"It's just an excuse to party, really," Wave replied dismissively. "Nobody complains because you get a free holiday out of it." Then, after a short pause: "Good luck with your test."

Kai watched her go, unsure if she was mocking him or genuinely wishing him luck.

"Don't mind her," Becky said. "You did great! You'll do great tomorrow too, I'll bet. No need to worry."

Kai let out a shaky breath. "So was that a pass, then?"

Becky grinned. "Slanting's still advanced theory, no matter how awesome it is. You failed."

As soon as he entered his room, Kai picked up his dossier of notes that he'd complied over the past three weeks and opened it up. He'd promised Felix he wouldn't go crazy on the revision that night, but it wouldn't hurt to just look over them before he went to bed. Especially now, when Valcor and Rafael were still in school and the room was peaceful and quiet.

The notes were an impressive collection of things straight out of the textbook, things he'd been told by his teachers in his lessons, and sheets he'd copied from what Valcor and Rafael had salvaged from when they were apprentices. It was now thick and heavy, at least a hundred pages long, and it sat on his bedside table for him to study whenever he had the chance.

He revised flat out for three hours. He vaguely registered Valcor and Rafael coming in and greeting him, but he couldn't remember replying, and he didn't know what they did after that. His mind was reeling and blurring dangerously as he struggled to pack in whatever would still fit into his memory. It was five to eleven when Rafael touched him lightly on the shoulder, dropping him into reality with a harsh thud.

"Kai, that's enough," he said seriously. "Get some sleep. You look like you need it."

"I've only got twenty pages left, Raf," Kai protested. "Then I'll go to bed."

"C'mon, Kai," Valcor agreed. "Take a break. You've done enough already. *I* didn't revise nearly half as much as this and I still passed."

"Yeah, but you've been learning this stuff for years."

Quickly, Rafael leaned over and swiped Kai's dossier from the desk while he wasn't looking. "No more revising," he said firmly. "I'm not sure if there's such a thing as death by revision, but I don't want you to be a victim. The test is easy. Now go and get some sleep."

"What's actually in the test? Like, what are we meant to do in the practical and stuff?"

"In the practical? Well, usually they'll tell you to go somewhere, typically to another island, in a set time period. They'll give you a map and bearings so you know where you're going. One of the teachers will follow you in the background, marking you on all the criteria, and if you get into trouble, they can come and help quickly, although it'll mean you lose marks. Also, they don't mark you on attack and defence, although it looks good if you slip it in somewhere. That's it, okay? They're not gonna ask you to do anything they know you can't do; it's not worth all this worry."

Valcor said gravely, "Rafael's right, Kai. You've probably memorised the whole thing already."

"I don't want to fail, guys. I really don't."

"If you fail, I'm happy to give you my dinner for the next month. With all the work you've done, I'd say your chance of failing is about as likely as the moon dropping clean out of the sky."

Rafael nodded in agreement and put Kai's dossier in his bedside table. "Confiscated. You can have this tomorrow. Don't look at me like that, Kai; you'll do fine."

SEVEN

The following morning brought a cold, greyish dawn, occasional whispers of wind drawing sharp bursts of bitter air through gaps under the door. Kai woke up with the beginnings of a headache, a bleary haze of sleep enveloping him, and the thrill of what was going to happen that day making his pulse race.

Everything around him seemed to be moving in slow motion. He kept glancing at the clock during his first few lessons, thinking ten minutes had passed, yet the second hand hadn't quite clocked a full sixty seconds. He couldn't concentrate on what the teacher was saying. It felt as if life were suddenly so far away. It felt as if he were looking down on himself from above. It felt weird.

Ms Greeve came to collect him halfway through geography. She didn't even bother knocking, just barging through the door instead, ruler in hand. Their geography teacher, Mr Ira, dropped his board pen as she marched in. He looked worried.

Valcor gave Kai a nudge as he grabbed his belongings and got up to leave. "Good luck," he said, and Sacha gave him an encouraging grin and a wave. Tess was already waiting outside, her gaze focused on the floor. They collected Felix from his natural science lesson in room

2. He looked excited but slightly nervous. Kai was just nervous.

"I'm moderating you three for the written paper," Ms Greeve said to them as they ascended the stone steps of the tower. She pushed the door of the library open and led them inside. "That means no talking, no communication, no nothing. If you make one noise you're not meant to, you're out. Got it?"

There was another door at the far end of the library, a door Kai hadn't previously noticed. Behind it was a small room with nothing but four desks with chairs and a moderator's desk at the front. Kai sat down, feeling worried. What if he opened the test and couldn't answer a single question? What if he forgot everything? What if . . . ?

"The test lasts ninety minutes," Ms Greeve announced, sliding a booklet onto their desks. "Start now."

There was the sound of rustling paper as the three of them opened their papers. Kai flicked through his, skimming the exam. He recognized the questions, answers already flicking through his mind. He forced himself to relax.

It's cool, he thought to himself. *I can do this.*

Picking up his pen, he started to write.

"Time's up," Ms Greeve barked suddenly. Kai looked up sharply, his head fizzing from all the brainwork. His hand ached too. He flexed his fingers, trying to lessen the dull, persistent throb it emitted as Ms Greeve swept around the room, deftly collecting their papers and storing them in her ageing rucksack. Beside him, Felix gave an exaggerated stretch and grinned.

"Glad that's over," he said. He sounded as if he were enjoying himself. "How'd you find it?"

"Tough," Kai admitted. Now that the test was over and collected, he felt a bit more relieved. He didn't know how he'd done. Sometimes he could sense exactly what kind of answer the examiner wanted. This time it was more of a shot in the dark. "You?"

Felix shrugged. "Not too bad. Although that section on night riding totally killed me."

"We're in the middle of a weather conditions topic in our theory," Kai said gratefully. "We just did a lesson on night riding. So I guess I've got something to be happy for."

"Lucky," Felix said enviously. "So how do you think you did?"

"Don't know. I can never tell. I think I did okay."

Felix grinned. "That's the spirit. A bit of optimism never killed anybody."

Ms Greeve rapped loudly on the desk with her beloved ruler, silencing them. There were many rumours about her ruler and how she never went anywhere without it. Some said she was given it as a present from the ruling family on Meridian for some adventurous deed or other. Some were adamant that it concealed a secret sword that she used to strike dead any pupils who disobeyed her. Some went as far as to say she slept with it at night and talked to it when she thought nobody was looking.

"Let's go, kiddies," she snapped. "We don't want to be late for the practical exam, now do we?"

The practical wasn't on the field, as Kai had expected. Instead, Ms Greeve took the three of them and their Talites off the school grounds and through the small town centre, where a ring of tall buildings sold a wide variety of products, from food and clothing to beautifully hand-carved decorative furniture and a bookstore. It was three in the afternoon, during the middle of the week, so it was rather quiet in the village. A few people were milling around, some admiring the decor on the mirrors or buying small loaves of bread.

Beyond the town was an open expanse of rolling plains, the base of a huge, looming mountain just in front of them. It was getting warmer that late afternoon, but the air still held a bitter tinge to it, and Kai found himself shivering.

The senior staff team were already there waiting for them. Mr Shorren stood in the middle, his sharp green eyes regarding the three wordlessly. To his left and right sides stood John as well as Kai's navigational science teacher, Mr Tanner. Mrs Snowe was the final teacher; Kai hadn't seen her before.

"Welcome," Mr Shorren said calmly, "to the practical section of your rider's exam. I hope the first test wasn't too difficult?"

Indistinct acquiescent murmurs were offered in response to his question. Mr Shorren nodded and continued, turning round to face the huge mountain in front of him.

"Summit Peak," he announced, stretching his arms wide. His scarf—emblazoned with the school's logo—flapped madly behind him in a sudden gust of cold air. "The tallest mountain in all of Keturah. For centuries, it has been the emblem of Tissarel; people come from all over the region to visit. Partway up the mountain is a platform cut into the rock face," Mr Shorren said. "Follow me up there and I will tell you what your task is for today."

Skyriders

Kai glanced briefly up at the mountain again. The peak looked staggeringly high, the craggy rock face imposing. A staircase had been carved into one side of the mountain about halfway up, but up until then, it was all free climbing.

Mr Shorren deftly mounted his Talite, and with an exuberant cry, it shot upwards, spiralling in a vertical line into the sky before levelling off into a horizontal plane, neatly landing on a platform-like ledge on the side of the mountain. Kai gaped at them. He was pretty sure he hadn't learned to do that yet, especially not that fluently. He was surely screwed.

The other teachers followed suit, their Talites smoothly ducking and weaving between each others' flight paths as they rose to join the head teacher. John whispered some advice to them just before he took off.

"Vertical flying's elite theory. You won't be expected to do that now. Just get there any way you can. Good luck."

Kai hastily clambered up onto Farrell's back. He gave an anxious whine, pawing at the ground, his tail waving uncertainly from side to side.

"It's okay, Farrell," he said reassuringly, leaning forwards to stroke his head gently. Beside him, Tess took off, ascending in uncertain circles to where the teachers were gathered. "It'll be fun. You'll probably enjoy it more than I will."

He nodded quickly at Felix, who looked rather pale, mouthed *good luck*, and took off, ascending slowly into the air. He felt Farrell start to calm down as they rose, and his Talite's growing confidence relaxed Kai too.

He landed shakily at the edge of the platform, Felix close behind. The view was stunning. To the northeast, he could see just about as far as Meridian. The school looked impossibly tiny, the pupils entering and leaving the building almost imperceptible.

"Wow," he murmured.

"This is certainly . . . high," Felix remarked.

Mr Shorren nodded. "The view is marvellous, don't you think? It's much better when you're right at the top. I would have liked to conduct the test from the summit myself, but we simply don't have time . . ." His voice trailed off wistfully, but he regained his composure. "But on to more important matters. To the northeast of here is a small island that, strictly speaking, is a shared territory between Tissarel and the nearby island of Tireya. Its name is Rakesh Isle, a small guard outpost. You should be able to see the guard tower there as you get closer. For your test, you will simply have to fly to the island and back, but Mr Tanner, Ms Greeve, and I will accompany you and monitor your flying ability carefully—as well as discreetly. We will mark you in three areas: your position, your methods, and the communication between you and your Talite. We expect you to utilize as much of the apprentice training you have learned as possible. Any questions?"

The three of them shook their heads. Kai couldn't see the island Mr Shorren was talking about, which concerned him slightly, but Farrell seemed to know what he was doing, and in the worst-case scenario, he could always simply follow the other two. Mr Tanner handed a map to each of them in turn, showing the location of where they were heading.

"You may leave when you're ready," Mr Shorren said. "Best of luck to you all."

Kai nudged Farrell into ascending, quickly feeling himself relax as the comforting familiarity of riding settled on him. He realised something with a start: riding had become commonplace for him now. At first, it had been unfamiliar and perplexingly difficult. Now he was used to it. A newfound confidence washed over his consciousness, and Farrell gave a pleased chirp, as if he'd been waiting his whole life for that to happen.

Fifteen minutes into the journey, Kai caught his first sight of the island: a mostly uninhabited small speck of rock floating just in front of the horizon.

"See that, Farrell?" Kai murmured. "That's where we're headed."

He said that mainly to focus his Talite, who seemed to be far more interested in the little flying bugs that occasionally flitted into view. Kai hoped desperately that Farrell wouldn't chase after them, especially not today. He tried to convey his worries to his Talite multiple times during the journey there. He wasn't sure if Farrell was getting the message.

But the journey there passed uneventfully. When they were within about five minutes of reaching the island, Farrell suddenly slowed down of his own accord, startling Kai out of an uneasy daydream he'd fallen into.

"What's up?" he asked, and then, figuring Farrell wasn't exactly going to come right out and tell him, looked up to see for himself. He felt his heart sink.

"Oh."

In front of Rakesh Isle was a field of floating rocks, varying in size from small rocks the size of his fist to rocks that were taller than he was. Negotiating their way through them would be a nightmare.

Things got worse when he neared the rock field and noticed a nest of the small bugs that had been worrying Kai through the journey. They were inside a hollow in one of the rocks, the insects flitting about without a care in the world.

"No chasing after those things, please?" Kai said uncertainly. "If we pass, I'll take you here myself and you can go as mad as you please. Just not today."

Kai wasn't sure if Farrell had got the message, but he started them forwards anyway, praying to some higher being that he'd understood. The rock field was as perilous as he'd expected. Felix and Tess seemed to be doing much better than he was, looping smoothly in and out of the rocks, while he stuck to first position all the way, guiding Farrell through them at a snail's pace. He was the last to reach the island, but that didn't worry him too much because he was more concerned about getting there in one piece. Mr Shorren and the two other teachers landed behind him.

"We'll take a short break before we head back again," he said. "You're all doing very well, I must say."

There wasn't much worth doing on the island. It was mainly barren, rocky landscape, so small you could see from end to end of it without trying too hard. The only things of interest were a small cabin at the opposite end, presumably empty, and a guard tower in the middle, built sturdily of stone. At an opening in the top, there was a wide window with what appeared to be the barrel of some kind of cannon, the faint silhouette of a man working the tower. He waved at them as they landed.

Kai mentally reviewed his performance on the journey there. He thought he'd done well so far, and Farrell seemed to be reasonably focused. It was easy enough to judge how well he'd been doing on the positions scale. He'd tried to cover most of the positions, with varying degrees of success. Method was harder to judge, mainly because Kai had no idea what it entailed. The last category, communication with his Talite, he wasn't too sure of either, although if what Becky and Rafael had told him was correct, he should do just fine.

Mr Shorren clapped his hands loudly, signally the end of their rest period. "All right, shall we get going? The quicker we get back, the better—"

He was cut off by the loud sound of a bell ringing from the guard tower. Mr Shorren froze midsentence before glancing around and talking to the students in a rapid, quiet voice.

"Get out of the way."

The three of them exchanged bemused glances, but Mr Tanner looked concerned as he ushered them behind one of the larger rocks.

"What's going on?" Kai asked.

"The man at the guard tower," Mr Tanner explained. "The bell means he's seen something."

"A Dracaen?" Felix asked anxiously.

Mr Tanner nodded grimly. "Most likely. Don't worry; the bell's just a warning. If it looks like it's coming close, the guy will take care of it."

They waited in a tense, breathless silence. Suddenly, there was a harsh, loud shriek that made Kai flinch, and a Dracaen swerved into vision. There was a sudden hollow pop from the guard tower and a flickering whirr of air, and then the Dracaen gave a furious growl. Unable to stop himself, Kai peered round the side of the rock. The Dracaen was on its back, legs thrashing against a net that had hopelessly snared it, weighted to the ground with metal balls.

They slowly got out from behind their hiding place as the man who ran the guard tower jumped out and hurried over to it, springing out of the way as the Dracaen tried to snap angrily at him, a long, silver sword gripped firmly in his hands.

"Are you gonna kill it?" Tess asked.

"I have to," the man said, bringing the sword down with a brief, violent thrust. The light in the Dracaen's eyes died as the sword pierced its heart. "It could have killed much more of us if it ever got to Tissarel—or anywhere else."

"Do you get many Dracaens passing this way?" Mr Shorren asked.

"Quite a few," the man said. "My job's gotten more interesting lately. They're thinking of upping the security around here to two or three guards if this keeps up. Well, you all have a safe journey back, won't you?"

He nodded a farewell and returned to the guard tower. Mr Shorren looked at the three apprentices. Kai glanced briefly at the dead Dracaen at his feet, feeling an inwards shudder of repulsion.

"Sorry you had to see that," he said. "Shall we continue?"

Kai managed to persuade himself to switch into third for brief, sporadic parts of the return flight, although he didn't trust himself to remain that way for too long. He was in one such reckless phase when suddenly something small and sliver flashed across his vision. Much to his alarm, Kai felt Farrell's muscles tense in anticipation for something. This wasn't good . . .

"Farrell, no!" Kai said in alarm, barely managing to adjust his position in time for Farrell to suddenly dash sideways, trying to snap at the tiny creature, veering away from the other two candidates, who looked at him with suitably startled expressions. Kai pulled desperately on his band, trying to get his attention, but to no avail. In a last attempt to subdue his Talite, Kai considered calling out to one of the teachers for help, but at that moment the bug wriggled out of Farrell's grasp and flitted out of range. Farrell stopped chasing it, instead giving an uncertain whine.

"I said no chasing things," Kai said sternly, his voice cracking with apprehension. He was probably going to fail for sure now. "Do you want me to fail?"

Farrell let out a joyful clicking sound and shot up into the sky, looping round in a large circle before returning to his somewhat more expected trajectory. Kai wasn't sure what to make of that, so he let it slide, blithely hoping that Mr Shorren and the other two teachers were simultaneously otherwise occupied during the escapade. But he couldn't stop the inevitable sinking feeling that descended upon him as they landed.

Mr Shorren beamed at them. "Very good. You've all done marvellously. I think that concludes your exam. You are free to leave."

Both Valcor and Rafael were in the room when Kai pushed open his room door, which, considering it was just past four in the afternoon, surprised him to no end.

"You're back," Valcor said eagerly.

"Don't you have a club today?"

"It was cancelled. Mr Tanner was with you apprentice kiddies."

"So," Rafael said. "How'd it go?"

"Okay," Kai said. He quickly added, "We saw a Dracaen on the way there."

"What, really?" Valcor asked. "Did you get attacked or anything?"

"Nah," Kai replied. "The guy in the guard tower killed it."

"Where'd you go?"

"Rakesh Isle."

"What, that little island?" Rafael said. "Must be running out of places."

"I thought they always went to the same place."

"They like to mix it up a bit, probably so you can't plan your route beforehand. Makes sense, although some of the places are a bit strange. I know someone who had to go all the way to Astlar and back in a one-hour slot."

"Where'd you go?"

Rafael grinned. "Meridian. We didn't stop for long, though, so it wasn't too exciting."

"He got lucky," Valcor chipped in. "*I* had to make do with the Firdes. We sat for two minutes right next to this huge swamp. By the time we left, we were covered in mud, and Ms Greeve wouldn't let us back inside until we'd washed the dirt off our Talites in the freezing cold and everything. I'd have traded it for Rakesh Isle any day."

"I probably screwed it up. There are these floating rocks in front of it, and we were this close to hitting a few of them."

Valcor shrugged. "I bet you did fine. At least you've done it now, so it's all good. And you've got the spring festival to look forward to next week."

"It's still on? I heard they were going to cancel it," Rafael said. "Because of the Dracaens and everything."

"They were thinking about it, but apparently everything's under control. They've got patrols going round, and the emergency response team are on high alert should anything happen. And it's such an important tradition, so nobody really wants to miss it. You should come with us, Kai," Valcor added. "Its good fun, and we get two days off school."

"Who's going?"

"I'm going—so is Sacha. Pretty much everyone goes, at least for one day. Since it's your first time, you won't want to miss it. You'll come, right?"

Kai said, "Yeah, why not?"

A loud rapping on the door snapped Kai awake from the lazy sleep he'd drifted into. Early morning sunlight streamed onto his face in square patches as he forced himself out of bed and over to the door, rubbing the sleep out of his eyes.

"Huh?"

"Kai, hey. Sorry it's so early. Were you sleeping?"

"Felix, it's seven o' clock. On Saturday."

"I'll be quick. This is yours."

It was a small brown envelope with his name written on it in smooth, slanting cursive. Kai was still half-asleep, so he didn't realize what Felix had given him until he'd half opened it.

"Wait, this is . . ."

Felix grinned. "And *now* he gets it."

"You woke me up," Kai said defensively. "You can't expect me to jump to conclusions already. Here, come in so I can read this. Do you have yours?"

"Yeah. Mr Tanner asked me to deliver them this morning."

"What were you doing up so early?"

"Observation club," Felix explained, following Kai inside his room. "It ties in with navigational science. You sort of go out and look at the stars and stuff in the early morning. You've got to wake up early, but it's fun."

Valcor had woken up by now and was blinking sleepily at them. "I thought you didn't like waking up early on weekends."

Kai brandished his envelope at him. "Got my results," he said, forgetting to be nervous in the wake of his excitement.

"Well, open it," Valcor said. "Let's see how you did."

Kai pulled open the envelope, taking out a single sheet of paper. His eyes immediately flicked to the bottom of the paper, where his final mark was, and he breathed a sigh of relief when he caught sight of the word PASS written there.

"What'd you get?" Valcor peered inquisitively over his shoulder.

"Pass," Kai said, surprised to feel his heart hammering even now.

Valcor cheered enthusiastically and clapped his hands; then realising that Rafael was still sleeping, he stopped abruptly. He cast a guilty look over at him, but Rafael hadn't stirred.

"What'd you get, Felix?" Kai asked.

"I passed too, which was surprising because I totally screwed up the practical. I was so nervous . . ."

"I was nervous too," Kai agreed. "And Farrell was being a bit jumpy. He kept chasing after stuff."

Felix and Valcor looked at him blankly.

"Who's Farrell?" Felix asked.

"Oh . . . That's just the name I gave him . . . uh . . . my Talite, I mean. Don't you name yours?"

Valcor shook his head. "It's not that common. I know a couple of people who've named them, but seeing as Talites don't always respond to voice commands, there didn't seem to be much point."

Kai nodded and then said to Felix, "You coming to the festival next week?"

"I was thinking about it. It's probably not much fun if you're on your own, though. Also, some people are saying it's dangerous, with all the Dracaens and stuff."

"Come with us," Valcor said. "Kai's going too. The more people, the better. And Rafael said they've got patrols going round, too, so you don't have to worry about it."

"That'd be cool," Felix said.

"Are we . . . riding there?" Kai asked.

"'Course," Valcor replied cheerfully. "Don't look so worried. It's not long from here to the Firdes. Besides, you're a rider now. Hey, does that mean you'll be in our class?"

Kai said, "I don't know. I guess I'll need a new timetable. Again."

"On the plus side, we're finally away from Ms Greeve," Felix noted. "Man, my life looks a whole lot better now."

EIGHT

Kai had never seen so many colours in all his life.

The place wasn't dissimilar to a steam fair. Kai had been fond of them when he was younger; he'd go with his mother and they would go crazy on all of the rides before crashing out in a candyfloss stall and doing serious damage to their dental health. The memory brought back a fierce wave of nostalgia.

A loud, jaunty tune warbled through the narrow streets of the town centre, distracting him. Rippling with the excited voices of the jostling multitude of people that crowded the paths, it gathered volume until it was soaring above their heads, the ground trembling beneath their feet in the wake of the pulsing beat, but even the inescapable melody couldn't beat the swirling mass of colours that surrounded him. There was every hue and shade, draped across buildings in garish banners or littering the floor as lilting confetti, sweeping and twirling in a crescendo of colour.

Valcor grinned at him. "You'll get used to the noise," he shouted over the incessant driving music.

"I really don't think I will," Kai said tentatively.

"This beats school by miles," Sacha said. "I love festivals. There should be one every month, at least. What're we gonna do first?"

Valcor shrugged. "Wander around? I'm sure you'll find something."

And that she did, less than a minute later.

"Val, guys! Look at this!"

There was a small crowd assembled in front of a wide circle of fenced-off ground. A group of four performers had just started up their act: an elaborate dance routine complete with a daredevil's touch—a long staff, the ends surrounded with glowing balls of fire. Kai watched, transfixed, as they deftly interlaced blazing trails of fire, mimicking their fluid movements.

"Wow," Sacha breathed. "I'd like to learn how to do that. How'd they manage not to get burned? Look how close the fire is to them!"

"Come back here when the sun's down," Valcor said knowingly. "This is just a warm-up. The good stuff happens when it's dark. You can see the fire better."

They moved on, merging with the crowds again. There was no lack of things to do: everywhere they turned, there were different stalls and performances. Everything one could dream of was there in some form or another: elaborate plays, craft sessions, stalls selling blown glass figures or samples of a variety of brightly coloured fruits, Northern dance lessons and fortune-tellers, and everything in between. Occasionally, Valcor or Sacha would meet people they knew well from school and start up conversations about which stalls were worth seeing, which usually resulted in their going to see what they were talking about, bouncing hysterically from place to place. By midday, Kai was exhausted, his feet already aching.

Valcor brought the four of them lunch from a nearby food shop, which they ate just outside by an ornamental rock pool. Kai was happy to listen in silence to the accumulated cacophony of at least twenty different conversations going on within his range of hearing.

Sometime during the course of the meal, Rafael arrived, accompanied by the girl with the hat who'd sat with them at dinner at school, and Valcor and Felix left with him a few seconds later to have a go at a game stall they'd spotted awhile back. Kai stayed with the two girls while he finished off his meal, his attention straying away from his companions to a heated conversation going on beside him.

"It hit him on the side, like, *wham*! Just like that. He hardly looked at it. It just attacked him."

"That's terrible! Is he okay?"

"Jaraiya took him to the medic. He said he'll be fine. But seriously, when's the last time you heard something like that happen?"

"Actually, there are a lot of stories going round like that."

"No kidding? Who else said that?"

"Mawyer. He says his girlfriend saw a couple off the side of Astlar. They didn't attack him or anything, but he saw 'em just the same."

"Remember Teklah? That old lady keeps going on about it. You know, the one who said she was there when the city got destroyed? She says we're all doomed to the same fate if this keeps up."

"She's crazy. Everyone knows she's crazy."

"You know, I don't think so. In fact . . ."

"Hey, Kai, Yoko and I are gonna go watch this guy throw knives at stuff. Do you wanna come?"

Jolted out of the doze he'd slipped into listening to the conversation next to him, Kai took a few seconds to adjust himself before replying. "Yeah, sure."

Sacha got pulled out to be a volunteer for the act, which mainly involved having a variety of knives thrown at her from impressive distances, to the great amusement of the crowd. She explained later, as they were walking away from the act, that her conspicuously coloured hair made her a target for such acts.

"You could dye it," Kai suggested.

"Sure I could," Sacha said. "But I quite like the attention. And some guys give you free stuff, you know, as a thank you for participating."

"Because getting tied to a chair and having knives thrown at you is totally worth a tiny stuffed toy that you'll probably lose by the end of the week," Yoko remarked wryly.

"'Course," Sacha replied. "C'mon, Kai, you haven't done much. Let's find some games to waste our money on. It's not worth coming if you don't bring something home."

"I haven't got any money," Kai said.

"What, nothing at all?" Sacha said, her tone implying that the previously stated was verging on the borders of completely impossible.' She paused, deliberating this fact. "You haven't been here long, though. That might explain it."

"Look, I'll lend you some," Yoko said, pulling out a handful of coins from a pocket.

"Thanks," Kai said, somewhat startled. "I-I'll pay you back. Somehow."

By the time the sun had set, Kai had learned how to dance a traditional Astlarian jig, made a kite in the shape of the sun, nearly shot an instructor while learning how to use a crossbow, brought a large elaborate map of Keturah for his room, and won a massive purple Talite by popping a line of balloons with a handful of throwing darts. They bumped into Valcor, Rafael, and Felix again in the queue for the fireworks show at the end of the day, which according to Sacha, was the only reason people came to the festival at all. The boys had been pretty busy as well, and the six of them swapped stories about their various antics throughout the day—until a red streak of light shot up into the air and erupted into a rather disappointing shower of sparks.

"It's starting, guys," Sacha said excitedly. "Shut up! Look!"

A line of yellow light shot up, tingeing the sky orange as it mingled with the dying remnants of the red light before it, but by now the crowd's eager chattering had dropped to an awed whisper, their attention focused on the black canvas of sky above them. The third flare was green; no sooner had the shot erupted into a flower of light than the sky seemed to explode in a flare of light that spiralled upwards and outwards in gleaming colours that seemed to sing with the vibrant energy that ran through them. More pulses of colour exploded into life, painting the sky with sparkles of silver and gold, streaking it with fingers glowing with light. For ten minutes, the clearly enthralled crowd watched as the fireworks continued, until finally the light died, the night silenced, and the eager voices of the assembled multitude quickly rose to replace it.

Kai looked nervously at the growing darkness. With all the excitement, he hadn't paid much thought to anything outside the festival, but now that he had a moment to think, he realised that he had stayed out quite late, and he still wasn't too keen on flying at night.

Kai left with Felix, who'd voiced that he'd been thinking similar thoughts, and Sacha, who said she had a big geography project to finish for their next lesson. They rode home in a sleepy, contented silence, the stillness of the night, marbled with bands of milky starlight, twining itself around them like an affectionate cat. Kai was feeling particularly drowsy by the time he arrived at the school, but he was not quite in the mood to go to bed, so he sat outside on the damp grass with Felix and their Talites, looking up into the sky.

"I love the nights up here," Felix said. "I could never see the stars back home; either the city lights ruined it, or it was too cloudy. But here the sky's so *clear*. It's like you could just reach up and grab a handful of stars if you wanted."

Kai nodded. He used to like staring out the window when he was younger, sneaking out of bed when he thought his mother was asleep and pulling up the blinds so he could see the sky. Most days the clouds obscured most of it, but sometimes they drew back, revealing a little patch of sky, scattered flecks of pure white gleaming against the darkness. He used to name them too, but there were so many, and they always seemed different from night to night.

"I used to make up constellations when I was younger," Kai said. "I can't remember any now, though."

Farrell made an inquisitive clicking noise and nudged Kai's shoulder. Felix smiled.

"Maybe he's asking you to make one up for him," he said wryly.

Kai patted Farrell's head affectionately. "He probably is. I'll see if I can fit you in, huh?"

Farrell gave an excited chirp and rested his head against Kai's arm, his eyes closing contentedly.

"Poor soul is probably tired," Kai said, getting to his feet and disturbing his Talite, who had quickly settled into a peaceful doze. "I'd better take him in."

Felix's Talite was already sleeping and took much more effort to rouse. It gave a half-hearted growl as it awoke, flattening its ears, its tail twitching in irritation. "Come on, we're going back to the stables," Felix told it. "It's a better place to go to sleep than out on the field."

Kai returned to his room after they'd dropped off their Talites, exhausted after the long day. He read for a bit from a book he'd borrowed from the library, but the need for sleep kept swamping him at intermittent intervals.

The lights out bell jolted him out of the half sleep he'd fallen into. For a few seconds, he looked around, disorientated, but gradually he realised where he was. He'd fallen asleep while reading, using his book as a pillow. Feeling somewhat embarrassed, he quickly closed the book and slid it into his bedside table drawer. He then padded over to the light switch on the other side of the room and flicking it off, plunging the room into a deep darkness.

The festival lasted two days, which meant they had Friday off as well. Kai didn't feel the need to visit again, especially since he was out of money, and he took the opportunity to lie in. Valcor left early, explaining to Kai—after he'd woken him up—that he might as well get the best out of the absence of school while it lasted.

Rafael replied that sleep satisfied that purpose almost as well, which sparked a heated debate while Valcor got ready to leave.

The rest of the morning passed without much of interest happening. Kai and Felix spent most of it racing each other at sudoku in his room until the bell rang for lunch. They went to the library afterwards to return Kai's book, which he'd managed to finish that morning. While perusing the aisles for new books, they quite literally bumped into Becky, whom Kai hadn't seen for a while. They were in the middle of an avid conversation when Wave appeared rather suddenly, brushing blue hair out of her face as she regarded them with cool indifference.

"Becky, Felix," she said sharply. "We've got an errand to run, so you'd better quit your talking and get a move on."

"What errand?" Becky asked, mystified.

"Jaz got a hit a while ago in a Dracaen attack," Wave said. "She's getting better, but her leg's broken, and they've run out of syipis for the treatment. Mr Feld asked us to get some for him."

Kai had learned about herbal remedies in his natural studies lessons and was pleased that he knew what she was talking about. Syipis was an herb used as a painkiller, often found on rocky slopes at high altitudes.

"Summit Peak's the closest syipis ground," Becky said thoughtfully. "But then we'd have to scale the whole thing."

"Summit Peak?" Felix asked faintly.

"Exactly, and that's a three-hour round trip, so we'd better leave now if we want to be back before sunset," Wave snapped.

"Can I come?" Kai asked, figuring anything would be better than passing the next three hours by himself.

Wave said, "Whatever. Let's move."

The mountain looked so much more imposing when one was at its foot. Looking up, the peak seemed impossibly far away, a dark silhouette against a clear blue sky. But Kai had been up the mountain, or at least halfway up it, in a much shorter time than the three-hour figure Wave had pulled out of nowhere.

The four of them ascended the mountain to the same platform where Mr Shorren had taken Kai and the others for their exam. A week later, Kai still felt the same rush of exhilaration he had the last time. He'd assumed that they were just stopping for a brief stopover, so he was taken aback when Wave and Becky jumped off their Talites and began securing them to stakes driven into the ground and surrounding walls.

"What are you doing?" he asked finally.

"What does it look like?" Wave said.

"There's no space to keep the Talites at the top," Becky explained. "We have to leave them here and climb the rest."

"Climb the . . ." Kai couldn't finish, for his voice was silenced by shock. Even halfway up, the peak still didn't look any closer. "All of it?"

"That's right," Becky said. "That's what the stairs are for." She motioned to a set of stairs etched into the rock face; the stairs continued spiralling around the mountain until they faded into the silhouette of the peak.

"Can't I just stay here?" Felix asked faintly.

"Of course not," Wave said incredulously. "What are you, mad? Come on; tie your Talite so we can go. I'm not spending any more time dithering around here."

"I can't go up there," he said desperately.

Wave stared at him blankly for a few seconds before a sort of revelation passed over her face. She smirked. "What's the matter, kid?" Her voice was edged with undisguised mocking. "Scared of heights?"

Becky looked over at him curiously as Felix nodded.

Wave snorted derisively. "Call yourself a rider and you're scared of heights? Pathetic. How're you planning to spend the rest of your life, then? Sit at home and cry all day?"

"Wave . . . ," Kai began hesitantly, but she ignored him.

"Look around you, kid," she continued. "We're in the middle of the freaking *sky,* like a hundred miles off the ground. What kind of half-brained *idiot* would be scared of heights in a place like this?"

Felix looked at his feet and didn't reply.

"He can stay if he wants, can't he?" Kai asked finally. "I mean, it's not fair to make him go if he doesn't want to."

"You don't get it, do you?" Wave said. "What do you have up in that head of yours? Wool fluff?"

"Get what?" Kai asked, genuinely confused.

Becky looked at him uncomfortably. "He . . . he *has* to go, Kai."

"What?"

"He has to. We're not allowed to leave anyone out on their own . . . because if something happens, we can't help them."

"I can stay with him," Kai offered.

She shook her head. "Anywhere else, yes. But up here . . . it's too remote. You need groups of three at the least. That's why Mr Feld asked for three people."

"Look," Wave cut in impatiently. "I don't know about you, but I want to get up there and back down before sunset. Those stairs are as dangerous as they look, and heaven help us if we're trying to go down them in the dark. So if you *really* want, we can sit here until you suck it up and climb the mountain, and if I accidentally push you off the edge in the dark, it was your own fault."

Felix swallowed hard. "All right, fine. I'm coming."

NINE

The ascent was every bit as daunting as Kai thought it would be. Half an hour in, his legs were aching, he was desperately thirsty, and he couldn't help thinking this wasn't such a good idea after all. His lungs seemed to be ripping apart with all the effort, and each step became a struggle in itself. The only thing that kept him going was the fact that Wave was walking behind him; she had a large stick in her hand and didn't seem to be suffering from any of the hardships that he was.

By the time they reached the summit, Kai was exhausted and couldn't help collapsing to the ground to get his breath back.

"What this mountain needs," Kai said to Felix, between gasping for air, "is an escalator."

Felix smiled then, but his expression hadn't changed much from the blatant fear it had held all through the journey. Wave was already at work, crouching beside a patch of wide-leafed plants with thin stems that ended in small white circular buds at the tip.

Once Kai recovered enough energy to look around without being in some sort of indescribable agony, he stared to calm down, taking less frantic breaths. Becky appeared next to him, a bottle of fresh spring water in her hand. She handed it to Kai.

"Here, Kai," she said. "You look like you need this."

Kai hastily gulped down the water. Becky motioned to him. "Come through here. You'll like this."

Reluctantly, Kai staggered to his feet, following Becky through a huge arch cut into the rock face to a small balcony-like ledge, which was fenced off to stop people from inadvertently falling off the edge. From here, the ground was terrifyingly far away, and the fence didn't look really strong enough to withstand any kind of impact. Kai wondered how long it would take for him to hit the ground if he fell . . .

"Don't look down," Becky said. Kai could hear the smile in her voice. "Look this way. Outwards."

It was bitterly cold, the swirling air somehow reaching all the gaps in his clothing and slowly turning his fingers numb, but Kai didn't notice as he gazed in awe at the scenery. From here, he could see all the way across Keturah, the islands floating merrily beneath him. They were so high up that it was like they were right under the roof of the sky; if he could just reach up a bit higher, he'd be reaching up into the folds of the upper atmosphere.

Becky was quivering with the cold, but there was a kind of gentle awe alight in her eyes as she spoke. "It's beautiful, isn't it?" she asked, her voice soft like the trailing winds. "I've always loved it up here. You can see everything."

Kai tried to picture his map in his head to decipher which island was which, but the image failed him. Finally, he turned to Becky for help.

"Well, this is Tissarel," she began. "You know that already. I expect you know Tireya as well; that's the little one to the side of this one. They build travellers ships that you can hire out for longer trips, like to the Deep Sky, for instance. And the ones to the south are the Firdes, but I expect you know that already, seeing as the festival was there this year. Did you go?"

Kai nodded. "Valcor took me."

"What'd you think?"

Kai winced. "It was a bit loud at first, but once you got used to it, it was pretty good."

Becky nodded. "I missed it this year. I was busy with some work yesterday. I was going to go today, but then we got pulled out on this errand. Never mind—there's still the winter festival later."

"There's another one?"

"Just the two," Becky said. "Although the winter one's not so good because of the cold. Anyway, where was I...? Oh, yes, okay. The big one in the middle is Meridian. I'd be surprised if you don't know that one. The island to the south of Meridian is Verran. They're known for supplying electricity: they go into storm clouds and collect lightning from the sky. I don't know how they do it; it's one of their most guarded trade secrets.

"The little island to the northeast is Astlar; that's where your water came from. See that waterfall coming off the side? That river's famous for its purity and healing powers. People come to Astlar regularly to buy the water; the spring's right at the top of the small mountain to the side there. The smaller island in the south is Ilyas. There isn't much worth seeing there, except that huge lighthouse in the middle."

"What is it for?"

"We call it 'the beacon'; it's for guiding travellers returning from the Deep Sky at night."

"The deep sky?" Kai asked. He'd heard the term used a few times, including from her a moment earlier, but he had never quite understood where or what it was.

"It's the area of sky east of Keturah. It's all too easy to get lost in there, and it's overrun with Dracaens because they generally live there. Well, they're supposed to, but apparently they've been roaming around Keturah lately..."

"What about that one, to the north of Meridian?"

"Oh, that's Teklah. It used to be a proper civilization, one of the great cities of the third cycle of Keturah's history, but Dracaens started attacking it, swarming without any apparent incentive, and destroyed the whole place in one night. They only managed to save a handful of people. Now all that's left is a bunch of ruins. Some smaller animals have moved in too; the Hunters' Guild goes there often for hunting errands; they sell the catches off to the shopkeepers. Sometimes they call region-wide meetings there, too, but they're *really* rare. Nobody I know remembers the last time one was called."

Kai nodded and looked over at Felix, who was hunched against the wall, head buried against his knees. "Come on, Felix," he said. "Take a look at this. It's really great, as long as you don't look down."

"That's what they always say," Felix replied miserably, but after a moment's hesitation, he shakily got to his feet and approached the edge of the ledge cautiously. He took a deep, trembling breath as he reached the fence and looked hesitantly out across the sky. His breath caught in his throat like a gasp. "Oh," he said, clearly torn between being terrified and captivated at the same time. "Oh, *man*..."

"There." Wave's voice sounded behind them, calmly triumphant. "That wasn't too difficult, was it? Come on, I have the herbs here, so we'd better get a move on. We'll probably beat the sunset if we leave now."

Wave was right: the sky was streaked with lines of faint pink and yellow as they reached the platform where their Talites were nestled. Most of them were asleep; Becky's was pawing at something on the ground, and Farrell, whom Kai had been too soft-hearted to tie down, was flitting eagerly through the sky, chasing after insects. By the time they reached the school, it was dark, the lights from the building casting long shadows behind them as they put their Talites in the stables for the night. They'd missed dinner, but Mr Feld had told the kitchen staff to save something for them for when they returned. The dining hall looked so much bigger when it wasn't crammed full of people; the lack of noise was almost eerie.

Wearily, he ascended the stairs, dreading the stiff limbs that were sure to result from the day's arduous efforts and desperately wanting to sleep, only to find Valcor and Rafael playing cards on his bed.

"Oh, hey," Valcor said, and then waved a crumpled document at him. "Tess dropped this off for you."

It was his new timetable, effective from the start of next week, which for some reason, made him feel a bit depressed. Not that he wanted to stay in apprentice school—indeed, he was willing to get as far away from Ms Greeve as possible—but once again, he was being hit with another sudden change that he had to adapt to.

Berating himself for being so pessimistic, he forced himself to look at the positives. He was clearly moving up in the world; he'd managed to pass the test after less than three weeks at the school. He was acclimatizing, settling in, getting the hang of it. This was *good*. And besides, being a rider axed half an hour from the total time he had to be in school, which was an added bonus.

Come on, Kai thought reassuringly to himself. *I'm worrying too much. It can't be that bad. It'll probably only get easier from here. I think.*

Kai bumped into Tess on the way to his navigational science lesson on Monday morning, and feeling it necessary to talk to her, seeing as they'd taken the test together, he greeted her and asked how she had done on the test. She gave a shrug and said nothing for a while. Finally, as Kai decided he wasn't going to get a response from her and would probably be late if he kept waiting any further, she spoke.

"I passed," she said shortly, but she didn't look particularly impressed by that.

"Congratulations," Kai said genuinely, but Tess simply scowled at him.

"Don't think it's going to get any easier," she snapped. "They'll think you can move mountains in your sleep now."

She walked off before he could reply, and Kai hastily remembered that he had a lesson to get to, so he simply filed the conversation somewhere in the back of his mind and forgot about it.

But as the week dragged painfully onwards, Kai realised that what she said was closer to the truth than he'd hoped. He was getting good marks in class, but most of his teachers seemed absolutely convinced he could do much better, just as a certain someone who so happened to be related to him had been able to. And as his life spilled into the next week and the next, he found himself locked in a never-ending struggle to prove to his teachers—and subconsciously, his mother—that they were right. He'd never worked so hard at school in his life, but something, some rampant desire forced on him to achieve the unachievable, pressed him on, past anything he'd ever done before, past the amount of work anyone should be expected to do in such a short amount of time, past any sort of logic and coherence of any kind.

He woke up one morning a few weeks later, feeling like a deflated balloon. He had a splitting, throbbing pain on the left side of his head, which only got worse when he tried to move. He couldn't walk more than a couple of steps before he was swamped with a fierce wave of dizziness, and everything around him seemed to be insanely loud. He managed to struggle through the early morning and up to breakfast before Valcor told him he looked terrible and should see the nurse. Insisting he was fine, Kai swallowed a few mouthfuls of breakfast and sloped off to his practical technology lesson.

"Kai, are you all right?" John, who taught the tech lessons, asked him, concern edging his voice as Kai entered the classroom.

"I'm fine," he muttered, sitting down. If he kept very still, the headache abated slightly. All he had to do was refrain from moving around too much.

"Are you sure? You're almost dead white. I think you should see the nurse."

"It's okay," Kai protested. "It only hurts when I move about too much."

"So you *are* ill," John said. "I know practical technology is a wonderful lesson, but I don't think I should let you do the lesson if you're sick, Kai, no matter how healthy you claim to be."

"Valcor said he looked sick earlier," Rafael commented seriously from behind them. He'd just walked in a few seconds ago.

"And I expect he's right," John agreed. "Could you take him to the nurse for me? Hopefully it's nothing serious, but it's always good to be sure of these things."

Rafael nodded and in silence led Kai down the corridor towards the medical room. The nurse, a young woman with long brown hair and a kind, open face, smiled at them as they walked in.

"Hello, boys," she said. "What can I get you?"

"Kai says he feels a bit sick," Rafael explained.

"Does he? Let me see . . ."

The nurse ran a few tests, took some measurements of his temperature, and asked for some symptoms. Finally, she took a step back and regarded him carefully.

"Have you been working very hard lately? Do you have any big projects or something similar?"

"Sort of," Kai admitted sheepishly.

"And then some," Rafael said. "He's been studying right up to lights out almost every night these days, probably more during the afternoons."

The nurse nodded. "It's probably a migraine. It shouldn't be too serious; all he really needs is a little rest. But as you've been working extremely hard lately, you should take a couple of days off school as well, just to get you back to normal. You'll be fine in next to no time. Let me just write a note for your teacher to tell him what's wrong . . ."

She walked off into a back room, leaving Kai sitting glumly on the bed.

"Why do you do this to yourself, Kai?" Rafael asked.

"Do what?"

"Work so hard. It's not even for anything big. It was understandable when you had the test, but this... Don't you think you're going too far now?"

"I'm not working *that* hard," Kai said, but he knew he didn't sound impressively convinced, and Rafael seemed to share that opinion.

"Come on, Kai. You made yourself *ill* because of all the work you're doing."

"It doesn't matter to you," Kai said darkly. "Why should you care?"

He sighed impatiently. "I don't want to see you do this. It's like you're bent on working yourself to death. Why won't you just take it easy?"

"Because everyone else thinks that I'm supposed to be amazing at this. Because nothing I do satisfies them," Kai snapped back, feeling everything rise up, all the stress and the frustration flooding out in one explosive climax. He took a deep breath, pain throbbing again just behind his eye. "Even if I got everything right, they'd probably find some way that I could reach up to my mum's standards," he said in calmer tones. "I don't want to let her down, Raf. I just feel like I'd disappoint her if I failed."

"But you're not failing," Rafael said. "You were doing fine before you went into overdrive."

Kai shook his head. "It didn't feel like it."

The nurse arrived then with a note for Rafael to take back to John and a cupful of syrupy medicine for Kai, cutting off any further conversation.

"Here, drink this," she said as Rafael left the room. "It'll help you sleep. You should feel better when you wake up."

Kai obediently drained the cup. The medicine scalded the back of his mouth and seemed to burn its way down his throat. Kai broke into a fit of coughing, which faded away as the medicine started to take effect. He vaguely heard the nurse say something, but he couldn't quite make out the words as the blackness around him engulfed his mind.

Most of the headache was gone by the time he woke up a while later, but the nurse insisted on keeping him there for a while longer. It wasn't quite dinnertime by the time he was let out, but he could smell the scent of something being prepared in the kitchens downstairs, the distinct aroma trailing through the corridors. The school was quiet at this time of day; students had no reason to be in the building unless they had clubs or detention. He could hear animated chatter and laughing in the mounting twilight outside, but he didn't really feel like talking to anyone. Sticking to the more obscure corridors of the school, he wandered aimlessly around the building until, by pure chance, he ended up in a huge red-carpeted room, a majestic staircase sprawled in the middle of it. He recognized the room immediately from his first day at the school. Instinctively, he found himself approaching the back of the room, where the row of photos ranged across the gold-rimmed walls, until he was face to face with the smiling picture of Faye Hunter.

For a minute, he stared numbly at her face, a montage of his life with her flashing across his eyes. He could see his mother's face superimposed over her eighteen-year-old self, still remembered seeing her hunched over one of the potted plants that reigned over the kitchen table, her red hair falling scraggily into her gentle smile as she watered it. She used to talk to plants sometimes, saying it helped them grow. At first, Kai had thought she was delusional, but after a while, the idea seemed to grow on him. Frederick the cactus became a fully integrated member of the family, and Kai never failed to give it a respectful nod before he left for school.

The reverie faded abruptly, leaving tears brimming in his eyes and a feeling of desperate desolation welling up inside him. He missed his mother. He missed her scatty sense of humour, her unfailing determination and her strange habits, the way the room seemed to be a little more vibrant when she was in it, the way she'd always give him a deep soil-scented hug when he came home from school, the way they used to have pointless fights about pointless things, then forgive each other and get out what she used to call the "forgiveness ice cream" to eat in front of the TV.

Kai, honey, why do you look so sad?

It was his mother's voice, unmistakably. Kai started then, wondering if he was finally going crazy.

What are you doing here? he responded mentally.

You look a little down, dear. Penny for your thoughts?

I don't think I can do this. I'd be better off back where I was. At least I knew what I was doing.

But you didn't like it there, hon. His mother sounded wounded.

I liked it.

Then why did you agree to come here?

There was no answer for that. Kai hung his head and stared blankly at the floor.

Anyway, you've got a great life here. You have friends, not to mention a magnificent Talite. What's not to like?

Everything, Kai responded bitterly. *Everyone expects me to measure up to you, just because you were great. They call you the best rider who ever lived. I can hardly ride to a decent standard.*

The best rider who ever lived? Well, that's quite a title. Although I must admit, I always used to envy Yel Drew's style. He taught me my elite theory . . . He'd probably have taught yours too, if he hadn't died in that terrible accident . . .

Are you joking? I'll never get to elite standard.

If you want it enough, you can. That's the moral I lived by, and look where it got me: "the best rider who ever lived". How I wish I were alive to see that . . . Kai, shall I tell you a secret? People always say things like "naturally gifted" or refer to genetics, but I think the only reason I did well in life is because I lived for myself. Not my teachers or anyone else. I set my own goals and worked to my own standard. Your teachers shouldn't mind—they'd probably feel better if you weren't running round giving yourself headaches anyway. And once you discover yourself like that . . . well, there's no limit, really. See if it works; I'll bet my newly found title if it doesn't.

The faint echo of the bell snapped Kai into reality. He looked at his mother's face one more time, smiling behind a thin sheet of glass, and turned away to go.

Bye, Mum. Thanks for the advice.

Oh, Kai, you'll do fine. You'll probably do better than I, if anything.

I don't think I'll get better than your title.

I wouldn't bet on it. You'll see.

Kai bumped into Valcor and Rafael on the way to the dining hall. He felt better, happier than he had in a while. He hadn't quite reached them when Valcor jumped on him with a barrage of questions without waiting for Kai to answer them.

"Kai! Where have you been? We were looking for you! Do you feel any better?"

"Hey, Valcor."

Rafael nodded at him. "You look better. What've you been up to?"

Kai hesitated, wondering how he could put it without condemning himself to the ranks of the certifiably insane. Eventually, he settled on his tried and tested tactic: the vaguely elusive response.

"You know. Stuff."

"Come on, we'd better hurry up," Valcor put in. "Someone said there was ice cream for dessert today. It'll all be gone if we wait too long."

Seeing Yoko at their dinner table reminded him that he still owed her some money from the festival. With no viable way to procure some, he turned to Valcor for advice.

"What do you want money for? I can lend you some if you want."

"No . . . Well, thanks, but I've already borrowed some, and I need to pay it back."

Valcor nodded. "Well, usually parents send their kids monthly allowances," Valcor explained. "Seeing as your parents aren't up here . . . uh, the only other way is through errands."

"Errands? Like the one we went to earlier?"

"What's this? You did an errand?"

"Well, strictly speaking, I tagged along, but Mr Feld asked us awhile back to get some herbs from Summit Peak."

"Ah, that's different. That's a school errand, so you don't get money for those. Sometimes citizens who live near the school ask us to do favours for them; that's when you get paid. But the school chooses people to take them, so it could be a while. The easiest way to get an errand is through Hunters' Guild."

"Ah. That's that club you go to, right?"

"Yup," Valcor said. "It's after school on Tuesdays. You should come if you want to get some money. Interested?"

Kai shrugged. "Yeah, why not? I don't have much to do with my afternoons anymore anyway."

TEN

The Guild members met in a large room underneath the main school building, which Kai had never seen before. It was low-ceilinged, a dim light hanging from the ceiling, with springy wooden floors and an impressive assortment of weapons ranged in display cupboards around the edges.

John led the Hunters' Guild—there didn't seem to be much he *didn't* do. The group was comprised of around twenty people, most of whom he vaguely recognized from his classes around school. Wave was there too; she gave him a brief nod of acknowledgement as he entered. After taking a quick register, they left the building, collected their Talites from the stables, and reassembled on the field for their session.

"In today's session, as the more perceptive of you may have guessed by the fact that we have our Talites out today, we'll be picking up again on on-Talite combat. This is a rarer form of attack and is mostly only used in mid-air, say, if you're attacked by Rayeds or Dracaens, but what with the increasing number of them running wild out there, I think it's more appropriate than ever. I know the last session on this was a long while ago, so I'll just go over the basics now, and then we'll get on with our practical.

"Now, attack and defence positions typically have little use in normal flying; if anything, they're just elaborate variations on second and third. When you are fighting on your Talite, however, these two positions are pretty much all you can expect to use.

"Your Talite is the core factor in this. Under all that fur and fluffiness, they're tough and sturdy, and they'll resist sudden impacts. You can use their tails to attack as well. Some people prefer to use weapons for an added kick—that's fine, but you need to pay attention to balance and weight shifting then, so we'll stick with plain mode for today. All right, guys, find a partner and we'll do some quick one-on-one battles. Kai, you're with me."

While the other kids paired off, John mounted his Talite and motioned for Kai to do the same.

"Seeing as it's your first time doing this sort of thing, I thought I'd do this one a little differently with you," John explained, taking off with smooth precision. "So imagine you're flying along on your way to another island, say, and suddenly a Dracaen appears out of nowhere. We don't have any Dracaens here for you to fight, so you'll just have to imagine I'm one. What do you do?"

"Run?"

"Yes, ideally that would be the best course of action. However, running doesn't make for very good combat training, so we'll assume you can't run away. Next plan is . . . ?"

"Try to fight?"

"Good. So I'm a Dracaen, and I'm about to kill you. Attack me."

"Attack you?" Kai asked, bewildered. "But—"

"Don't worry; I just want to see how you fight. This is part of your lesson. Attack me."

Skyriders

Kai hesitated, not knowing what to do. He couldn't see how he was supposed to fight John; he had years more experience and, in the best-case scenario, could probably knock him clean off his Talite if he wanted to.

He relaxed his grip slightly, dropped into a half crouch, and lunged the Talite forwards at John, who dodged effortlessly.

"Predictable. If I were a Dracaen, you'd be dead," he said. "Try something I don't expect."

He lunged forwards again but at the last minute ducked to the side as John dodged, before sweeping upwards again and lashing out with Farrell's tail. It hit John's Talite across its body, but John quickly retaliated with a driving jab forward, smashing into Farrell's body and knocking him off balance.

"Dead," John said. "Although you were doing fine until you stopped doing anything. Keep on moving; never stop."

The third attempt was another fail. He'd tried to attack him from above, but John quickly batted him away with a powerful swipe from the wing of his Talite, sending him flying backwards.

"Dead. Not to mention some nasty facial wounds, I might add."

Kai stared at John in fierce contemplation. He couldn't see how he could get the better of him. He advanced for the fourth time cautiously, slowly inching forwards until he was within striking distance. As John's Talite raised a wing to bat him away again, he quickly twisted and Farrell flipped over and slid underneath it, before kicking at its underside. John sprang sideways, his Talite yelping in pain, and Farrell sent its tail in a sweeping curve, catching the Talite on the side of its face.

John recovered quickly, though, springing sideways, crashing into Farrell's body to knock Kai off balance, before spinning round and slamming the full weight of the Talite at him, the force sending Kai rushing backwards like a missile. By the time he'd regained sufficient control to stop moving, he was several metres away from him.

John brought his Talite to a graceful landing at the edge of the field and jumped off, Kai quickly following suit.

"This isn't fair," Kai said dejectedly, rubbing Farrell's head where he'd been hit. "I can't beat you. I don't think I could come close."

"Naturally," John said. "But that wasn't the idea. I merely wanted to see how you formulated an attack plan in your mind. You were very good, I must say, that last one especially. That took me by surprise." He paused, running a blade of grass across his fingers, and then: "You know, Kai, you fight a lot like Becky."

"I do?"

John nodded. "It might be pure coincidence, or you might have seen her ride and just picked it up, or something . . . I picked that up quickly. It's easier to formulate a counter-attack when you've got a good idea of what they're going to do."

"She taught me how to ride," Kai said. "Well, for the most part. Before the exam."

"That explains it," John said. "It's not necessarily a bad thing, but it has a few dangers of its own. The thing is, Dracaens are extremely hard to kill. They'll run away if they're injured enough or if they feel they're outnumbered, and most people don't pursue them because they feel they were lucky to get out of that alive. They're also adaptive and pick up things quickly. Fall designed all his species to be able to pick up their riders' styles quickly to make training quicker, so it'll pick up an opponent's quicker as well. That's why the longer you battle with any of the Fallite species, the harder it'll be. It's also dangerous fighting with someone with a similar style as yours for the same reasons. We tend to pair people up with greatly contrasting approaches, like Valcor and Rafael, for example. Have you seen them fight?"

Kai shook his head.

"Well, there's an example anyway. Ideally, what you should do now is try to develop a style of your own."

"How do I do that?"

John got to his feet and vaulted back on his Talite. "More fighting. But this time, forget everything Becky taught you. Just look within yourself and ride."

They sparred again for a while, until John clapped his hands again to signal the end of the session. "Good job, guys. I've seen some good work today. So for our final death match today . . ."

The members of the crowd immediately lowered their eyes, plainly trying to avoid eye contact for fear of being chosen, but trying not to make it too obvious.

"I think seeing as Kai's here, he deserves to see you fight, Valcor," John said. "And your opponent . . . Uh, all right, Abby, come on up. We'll go on the floor this time. First person to knock their opponent off their Talite wins."

Valcor gave Kai a cheerful two-fingered salute as he climbed atop his Talite. His opponent, a tall girl who looked to be around sixteen, with golden swirls of hair falling down her back, also mounted her Talite, and the two circled warily for a few seconds.

"This should be good," John said to Kai. "Abby's just been promoted to elite, but I reckon Val can hold his own on this one. She's a cautious fighter, though. It'll be interesting to see whether he can break her defence."

The fight had started, most of it limited to flashing blurs of creamy yellow and white as well as the snarls and yelps of the Talites and cheering shouts of the other Guild members. Valcor kept up a relentless offence at breakneck speed, barely giving Abby time to block one strike before launching another. But John was right; she kept up a strict defence and didn't seem to be fazed by the onslaught, merely biding her time, searching patiently for an opening.

How she found one, Kai couldn't tell from outside the fight, but one minute she appeared to be being forced into a corner, and the next there was a flash of movement and she jabbed forward, blocking one attack and deftly twisting round, a slashing tail hitting Valcor's Talite across its face. It backed up a few steps, giving Abby all the advantage she needed. She took a step forward, her Talite's powerful wings looming high, ready to attack.

She hit hard across his Talite's body, and again, but as she prepared the third strike, Valcor dodged. The wing hit the ground where he'd been standing a moment ago as he whirled round in a huge circle, slashing the tail across her body, knocking her off.

The crowd burst into enthusiastic applause as Valcor leaped off his Talite. He shook hands with Abby, as was the traditional custom with these "death matches", and with that, the group dispersed in groups of twos and threes, talking eagerly amongst themselves.

"So what'd you think?" Valcor asked enthusiastically.

Kai nodded. "It's interesting. I liked your fight at the end."

Valcor grinned. "I was good, wasn't I? It's a little tradition we have; we always have a one-on-one fight in front of the whole group. Although if you want to see something *really* impressive, you should see Wave fight. It's totally crazy. She once beat some kid in less than three seconds. You could've blinked and missed it."

If everything he'd heard about Wave was true, Kai thought reflectively as they dropped their Talites off at the stables, then she'd be on par with some sort of deity. He could still remember seeing her while he was training with Becky, performing a loop flawlessly in mid-air as if it were something she did naturally. He often fantasized about that, wondering how long it would take *him* to be able to ride like that.

Valcor flicked a hand in front of his face, distracting him. "You okay?" he asked. "You're just sort of staring into nothing."

Kai looked up quickly. "Oh . . . what? No, I was just . . . thinking."

"Oh, good. So, you're coming back next week, right?"

Kai nodded. "'Course."

Mrs Snowe pointed at the impressively lifelike picture she'd just drawn on the board in front of them. "In today's lesson, we're continuing our Fallite anatomy topic," she informed her sleepy-looking class. "So . . . Dracaens. What do you know about them? Come on, I'll take anything."

It was the last class of the evening, and Kai was starting to feel the fronds of tiredness pulling at his consciousness. Natural science didn't usually bore him, but he'd been working hard all day, and right now he wanted more than anything to lie down and get some rest.

"They're dangerous," someone offered.

"Good, there's a start," Mrs Snowe said, writing DANGEROUS in bold lettering above her picture. "Anything else?"

"They've got lots of spikes on their tails—and their wings too."

"They're omnivores, although they do prefer meat."

"They can rip a Talite to pieces in five seconds with their claws."

"What a delightful piece of information," Mrs Snowe murmured, the words RIPS TALITES TO PIECES forming under her pen as it squeaked across the whiteboard. "Keep it coming."

"I heard Mr Shorren rode a Dracaen once," someone piped up. Kai looked up sharply, all trace of tiredness gone. A ripple of interest spread across the classroom, rising in a crescendo of voices until it seemed everyone was talking at once.

"Impossible. You can't ride a Dracaen."

"Mr Shorren rode a Dracaen? Mr *Shorren*?"

"Yeah, I heard that one. He rode it all the way from Ilyas to the Firdes, no joke."

"She's lying. Of course she's lying."

"He doesn't look like he rode one. I mean, he doesn't seem to do *much* . . ."

"Of course he does. He's our *head teacher*, for crying out loud."

"I heard he did it blindfolded while juggling a bunch of porcelain teacups."

"Don't be *stupid.*"

"Could you *actually* do that? Why didn't he die?"

Admittedly, Kai hadn't thought much of his head teacher. Sure, he was the head teacher, and from what he saw of him during his apprentice exam, he was an elite too, but there was a big leap from the short tawny-haired man with sharp green eyes hidden behind a pair of wire-rimmed spectacles to what he was hearing now.

"How did he do it?"

"But, Mrs Snowe, you *can't* ride a Dracaen."

"All the Fallite species were initially designed for riding," Mrs Snowe said, amusement evident in her voice. "You can ride each and every one of them."

"But what about positions and everything? It wouldn't respond to any instruction. You wouldn't be able to control it."

"That's only in conventional riding, though," the same girl who'd started the conversation said. "If he was free riding, it'd work."

Kai had never heard the term before, but there was no way he could ask while the class were this excited.

"You're saying he was *free riding* a *Dracaen*?" someone spluttered incredulously after a moment of stunned silence. "*Now* you're crazy."

More opinions were offered, rejected, debated, until Kai couldn't pick out individual words anymore, just an incoherent mush of voices.

"Quiet class!" Mrs Snowe shouted. "I can't even hear myself think anymore."

The voices dwindled to an expectant hush but didn't fade altogether.

"Is it true?" someone asked, finally coming out with the most obvious question.

"Yeah, you're a senior, Mrs Snowe, so you should know. Did he really?"

Mrs Snowe smiled. "Oh, yes, but I think the claims of his juggling blindfolded are a *little* far-fetched."

The class gave a sort of collective awed gasp before launching into avid whispered chatter again. Mrs Snowe rapped on the board with her pen. "Focus on the *work*, class. We don't want to waste time. If we've got any time at the end of the lesson, maybe I'll tell you about it. Now back to Dracaens . . ."

When Mrs Rawthon popped out to get some textbooks during his next theory lesson, Kai asked Becky about free riding. The room was cold, fierce winds rattling the fragile windowpanes. Outside, the wind had whipped itself up into a raging flurry of fury, streaking through trees and ripping their leaves clean off the branches, flinging small branches at the window.

"It's the ultimate form of riding," Becky said. "No gear, no positions—just you and your Talite."

"It sounds difficult."

"It *is*. People have strived over lifetimes to be able to master it. They teach a vague outline of it, but that's really advanced elite theory. It marks the ultimate feeling of trust and coordination between the rider and the Talite."

"Can you do it?"

"Me?" She shook her head. "No. The only people I've heard who could pull it off decently were the legends in the hall of fame."

That included his mother, Kai supposed.

Mrs Rawthon came back then, so Kai buried the conversation somewhere and concentrated on his schoolwork. But it bothered him still, so he dragged Felix to the library to look up the subject in depth.

"Free riding?" Felix asked as Kai browsed the labyrinth of bookshelves in search of something that could help. "I've never even heard of it. Are you sure that's what it's called?"

"Sure. Becky told me about it," Kai said without turning round. "Hang on, what's this . . . ?" He pulled out a battered-looking hardback, several inches thick, with the word LORE engraved in gold lettering on the front. It'd been stuffed behind one of the isles, inadvertently concealed between piles of old weather reports, gathering dust for an indefinite amount of time.

"Is this about free riding?" Felix asked doubtfully.

"I don't think so. I just found it behind the bookshelf."

"It looks a bit suspicious," Felix said.

"I'll say. Dusty old obscure book, hidden behind some aisles with no other relevant information. What're the odds that a portal will appear and suck us into it if we open it?"

The book had no background information, no blurb, not even a picture on the front to describe what it was about. It had no library sticker on it, so the school probably didn't even know it was there.

Kai flipped it open. There was no portal, no trans-dimensional travel, just a plume of dust that floated into his face and made him cough.

"I can't read it," Kai said. "It's all in code or something."

"Let's see," Felix said. Kai handed the book to him. For a moment, there was silence as Felix studied the text.

"It's one of the old languages from the first cycle," he said after a lengthy pause. "Ilyasi or Astlarian, I'm not quite sure."

"How did you know that?"

"Cultural studies," Felix said.

While it was compulsory to take them as an apprentice, cultural studies, weather tracking, and alternate civilizations were enrichment subjects you had the option of either continuing or dropping once you moved up to rider. Kai had been all too keen to drop the subject when he moved up, feeling it was no use to him, but now he was wondering whether it held more relevance than he'd originally anticipated.

"Can you read it?"

Felix shrugged. "I'll have a go. It might take a while."

While Felix struggled through the book, Kai resumed his searching. By the time he'd found a book, Felix had managed to get the first sentence translated.

"'From the first cycle of Keturahn history, Kaitou Lethem, seer for the ruling family.' See, I was right—it's in Ilyasi."

"Anything else?"

"I don't quite get the rest of it," he admitted. "I'm not too good at languages. Something about records and mythology, really."

"So it's just a book of stories?" Kai asked.

"It could be. Like I said, I'm not that good with languages . . ."

"What are we going to do with it?"

"Leave it here, I reckon. If it's just a book of legends, then it's not much use to anyone. Put it back where you found it. So you found a book on free riding, then?"

"Yeah. Come have a look."

Free riding is a concept formed by elite extremists late in the fourth cycle, based on the notion of riding without limits, without restrictions. One of the most extreme and dangerous forms of riding, free riding soon became a goal for very few to achieve; in essence, the instinctive joining of the mind between the rider and steed.

Part one: Initiation and Integration . . .

"It sounds mad," Felix said.

"Becky says it's hard."

"Yeah, and Becky's an elite, so it must be."

"It sounds awesome. I'd love to be able to do that."

"I don't think I could. I'm having enough trouble with riding already."

Kai shut the book. "So what do you propose we do this afternoon? More sudoku?"

"Yeah, sure."

"Okay, guys, today we're moving on to armed combat."

They were inside today for their Hunters' session. The room had a chilly bite to it, and Kai couldn't help shivering as he listened to John outlining the basics of their session.

"We'll start off simple: the staff. Essentially, it's no more than a piece of wood, but with the right techniques, it's a formidable weapon. Ideally, we shouldn't really try to cripple each other too seriously while we're in a club, but we're training for practical applications here, so when we partner up, you'll have to wear body padding and helmets.

"Each staff has a maximum range it can reach, but if you're planning to attack, you'll have to step within that range, so most of the defensive moves are simply raising your staff to block any incoming impact. Max, come out and volunteer for me, please."

He tossed a long pole to one of the boys in the group, who reluctantly shuffled over to where John was standing.

"Now, if Max swings his staff in a downwards motion, like this, you can block it easily by twisting your body slightly, standing horizontally, and moving your staff to block it. Of course, this is no use to anyone right now, because if you just keep blocking attacks, chances are you'll slip up and get hammered. So whenever you block, make sure you do it in such a way that will maximise your chances of getting in a good counter-attack, like so . . ." John used his staff to move Max's pole into an upwards position, pushing it slightly aside before jabbing it dramatically at his face.

"There, see? Attacking with a staff is mainly limited to swinging motions, which should keep an unarmed enemy at bay, and thrusting motions, which with a lot of power can do a lot of damage." He demonstrated the two moves with elaborate, fluid movements, poking and slashing at an invisible opponent. "If you're fighting opponents in life-or-death situations, try aiming at the hands and feet—because if they can't stand up or hold their weapons, they're not really doing much. If you're fighting smaller animals, say, in a hunting situation, then you can simply swing at them, aiming for their bodies and heads most of the time."

John continued for a while, avidly detailing different techniques, he and Max giving little demonstrations. After pulling on some padded gloves and shin pads and retrieving a staff each from the rack at the back of the room, he finally let them pair up and try some one-on-one sparring. Kai's partner was Valcor, on account of his being pretty much the only person he knew well enough to talk to in the club.

Valcor was certainly a formidable opponent, employing a fierce, unrelenting blur of lightning-quick attacks that seemed to emerge from nowhere, keeping Kai constantly on his guard. His boundless energy gave him even more of an edge; while Kai started to tire after a couple of minutes, he was still going strong and still as fast.

John came round in his slow circumnavigation of the room, observing pairs and doling out constructive criticism and advice. With a calm interest, he observed Kai and Valcor fighting. Finally, he spoke up: "Don't you think you're being a bit hard on him, Valcor?" he asked finally, light humour outlining his voice. "He's barely been in this club two weeks."

Kai took the opportunity for a break, staggering a few steps backwards and taking a couple of exaggerated breaths, fighting a huge stitch down his side.

"He's good," Valcor said, impressed. His face had a red flush to it, but he appeared to be enjoying himself. "I haven't managed to get a hit in yet."

John looked over at Kai, who had managed to regain nearly enough composure to be able to breathe normally. "Try not to be too overwhelmed," John said. "He's pretty fast."

"That's putting it lightly," Kai said. "I couldn't see half the attacks coming."

"Try to find a gap," John advised. "Valcor's fast, but he puts all his focus on his offence, which leaves him open. Remember how Abby fought last week? She wasn't being backed into a corner; she was simply waiting for an opportunity."

"Do I get any tips too?" Valcor asked.

"Work on your balance a bit more," John said. "You're not recovering fast enough on your stronger attacks. It's fine with Kai because he's still inexperienced, but on a faster, more adept opponent, it'll have some serious consequences."

Realizing that his conveniently placed break was coming to a close, Kai took a couple of deep, measured breaths to clear his mind, and he and Valcor started up again, staffs clashing against each other, the reverberation of wood against wood filling the room. Valcor was still as fast, but now that he wasn't just trying not to get hit, it didn't seem to be as hard to deflect his unrelenting onslaught. Each attack was patiently blocked, Kai twisting out of the way like it was second nature, searching for the opening that John had advised to look for . . .

There!

Kai darted forward, twisting the staff forwards so it locked behind Valcor's oncoming attack. With a deft flick, he pulled the rod out of his hands, sending it clattering to the springy wooden floor.

Kai grinned at him jubilantly and breathlessly. "Does this mean I win?"

Valcor bent to pick up his staff. "Best two out of three."

By the time John called the session to a close, Kai was exhausted, a rush of inane adrenaline-fuelled elation running through him like crackling electricity.

"All right, for our final death match today . . . Uh, Kai, you've shown a lot of promise today, and you can take on . . . Wave, I think."

Kai blinked. He hadn't been expecting this. Valcor let out a low whistle.

"He really thinks you're good, Kai," he said, impressed. "Everyone else would get hammered."

"I think I'll fall into that category," Kai muttered, picking up his staff.

"Nah," Valcor said dismissively. "You'll do fine."

"We'll just do a timed match today," John said. "Three minutes. You win if you get the other to submit; otherwise, it's a draw."

Wave flicked a couple of strands out of her face, a calm, hard expression on her face as she circled him warily. Kai mimicked her movements, not sure how to go about this, watching her almost as carefully as she was watching him.

Then she attacked.

This was nothing like fighting against Valcor. She wasn't as fast as him, but what she lacked in speed she made up for in precision and power. The first strike hit him hard across his shoulder, the second a lancing blow across his arm, the force of it taking him completely by surprise. He staggered backwards, pain exploding across the impact line. She swung her staff again, but he was ready this time and blocked it, quickly moving in to counter-attack. Each strike was met by a block. It was as if she expected what he was going to do and had already figured out how to deflect it before he'd even made the move.

He quickly set into a rhythm, moving lightly, deftly, but he couldn't see how to get the upper hand in this game. She seemed to cover everything at once; her defence was solid but her attacks were still enough to leave him winded. She was fast, agile, and recovered too quickly for him to land more than a few hits at any one time.

Kai spotted an opening and went for it, swinging his staff low, locking it around her feet. She stumbled, but it wasn't enough to knock her over, and while Kai hesitated, she quickly used the opportunity to swing her staff hard across his body. Instinctively, Kai flinched, and Wave moved in quickly, sweeping him clean off his feet before he knew what was going on. By the time he was aware of what was happening, he was lying on his back with Wave's staff pressing into his chest and the crowd around him strangely silent with anticipation.

Moving purely on instinct, Kai slid his staff behind Wave's and pulled it towards him, disrupting her balance and sending her tumbling forwards. Kai rolled sideways just as she collapsed where he'd been just a second ago, scrambling to his feet and lashing forwards with a sharp blow across her back. She met his second blow with her staff in a neat parry; even while she was down, she seemed no less adept in blocking his attacks.

By the time John called for time, Kai was shattered, and he seemed to be hurting in fifty different places. He shook hands with Wave as the crowd broke into spontaneous cheering and applause.

"Good match," she said, although Kai wasn't sure whether she was saying that genuinely or out of tradition. He murmured a similar response before storing his staff away at the back of the room and joining Valcor, who'd been loyally waiting for him to finish.

"That was *awesome!*" Valcor said enthusiastically, barely waiting for Kai to come within hearing distance before launching into a lively torrent of words. "For a minute there I thought you were going to get killed . . .

but then you were like *whoosh* and . . ." He made some obscure hand gestures to describe this, should Kai have somehow missed the meaning of the original context.

John, who'd been lingering around to tidy up the room before locking it up for the afternoon, nodded in agreement. "It was a good match," he said. "I'm impressed you managed to hold your own against Wave, to be honest. You have a real talent with that staff, Kai. It's a shame we only do one session on staff fighting in Guild; with proper training, you could be really good at it."

"I got hit *loads,*" Kai said. "I can't even feel my arms anymore."

"You'll have a nice collection of bruises by tomorrow," Valcor said. "You should make up an impressive story to impress people with. Say you were walking down the road one day and suddenly this group of armed bandits jumped out at you . . ."

Valcor was right; by the next evening, his skin had developed a group of purpling bruises. Sacha asked him about them while they were at dinner, in between talking loudly to Valcor about why people generally don't try to walk a tightrope over high structures. Rafael was occupied with something that he wouldn't let anyone see, which typically turned out to be his homework, so nobody really took much notice.

"He was attacked by bandits," Valcor put in, before Kai had a chance to answer.

Sacha laughed. "And I suppose he fought them off blindfolded, with one arm tied behind his back?"

"How'd you know?" Valcor asked, totally deadpan. "You must be a psychic or something."

She grinned. "Lucky guess. Give over, Val. What really happened?"

"Kai was fighting against Wave at Guild yesterday," Valcor said.

"Wow, Kai, that's awesome!" Sacha grinned, patting him on the back. "What were you fighting with? Machetes? Did you get stabbed?"

"Nah, just staffs. They wouldn't let us fight with machetes anyway," Valcor said sardonically. "Think of all the casualties it would cause."

"I don't think we even *have* machetes at the school, Sacha," Rafael added with a laugh. "Did you win, Kai?"

Kai said, "It was a draw."

"John says he'd be really good if he got training," Valcor continued enthusiastically.

"That'd be pretty cool," Kai agreed. "But we don't get extra sessions."

"Staff fighting is quite popular in some places," Sacha said thoughtfully. "You could get lessons on Meridian, I bet."

"If you want training, you could talk to Yoko," Rafael said after a moment of quiet deliberation.

Kai looked around the table, realizing all of a sudden that their somewhat obscure companion appeared to be absent. "Where is she?"

"Out somewhere," Sacha replied vaguely.

"She trains people?"

Rafael shrugged. "Not usually, but if she thinks you're good, she'll usually try. She taught Valcor a few tricks at one point. If you want to ask, try to find her in the gym when she's training. She gets up really early, though."

Skyriders

It was not quite seven in the morning when Kai quietly pushed open the door of the gym. He'd only been there twice so far, and the room felt odd when it was so empty, a stark contrast to the constant chatter and noise he had become accustomed to.

Yoko was there, just as Rafael had said, warming up by practising different attacks on a flaccid punchbag in the middle of the room. Not wanting to disturb her while she was so focused, Kai watched her from the stairs that led down onto the floor. She fought as if she were dancing: elegant, fluid movements with deft, flicking strikes, moving so lightly he never heard her feet against the ground. She finally finished with her warm-up and tapped her staff lightly against the ground to get his attention.

"Kai, huh? What do you want?"

"Uh . . . I was hoping you could . . . teach me how to fight with the staff," Kai said hesitantly. She tilted her head slightly, giving the appearance of deeply scrutinizing him, although her hat covered most of her face so Kai couldn't see what the verdict was.

"You ever used one before?"

"Once."

"Let's see you fight, then."

"W-we're fighting now?"

She grinned at him, taking off her hat and tucking her hair securely behind her ears so it didn't fall into her face.

"Yeah. What're you scared of?"

Kai got to his feet and retrieved a staff from the back of the room. When he returned to face Yoko, she struck quickly, a low forward jab at his legs. Kai sidestepped, blocking her next attack before employing a swift counter-attack. The familiar rush of adrenaline set in as the fight continued, taking and dealing attacks with an odd, quiet determination that he'd never felt before.

Yoko wasn't blatantly more skilled than either Valcor or Wave; on the surface, you would have never been able to tell. But after a while, Kai realised she was much better. Most of what he'd seen of her earlier was merely the tip of an unexpectedly large iceberg: whilst on the exterior her strikes seemed fluid but rather flimsy and more for show than anything else, underneath was a reserve of pure finesse, a quiet flair that took Kai completely by surprise. She didn't seem fazed by anything; she was totally relaxed and coordinated. Although most of her attacks weren't obviously strong or fast, she employed devious tactics, deft flicks of her staff leaving stinging marks across his arms and neck, often appearing to be readying for one move before suddenly switching to another.

Kai soon lost track of time. He had no idea how long they'd been fighting or when it would end. He'd realised a while ago that she wasn't specifically trying to defeat him, although Kai was sure she could have multiple times if she'd wanted to; she was merely testing him to see the limits of his skills. And while it was exhausting, he found himself admitting that he was in fact enjoying this.

The morning bell sounded, breaking up the fight. Yoko retrieved her hat and pulled it back over her head, obscuring the expression from her face once again.

"You coming back?" she asked him finally.

Kai felt a rush of emotion, a mix between pride and exhilaration. "Yeah. When?"

"Tomorrow."

He trained with her most mornings from then on. The lessons were the same most of the time; warming up by drilling offensive and defensive moves before she taught him a few techniques to try out. Then they fought for the rest of the session—until just before the morning bell sounded, when Kai went back to his room to get ready for school. Yoko had started rather gently on him, until he could beat her, then upped her game, waiting until Kai could match her level before moving up.

One morning was dull and crisply cold, but once Kai warmed up, he didn't notice the cold. After nearly a month of training, Kai was pretty sure he was at about the same level as Yoko. The two of them had been locked in a fierce, fast-paced battle for a while, each vying to get the better of the opponent. Kai heard the door to the room closing, but he had his back to it and couldn't see who'd entered.

Yoko pounced on his momentary distraction, quickly driving forwards while his concentration wavered, forcing him a few steps backwards. Berating himself for getting sidetracked, Kai threw himself once more into the battle, blocking all other thoughts out of his mind until the bell's reverberating echo resounded throughout the room.

She nodded at Kai, leaning her staff against the wall. "Nice work today. Don't get distracted next time."

Kai nodded, turning to the door to see who had been watching them. He recognized the figure of his head teacher, leaning against the banister of the stairs, a sharp interest reflected in his eyes.

"I see you've found a new training partner, Yoko," he remarked. "Is he any good?"

Yoko nodded. "He's very good at this. Picks up stuff quickly. Best partner I've had so far."

Kai felt a rush of pride at the praise from Yoko, which from her was generally unexpected.

"Kai, I don't suppose I could have a brief word with you?" Mr Shorren said to him.

"I'll put your staff away," Yoko said, taking it from him as Kai followed him out of the room. Mr Shorren gave no clues as to what he wanted as he led Kai up a tight spiral staircase, pushing open the door that led to his office, leaving Kai to invent wild theories about what was going to happen.

The room was small but cosy, the huge floor-length window giving him a bird's eye view of the school grounds. Kai didn't see anybody yet—the morning bell had just rung—but he could see the flickering lights in some rooms, indicating that people were just getting up.

"So I see you've taken up staff fighting," Mr Shorren remarked conversationally.

Kai nodded, not entirely sure how to reply.

"Incidentally, I recall that your mother was an adept pole fighter," Mr Shorren said, "and judging from what Yoko told me, you seem to share the same quality. As a parting gift, she gave me her staff before she left for Earth."

Kai paused for a moment, surprised. "Can I see it?"

Mr Shorren smiled. "Of course."

He pulled open a long, flat box from somewhere behind him, polished deep brown wood fringed with gold gleaming at him. The head teacher open it, revealing a beautifully handcrafted staff nestled in rippling layers of pure velvet fabric. A scarlet gem was inlaid inside it, catching the early morning sun's rays and scattering them shamelessly across the room, streaking the very air around it with a dim red hue. There was a spearhead on the side, which fitted comfortably around the top of the staff, making it a more effective weapon.

"She made this herself for a practical technology project," Mr Shorren said. "I think I speak for both of us when I say that I think you should have it."

For a minute, Kai was too stunned to speak. "Me?"

"No, I was talking to the potted plant in the corner there."

Feeling slightly embarrassed, Kai continued. "But... I-I couldn't..."

"Nonsense. I can think of nobody else I'd rather give it to."

Go on Kai, sweetie. Take it. A warm, familiar voice echoed in his mind. *You deserve it.*

Kai took the box from Mr Shorren. "Thank you," he said gratefully.

"No worries. Have a nice day."

ELEVEN

Seasons shifted, the receding winter finally melting into the soft hues of spring, and the weather suddenly took a turn for the better. Kai welcomed the spring as much as anyone else, and because he felt he hadn't seen much of Farrell lately, he decided to let him play around for a bit after his riding classes in the evenings. Kai clambered onto Farrell's back, letting him take off, hearing his happy clicking sounds as he soared freely through the air.

It was the moment between dusk and true night, the moment when the sun was just out of view and a few early stars were already shining in the half-dark sky, the moon just rising over distant treetops. It was the moment when everything was silent, awed by darkness. By the time he landed again, he felt elatedly happy and relaxed.

Farrell was a flurry of activity, shredding errant weeds between his paws and then flitting round in the sky above Kai's head, chasing after bugs, before settling down beside Kai and slipping into a gentle doze. It was impressive how easily Talites found it to get to sleep, Kai thought, absently stroking Farrell's head. A flickering movement in the air caught his eye. For a minute, he tensed, expecting the worst, but he could make out the familiar figure of a Talite and its rider streaming vertically upwards and relaxed again. The two figures climbed higher, slowing down until they seemed to simply hang in the air.

Then they started to fall.

Kai panicked, wondering if he could wake Farrell and jump to the rescue, but they levelled off again with ease, flying flat out in a straight line. But it was shaky at best, and in some places, the Talite tilted so much he was worried the rider would fall clean off it. Basic manoeuvres went to pieces; the Talite wouldn't fly straight, wouldn't turn, and generally seemed to be resisting every movement.

Finally, the rider let out a cry of irritation clearly audible from where Kai was sitting, swooping downwards and landing heavily on the ground just in front of them. Kai had been expecting some sort of apprentice—who was somehow well versed in the ways of elite theory nonetheless—so he was shocked when Wave jumped off the Talite, her face tight with barely suppressed fury.

"Hi," he said awkwardly. Farrell woke up at this, gazing sleepily up at her. "What're you up to?"

She stared at him as if all she really wanted to do was kick him in the face. Kai wondered if he should make some polite excuse and leave. He was just formulating how best to phrase this when suddenly she spoke.

"You know about free riding, right?"

Kai nodded, something starting to make sense.

"I've always wanted to be able to do it—to ride like that without restrictions, without limits, without rules. All my life . . . since I was eight. But no matter how hard I try it, *this* pathetic excuse for a Talite—" she broke off to glare at her Talite, who pressed itself against the ground whimpering "—keeps screwing it up. *Every* single *freaking* time. It's nothing more than a stupid, *stupid* waste of—"

She stopped again, eyes dark with anger, clenching and unclenching her fists. Farrell gave an anxious whine and buried his face in Kai's arm. Kai wondered why she was telling him this.

"Maybe you should . . . be kinder to it?"

"Why would I want to do that after all it's done is let me down?" Wave demanded incredulously.

"Well, it's meant to be about the . . . bond between the two of you."

"I know what free riding is. I don't need to be lectured by the likes of you," she snapped. Then she seemed to change her mind and continued: "I don't hate him; just remember that. I'm not normally like this. When I stop doing positions, it just panics. It goes mad." She sighed. "I guess it's frustrating when I've wanted this for so long and it's still just out of reach."

Silence descended as her words faded into the clutches of night.

"You know, since I've been here . . . I've wanted to ride . . . like you," Kai said, suddenly, quietly, not looking at her.

"Seriously?"

"I saw you ride once, when I was training for my exam. You were doing it so . . ." He shook his head, words failing him. "I don't know. It was so cool. I've always wanted to ride like that."

She looked at him cautiously, as if she didn't know whether or not to trust him. Then she grinned. "Actually, you're not too bad yourself. That crazy stunt you pulled with the vertical drop was kinda impressive."

"You think so?"

"What? I said it, didn't I?"

Kai was surprised at the unexpected compliment. "Thanks."

After another prolonged silence, Kai got to his feet. "Well, I think I'll be going inside now. It's getting late."

Wave nodded. "Yeah, you're right."

After leaving their Talites at the stables, they returned to the reception area at the school. Meg was busy at her desk, filing some documents. She murmured a greeting at them without even looking up.

They'd barely entered the room when the door was flung open behind them, nearly hitting Kai in the back. Somebody was crying, a terrifying, urgent wailing which merged with agonized screams of pain.

Kai spun round and instinctively flinched. "What on earth . . . ?"

Two girls had entered the room, one sobbing hysterically, her face marked with scratches and cuts that mingled with her tears, watery red rivulets running down her face, and a long, thin scratch down her arm. Her friend was slumped in her arms. She'd been hurt badly. A huge gash ran up her leg, blood soaking her clothes and quickly pooling onto the floor of the reception area as her friend lowered her to the linoleum floor. There was blood everywhere, streaking her face, matting in her hair, and coating her arm, which had been twisted into an insanely awkward angle so that it was almost bent back on itself, splinters of bone sticking out at the edges.

Kai took a few steps back, feeling sick. He'd never seen so much blood in all his life, and it scared all sense out of him. He could only stare, dumbfounded, as Wave and Meg jumped in to help.

"Rae, what happened?" Meg asked urgently, crouching next to them.

The girl attempted to speak, but most of the story was obscured by her choking sobs, and the injured girl was in far too much pain to hear the question.

Meg looked over at Wave. "Take Renee to the medical room *fast*," she commanded, and Wave quickly obeyed, assisted by some other pupils who'd come to see what the commotion was about. She turned back to Rae. "Look, we need to help her, but we can't if we don't know what happened, okay? Stop crying for just a minute and tell us what you did."

She shook her head as if desperately trying to forget what she'd seen. Finally, she screwed her eyes shut, clenching her fists. "Dracaens," she said, forcing back more tears. "Two . . . two of them."

"Go on," Meg said, her face a mask of concern.

"W-we were outside . . . o-on the ridge by Summit Peak. We were just walking, you know . . . then these two Dracaens appear . . . like, totally out of nowhere. We didn't see them or anything. They attacked us . . ." She shook her head again, desperate, heart-wrenching cries emitting from her. "It was terrible. One of them grabbed Renee and started shaking her. I managed to make it drop her, but they kept on attacking. Renee was out for most of it, but she woke up and kept screaming all the way back here about how bad the pain was. Her Talite's dead; it tried to protect her, but the Dracaen just . . ." Her voice trailed off again. "I managed to get her onto my Talite and fly her here . . . Will she . . . ? Do you think she'll be okay?"

Skyriders

Meg looked away. "Maybe, kid. We'll have to see."

By this time, the commotion had drawn several other people into the reception area. The noise was deafening; people were screaming in shock and fear, shouting, shoving to get a better view. The room was a deluge of activity, and the noise was giving Kai the makings of a headache.

"*Quiet!*" Meg shouted at the assembled crowd. "Get away, all of you. Kai, keep a lookout at reception for me for a few minutes. I'm going to talk to Mr Shorren." The pupils dispersed reluctantly, their avid conversations still lingering as they left.

Meg returned half an hour later, looking haggard and tired, with one of the sanitation staff to clean up the pool of blood in the foyer. Kai could hear him mumbling under his breath: "Dirt tracks or something—*that* would have been plausible. But *this* I didn't expect."

"Thanks, Kai." She took her seat once more and moved the documents she'd been filing to one side before producing a pen from nowhere and writing something on a new sheet of paper. "This has made my day a whole lot worse."

"What happened?"

"You don't need to know," she replied sternly. "Lights out is in a couple of minutes, though; you should be in bed."

Disappointed, Kai made his way up to his room, trying not to think too hard about what he'd just seen. Judging by the severity of the event, the news should have spread round the school by tomorrow at the earliest, he reckoned, pushing the door open. That at least gave him the night to try to block out the image from memory.

"Kai! Did you hear the news! Some kid got viciously attacked by a Dracaen tonight!"

Mentally cursing the stupidly efficient news transfer system of the school and Valcor's general lack of discretion, Kai sat down on his bed. "Yeah."

"You don't seem surprised," Rafael said.

"I already heard about it. News travels pretty quickly round here."

Thankfully, the bell rang for lights out then, so they didn't pursue the conversation any further. As Kai predicted, everybody seemed to be talking about it the next morning. The teachers were having a hard time getting anything done because of all the whispered conversations going on, the conversations growing wilder and more exaggerated as the day progressed. By that evening, there were at least seven Dracaens involved, and Renee had been swallowed whole at one point during the attack.

The school remained excited about the topic for the next couple of days, but eventually it slowly started to fizzle and die out as normality regained a hold over their lives. Kai was starting to wonder whether the whole thing would simply be forgotten when Valcor came into their bedroom one evening in a good mood. He was generally always in a good mood, but today he seemed noticeably pleased about something.

"School's cancelled for tomorrow," he said happily, flopping down onto his bed.

"Cancelled?" Kai echoed, looking up from the book he'd been reading.

Valcor nodded. "Yeah. Meridian has called an emergency meeting on Teklah to discuss the Dracaen problem, and seeing as most people'll be there, including the teachers, the school's closed."

"An emergency meeting? Aren't those rare?"

"Yeah, they are. The last one was ages ago. But seriously, no school! How great is that?"

For Valcor, anything that involved getting out of school was a reason to celebrate.

"Are you going to the meeting?" Kai asked.

Valcor paused. "Maybe. I don't know. I might go down later in the day, like in the evening or something."

Kai nodded.

"Why, did you want to go?"

He shrugged. "Yeah. It sounds like something worth listening to."

Valcor grinned. "It'll be all over the school the day after. You'll probably be able to piece it together from the gossip alone." He leaned backwards against the wall. "Rafael will be pleased. About not having school, I mean. He likes sleeping in. Where is he, anyway?"

Kai said, "Haven't seen him today."

"Fine. I'll tell him when he gets back."

Kai ended up going to the meeting with Becky and Felix in the late afternoon. They arrived at Teklah with the vivid sunset splayed across the sky. After securing their Talites near the front of the island, they hurried up a coarse, rocky path that rose slightly on a slope. The island was mostly uninteresting. Piles of rubble were carelessly strewn around the place, bricks crumbling with age lying dejectedly on their sides. There were fragments of once-proud buildings, reduced to mere ruins, and trailing vines of plants looping in and out of the gaping cracks in the stone. Occasionally, the furry head of a small animal would pop out from behind a wall or from a hole before quickly disappearing again, fleeing into the shadows. The place resonated with the desolation of a previous disaster. It had a sinister undertone to it, and Kai couldn't help feeling slightly apprehensive.

They finally reached the meeting place. A raised platform had been built in the centre, and that's where a person stood yelling and pointing dramatically at the crowd that had assembled. Four tall poles were arranged in a diamond shape around the stage. At the top, a large deep red gem had been mounted, glowing in the approaching dark with such ferocity that it seemed to be on fire. Kai could almost feel the energy they gave off trembling through the atmosphere.

There was no way they could get closer than the very edge of the crowd. From this position, he couldn't see what was going on, but he could hear the comments being fired from place to place. They met Yoko at the outskirts. She'd made herself comfortable, sitting down on a rare patch of grass with her back against an old doorframe.

"Hey," she said, as they sat down near her.

"What've they been doing so far?" Becky asked.

"Not much. Everyone's agreed that the Dracaens are a problem. They've also agreed that they should up their defences, but on the topic of actually stopping them, they seem to be out of ideas. They've been arguing about it for the past two hours or so."

"We should make a fleet of armed ships and sail right into the heart of the problem. If we take out the Dracaens on their turf, they'll think twice before messing on ours!" a man shouted loudly from somewhere within the crowd.

"They're animals. They don't *think*."

"We shouldn't attack them," somebody else countered. "That would only make them angrier. We just need to lure them away from innocent people."

"What about the ERT? It's *their* job to do this kind of stuff!"

"The ERT?" Kai asked Becky blankly.

"Emergency response team," Becky explained. "They're a group of highly trained officers who protect and serve the citizens of Keturah. There are small squadrons on each of the islands; they help with things like fires, burglaries, and people lost in mountains or something. Their main base is on Meridian. There are around five hundred of them in all."

"The ERT are already on a state of high alert," a woman said loudly.

"She's the chief of the ERT," Becky told Kai.

"The Dracaen attacks mean that there are more emergencies than usual. All ERT members are either involved in rescue work or manning guard towers around the islands."

"All you are doing is responding; we have to get to the bottom of this!" somebody screeched. "If you just pull the surface of a weed, it will grow back again and again. We have to find the *root* of this problem: Why are they swarming? What caused this?"

There were tense mutterings, offered suggestions, irritated responses—people shouting and waving their arms around, gesturing furiously to get their points across. Kai listened, half amused, half distressed, at the mounting volume of the arguments zipping back and forth between the crowd.

"Ah, what's the use?" somebody yelled out. "We're not getting anywhere with this. We'll be better off if we just let them be. Maybe they'll just up and leave, same way they started. We should give them their own time and place."

The crowd paused then, considering this.

Suddenly, a hard, raspy laugher, much like a cackle, broke through the fallen silence. The group shifted as they turned to scan the area for the person responsible.

"Never in my life did I think I'd hear those words repeated again."

Yoko looked up, interested.

"What?" Kai asked, sensing a change in atmosphere.

"That woman," she said quietly, a kind of hard satisfaction in her voice, "is the last surviving person who escaped the fall of Teklah."

Becky said, "Now there's a piece of history I don't want to repeat."

"Everyone says she's crazy," Felix frowned.

Yoko grinned. "She probably is. But she knows what she's talking about. This might actually be worth watching."

After searching for a while, they managed to find a place where they could just barely see the stage. A wizened old woman was being helped up onto the stage. Her expression was stern, her face stark white except for dark eyes that seemed to pierce straight through anyone caught in their steely gaze. Leaning heavily on a stick, she slowly made her way to the centre of the stage, waiting until she had the crowd's full attention before plunging into a dramatic, well-oiled saga.

"I remember it like it was yesterday." Her voice seemed almost as frail as her body was, but it held an inner strength that reverberated across the crowd. Even from where he was standing, Kai had no trouble hearing her. "We were young and innocent back then, stupid fools who couldn't see a disaster coming if it hit us in the face. We saw the Dracaens increase in number. We heard the stories of them picking off workers in the fields and dragging them, kicking and screaming, off the ground before devouring them in the air. But we lived in the city—Teklah, the greatest isle on Keturah. We thought we were safe. We didn't do anything." She laughed again, softly and bitterly. "We were stupid. We could have done something to stop the disaster from happening, but we all thought they'd eventually just give up and go home. My brother said to me what you just said, that if we give them their space, they'll up and leave. Huh. If we'd had more sense, he'd still be alive."

The person who'd spoken earlier looked at his feet, clearly embarrassed.

"When they attacked, we weren't even ready. They were ruthless, frenzied, and hell-bent on causing some kind of damage that night. I've never seen so many Dracaens in one place before. They tore down the defences—our great city walls that had kept invaders out for centuries—like they were made of paper. People screaming, shouting, hugging their children . . . They destroyed the ships. There was no escape. We were trapped.

"For three or four days, they ravaged the island, tearing down everything. Lord only knows how I managed to get out alive. By the time it was over, there were only a handful of survivors left."

Here she paused, taking a moment to compose herself before continuing. Her words echoed into the sudden silence that followed it. Kai blinked. He'd been engrossed in the story, hooked from the first line.

"She's good at this," he murmured.

"She made a fortune telling this story to people since the incident," Yoko replied. "She's probably set for life now."

Becky nodded sombrely. "So many people died," she whispered. "It was terrible. I can't imagine what it would be like to actually experience it."

The old woman turned to the crowd, her voice rising. "Do you see what I'm saying? We can't afford to be fools like we were back then! History has a habit of repeating itself, and I can see the signs coming. It will be like the third cycle all over again, just you wait! If we don't put an end to this now, we probably won't live to regret it!"

The crowd launched into another bout of tense debate.

"We know of the danger!" somebody shouted. "But what are we meant to do? Why are they attacking?"

Kai turned to Becky. "What happened afterwards?" he asked over the sounds of people talking and arguing.

"After what?"

"After they attacked."

She paused. "Well, they sent out some rescue teams once the Dracaens left the island."

Kai shook his head. "I mean, what happened to the Dracaens after they attacked? Did they leave Keturah altogether?"

Becky hesitated. "I *think*," she said, although she didn't sound convinced. "I'm not sure. They haven't been around for a while, that's for sure. The attack on Teklah must have been around seventy or eighty years ago now. They only started getting serious recently."

They left the meeting soon after. It had all dissolved into more arguments and nothing being done. Kai felt like pursuing his initial thought further before he retired for bed, but when they touched down at the school, he realised how exhausted he was and changed his mind. He had time; he could pick it up tomorrow or some other time.

But things kept cropping up: urgent things like the ever-present mounds of homework on his desk, or huge gaping projects that swallowed up great chunks of his time without his even noticing, or errands that he *finally* got to run from the Hunters' Guild. A couple of weeks passed before the thought about the Dracaens disappearance even crossed his mind again, and by that time, he was too wrapped up in his navigational science homework to do anything about it.

So the thought hovered listlessly in the back of his mind like a ghost wandering around aimlessly, hoping that something would happen to trigger the memory that would prompt Kai to take relevant action. But nothing of the sort occurred, and it just seemed to fade away over time. Nothing happened.

At least not for a while.

TWELVE

"You know, Kai, I never took you to Meridian."

It was Rafael who'd spoken, rather out of the blue. It was breakfast, which was generally one of the quieter meals of the day, owing to the fact that Valcor and Sacha were usually too tired to argue about anything, and nothing much of interest really happened on the weekends.

Kai nodded. "You didn't," he agreed. "Things kept popping up."

"Do you want to go? I mean, I've gotta pick something up from the post office, and it's probably better if I go with someone, and you haven't been yet, so . . ."

"Yeah, sure."

"You're going to Meridian today?" Sacha asked, a serious expression on her face. She looked worried.

Rafael shrugged. "Why not?"

"It's dangerous out there," Sacha said pointedly. "I don't want you guys to get hurt like that kid did."

"Renee," Valcor corrected her. "She's my partner in natural science. I wonder how she's doing. I tried to visit her, but the nurse said she needs peace and quiet."

Sacha nodded. "Otherwise, everyone would be crammed in there to visit. But that's not the point."

"It shouldn't be too bad, Sacha," Rafael said.

"I'll bring my staff," Kai added.

She shook her head, ripples of ginger hair falling into her face. "Please don't go, Kai. I have a bad feeling about this."

Kai looked away. He didn't want to disagree with her openly, but he still wanted to go, despite the danger. Anyway, what were the odds of two big attacks like that in less than a couple of weeks?

"It'll be okay," he replied uncertainly.

Meg at reception held similar concerns when they told her where they were going.

"Meridian? After what's happened? You'd be better off here, I think." But after a couple of minutes of fierce persuasion, she let them go. "But be careful out there," she said, looking at them seriously over the rims of her glasses.

Rafael stopped outside the stables as they mounted their Talites.

"Are you sure you want to go? We don't have to, if you don't . . ."

"I want to go. I've never been before."

It was a clear, balmy day, the kind of day you wished you could cut out and stick on a postcard and send to your relatives to make them jealous. The sun was shining, the wind swirled languidly in the warm air, and although Kai remained vigilant, restlessly searching for any signs of trouble, the journey to Meridian passed uneventful.

The island was huge. It looked big from the map he had in his room, but being there was a completely different matter. The streets, crammed with tall houses and large shop fronts, were swarming with people shouting, yelling, and chatting about the weather.

Kai instantly preferred the calm atmosphere back on Tissarel.

Rafael pushed open the door of the post office, a light jingle of a bell announcing his presence as he walked in. There were a small number of people in the room, including an elderly couple at one of the desks. It was the only post office open on the weekend, so they had to wait fifteen minutes to be helped. An employee gave them a sheet to fill in, pointing them towards a desk and two comfortable-looking chairs.

Rafael gave Kai a scrunched-up letter as he started filling in the form with a pen that was on the desk. "Don't read it, okay? There should be a number at the top of the letter."

"Yeah . . . five-one-two-three."

"That's the one," Rafael replied, writing down the number where it said REFERENCE ID on the form.

"Why can't I read it?" Kai asked.

"'Cause it's personal," Rafael said. "There. Done."

After a brief check of the letter, the assistant retreated into a back room, returning a couple of minutes later with a small squarish package securely wrapped in thick brown paper and tied with string. "I believe this is yours," she said, handing it over. "Have a nice day."

"What is it?" Kai asked as they walked back onto the main street of Meridian.

"It's a present from my sister," Rafael explained, gently prising open the packaging. "She went to work in Verran a couple of years ago, so I don't see much of her. I asked her to get this for me."

It was a book, neatly bound with leather, dictating the chronicles of the great battles of ancient history, or words to that effect.

"History," Kai said with a grimace. "I hate history."

"Aw, history's not too bad," Rafael said mildly, tucking the book into his backpack. "It's like a huge storybook, except everything's true. Or, you know, exaggerated but based on truth. Interesting stuff. Want to try your hand at some fishing? Damon usually lets you go free on your first try."

Rafael skilfully weaved his way between the crowds, following a concise, well-rehearsed route to a small ramshackle hut at the edge of the island. Here it was quieter, although the lively bustle of the town could still be detected at the edge of their hearing.

"Ah, Rafael," the owner of the hut said. He was a large, boisterous man with unkempt hair and an odd-looking tattoo on the side of his face. "Haven't seen you for a while."

"Things happened," Rafael replied vaguely.

"Such is life. Who's your friend?"

"Kai. It's his first time here. Kai, this is Damon—he runs this place."

"Oh, new to this, eh?" Damon said with a sideways grin. "First go's on the house for you, kid. Hopefully you get hooked like my friend Raf here and keep coming back and spending half your life at this place. He's probably supplied half my life's savings by now. Don't you have friends where you come from, huh?"

Rafael said, "I've got friends. It's just nice to get out."

"So . . . what's it going to be?" Damon asked, already rooting around in the back of the hut for some equipment.

"Same as always," Rafael said, fishing a couple of coins out of his pocket. He gestured to Kai. "Come on, I'll show you how to fish up here."

They spent most of the morning baiting unfortunate birds and reeling them up to be sold later, and then they stopped off for lunch in an obscure café on a high outcrop overlooking the bustling centre of Meridian.

"What's with the castle?" Kai asked. He'd finished his lunch a while ago and jumped on the first topic he could as a means of entertainment.

There was a ridiculously opulent castle in the dead centre of the island. Kai had seen the turrets of it as they'd entered the marketplace, towering gold structures looming over the city. The walls were a pure white, all other colours around it dimming in its wake.

"Oh, that. The ruling family live there, although they generally don't do much anymore, seeing as the running of Keturah is mainly left to the council in Meridian. But the castle is hundreds of generations old, and the ruling family trace right back to the first ruler of Keturah, back in the first cycle, so people like the castle as sort of a reminder of past times."

Kai nodded. "Are we going soon?"

"When I finish this," Rafael said placidly, showing no signs of speeding up. "Patience is a virtue, you know. You're just like Valcor."

Presently he finished his lunch and stood up. "Do you wanna see anything else?"

Kai said, "I've got stuff to do back at school. I'll check the rest out another time."

Rafael nodded. "I thought you'd say something like that."

They'd covered half the distance of the way back when Rafael paused in mid-air, looking slightly concerned.

"What?" Kai asked.

"I thought I heard something," Rafael replied. "Be quiet for a second."

The afternoon seemed to hold its breath as they descended into silence, listening intently for anything out of place. Kai could almost hear the seconds ticking by.

Finally, Rafael shrugged. "Perhaps I'm just going senile in my old age," he said wryly.

Then Kai heard something, an odd rasping, shrieking sound at the back of his mind. "I heard something too. It was like—"

A flash of a dark, rippling body streaked past him, razor-sharp wings tearing across his face. Kai yelped in pain, feeling blood flow down his face. Instinctively, Kai reached for his staff, but the Dracaen was moving too fast for him to be able to hit it, and he was stabbing hopelessly at the air.

"Kai!" Rafael shouted at him. "Get away *now!*"

Kai heard Rafael's shouted command, but before he could act on it, the Dracaen's tail slammed into him, the force of it knocking all the breath out of his lungs.

Instinct kicked in a little late, and he quickly dodged the next attack, giving him time to escape to a safe distance, panting for breath.

"Are you okay, Kai?" Rafael asked.

Kai shook his head, keeping one eye on the Dracaen. It lunged forwards again, but Kai had been expecting it and jabbed his staff forward, the spear point embedding itself into its body. It gave out a high-pitched squeal as it recoiled, blood spurting out from the wound, but it was shallow and unlikely to do any sort of lasting damage.

Rafael swore under his breath. "This isn't looking good."

"Quick," Kai said to Rafael, his voice blurring. "That won't distract it for long."

But even with the creature injured and their having a ten-second head start, the Dracaen was too fast for them to outrun it. Already Kai could see it in the corner of his eye. It was gaining on them with every passing second, grating screeches of pain and fury echoing throughout his racing mind. Soon it would have caught up with them, and he was fast running out of any kind of helpful energy.

Kai ducked just as the Dracaen's tail swiped across the space where his head had been a couple of seconds ago, but the next attack came too quickly for him to react. A sharp pain exploded across his body as his vision reeled, his consciousness fading slightly before righting itself again. Just in time for the next attack, Kai tightened his grip on Farrell's band; the poor thing was whining in fear. He barely managed to hold on to the band as the pain smashed into his already weakened consciousness.

He was in too much pain to think, let alone do. He could see the Dracaen readying for a final strike that would undoubtedly send him falling helplessly, plummeting through the sky to a messy death, but he couldn't summon the energy to move. *This is it,* he thought, feeling an odd kind of calm seep over him.

The last thing he saw was a flash of red light, of pure energy, erupting from behind him, and then the world around him faded into a deep darkness.

THIRTEEN

Kai awoke sometime later feeling dizzy and lightheaded, his head throbbing painfully with a dull incessant pulse. He opened his eyes hesitantly, trying to make sense of where he was.

He recognized the room immediately, even though he'd only been there once in his life: he was in the medical room back at school. Which meant . . . he'd survived?

"What happened?" he murmured to nobody in particular, for the room was empty, quiet. Oh, no, wait, somebody was coming in.

"Kai, you're awake," the nurse said, smiling at him. "How do you feel?"

"Hurt," he said dully.

"I can imagine. From what Rafael said, you are probably the luckiest person alive. It's a miracle you're still here. Just a few bruises and cuts is all. Mild concussion, I think. You'll probably be fine for school in a day or two."

Things just kept getting better, Kai thought wryly.

"Where is he?"

"Who, Rafael? He's fine. He's in class now."

Kai looked over at the clock; it was just past eleven. So school had started, and Rafael appeared to be fine. He breathed a sigh of relief.

"How . . . ?"

"Shh now, Kai," the nurse said, cutting him off. "Take it easy for a while; try not to talk too much. I expect you'll get a lot of people coming once school ends. You can read this book if you want to."

"*The Complete Guide to Herbal Remedies*"? Kai asked incredulously.

"Give it a go," the nurse replied with a coy smile. "You might like it."

Kai was engrossed in a chapter about sedatives and tranquilizers when the door opened a few hours later and Becky entered the room.

"Oh, Kai, thank goodness you're all right," she said, wrapping her arms around him and hugging him tightly. Kai felt his face burn, cheeks flaring crimson.

"Th-thanks," he replied, somewhat startled.

"I was so worried. I thought you were going to die," she continued, her voice edged with genuine concern. "How're you feeling?"

"Better," he responded gratefully. "What happened out there? I thought I was done for."

"Rafael wouldn't tell me," she said, twisting her hands together awkwardly. "He said he wanted to talk to you first."

That just means more waiting, Kai thought. He desperately wanted to know what filled in the gaping void between his passing out and waking up in school almost completely unharmed.

Valcor was next to arrive, slinging his schoolbag down by the door and greeting him with no less enthusiasm than he'd come to expect from him.

"What're you reading?" Valcor asked, looking at the title with a smirk.

"There wasn't anything else to read," Kai said quickly. "It was either that or more sleep."

Valcor grinned. "Well, here's something to cheer you up. I've got your geography homework here, straight out of the lesson. Mr Ira doesn't want you to miss any of the highly fascinating work we did on anticyclones last lesson," he said, unceremoniously dumping a pile of slightly crumpled worksheets of the bedside table.

Kai smiled. "*The Complete Guide to Herbal Remedies* or geography homework. I'm not sure which one I'm more excited about."

He had a steady stream of visitors that day, including Sacha, who told him that she *had* warned him about going out, and Felix and Yoko. And finally, John and Rafael visited later in the evening.

"Hello, Kai," John said. "Feeling any better?"

Kai nodded. "Yeah."

"That's good. You were very lucky, I must say. I've seen too many people who tangled with a Dracaen and came out with more than a few cuts and bruises."

The nurse appeared, looking disapprovingly at John and Rafael. "It's quite late, and Kai needs to rest now."

"Sorry," John said diplomatically. "We'll be just a few minutes."

The nurse nodded. "Fine. But please be quick."

John turned back to Kai. "What happened?"

Kai looked over at Rafael. "What *did* happen?"

"How much do you remember?" Rafael asked him.

"Well . . ." Kai hesitated. "We were flying from Meridian . . . The Dracaen attacked us, and . . . there was this . . ." He paused, struggling with words to explain it. "It was like a red light, but I could feel it, sort of. Like an energy pulse, if that makes sense . . . That's it, really. I passed out after that."

Rafael nodded. "It came from your staff," he explained. "You know that red gem in the middle? From there."

"That staff probably saved your life," John said, intrigued. "Where'd you get it?"

"Mr Shorren gave it to me. My mum made it."

"Ah, *that* staff. I do remember it after all. She made it in one of her tech lessons."

"What happened next?" Kai asked.

"Everything seemed to be panicking. The Dracaen ran away; the Talites were clearly disturbed by something. I managed to get mine under control after a while, but it was difficult. Yours nearly dropped you; it took me ages to calm it down."

John raised an eyebrow. "The Dracaen ran away?"

He nodded.

"Are you sure? It didn't just spot another tastier looking thing and go after it instead?"

"No. I'm pretty sure it ran."

"How sure?"

"Almost certain."

John leaned back on his chair, clasping his fingers together.

"We might be on to something here," he said finally.

"What do you mean?" Kai asked.

"The only time a Dracaen will run from a situation is if it's completely outnumbered or if it's dying. And then you tell me Kai's staff can scare them away. So here we have a mounting Dracaen problem and claims that they will destroy towns and cities and kill everyone in them. And here we have something that seems to scare said Dracaens so much that they flee."

"Can we stop this?"

John sighed and got to his feet. "No. Not yet, anyway. But it's a start."

The nurse let Kai out late the next afternoon, telling him to take it easy for the rest of the day. He was milling around aimlessly in his room when Felix appeared, and undoubtedly, the conversation turned towards recent events.

"So you're saying you found a way to scare off the Dracaens?" Felix looked less than ready to believe this statement. "Why haven't you jumped into action and saved Keturah from imminent chaos yet?"

"Well, theoretically . . . there are some, uh, *complications*," Kai replied.

"Like . . . ?"

He shrugged, spinning his staff thoughtfully in his hands. "I don't know. It's like that phrase: 'From tiny acorns mighty oaks grow'. We just need more information, more leads. Less headaches too," he added, rubbing the back of his head. "This concussion isn't all it's cracked up to be."

School let out for three weeks in the middle of springtime. The air was laced with an expectant finality as the date approached: displays were taken down from walls; projects were finished and handed in; teachers hurriedly finished off topics, and the nicer ones let the kids organize end-of-term parties in the classrooms.

Valcor, Rafael, and most of the other people he'd become acquainted with went home over the break, along with pretty much all the teachers, departing the school in clumps, their excited chatter packed round them like a crowd of people. Kai didn't have the privilege of knowing of any close relatives on Keturah—or anywhere else, for that matter—which meant that he had to stay at the school for the holiday. The school felt much larger and lonelier when there was practically nobody there to fill the long corridors with avid chattering and energized laughter.

"Well, it could be worse," Felix remarked conversationally on the third day of the holiday at breakfast. Kai was bored already. "We could still have lessons."

"With, like, five people to teach? That'd be fun," Kai answered drily. He looked around the dining hall. The unfortunate others who for various reasons couldn't go home were sparsely dotted about the room, not really saying much. Kai counted about twelve people altogether.

"Hey, isn't that Becky?" Felix said suddenly, motioning to a figure on the other side of the room. Her back was to them, and she was collecting some cutlery.

"It looks like her hair," Kai agreed. "But I thought she went home."

She turned around then, proving beyond doubt that it was indeed Becky. Kai waved her over.

"Didn't expect to see you here," he said to her as she sat down.

"My mum works here," Becky said. "She's the nurse, so she has to stay in case someone gets hurt during the holidays. Tess is staying with a friend this time."

Kai nodded. "What do you do during the break, then?"

"Not much, really. It's surprising how doing nothing can stretch to three weeks."

"Sounds like fun," he said with a sigh, the life ahead of him becoming less and less interesting the more the day progressed. Then, something occurring to him, he continued more earnestly:

"Hey, Becky, you're good at languages, aren't you?"

Becky nodded hesitantly. "Yeah . . . I guess. Why?"

"We found this book the other day in the library," Kai explained. "We couldn't read it. It was in some ancient language—what was it called?"

"Ilyasi," Felix said. "It was a book of legends and stuff. Why are we going back to it now?"

Kai shrugged. "Well, I want to look up some stuff in the library, and it seems convenient. And you never know; there might be something interesting in there. I mean, it wasn't a normal book or anything. Probably shouldn't have been in the library in the first place."

Felix nodded slowly. "Valid point."

"You've lost me," Becky said, confused.

"We found this book in the library," Kai repeated. "There wasn't a stamp on it or anything, so we're not completely sure how it got there. It was in Ilyasi; Felix translated the first bit of it."

Becky frowned. "It was? Nobody uses that language anymore."

"It's from the first cycle," Felix added. "You'll understand better when you see it. What're you looking for, then, Kai?"

"I want to read about Teklah," Kai responded.

"Why?"

"Just following up on a hunch," he responded vaguely. "You guys ready?"

FOURTEEN

The library was the only place that hadn't changed since school had let out; it was still as quiet as ever. The book was where they'd left it last, wedged between two aisles. Kai pulled it out, dust flaring into his face.

"How'd you find this?" Becky asked, intrigued, as Kai broke into a fit of coughing.

"Pure chance," Kai said, sitting down at a nearby desk. "Can you read it?"

Becky studied the text for a couple of seconds. "Yeah. It might take a while, though. Do you have a pen?"

Kai left Becky and Felix translating the book while he hunted around in the history section, pulling out books that looked relevant to his research. By the time he returned to the desk, the two of them were a page or so into the text, the paper next to them fast filling up with the translation.

"What's this?" Felix asked, looking up at Kai. "History books? I thought you didn't like history."

"I do today," Kai replied with a flourish, opening up the first book and flipping the pages until he found the chapter he wanted. "Okay, let's see what's in here," he murmured to himself, delving into the folds of history.

Half an hour later, he emerged back into reality, the words of seven different authors spinning around in his head but no more knowledgeable about the subject than he'd been when he'd started. Feeling somewhat frustrated with his lack of progress, he leaned over to see how Felix and Becky were doing.

They'd had slightly more luck, having cleared around twenty pages. It was a small dent in a big book, but at least they were making progress.

"It's actually quite interesting," Becky said, scribbling things down in remarkably neat handwriting on the paper next to her. "They've got some really good stories in here."

"How 'bout you?" Felix asked. "You got anything?"

"Not yet," Kai replied, gathering up his books and heading back to the history section to collect some more. After a while, though, reading the same story over and over again got tediously tiresome, and Kai was beginning to feel his concentration flag. *Last one,* he said mentally to himself. *Then we'll call it a day.*

He opened the book.

> *The first noted appearance of Dracaens in Keturah was a year and a half before the fall of Teklah. With so few of them, however, the council turned a blind eye, believing there were not enough around to do any damage, and that their twice-fortified walls, the strongest at the time, would be sufficient to ward off any attacks.*
>
> *The fall of Teklah marked the end of the third cycle of Keturahn history. Dracaens swarmed Akkek, the largest city at the time, razing the city to the ground within mere days. Over one thousand people were killed, and it is estimated that only eight people survived the incident.*

Kai sighed. He'd read it all before. But what happened afterwards?

"Hey, Kai," Felix said suddenly, breaking into Kai's thoughts. "You found anything yet?"

"No. Why?"

Felix handed over the paper containing the last few pages they'd just finished translating. "You might want to take a look at this. I think it explains what happened to you the other day."

> *A poor trader by the name of Erith had fallen on hard times and was making his way from Tireya to the Firdes, hoping to reach the main isle and trade with the citizens there. It was a treacherous winter, and a snowstorm soon blew up like none ever seen before as he reached Stormaker's Pass. He could not see the town before him, nor anything behind him, save for the whirling storm. He was soon cold and exhausted and feared for his life.*
>
> *Suddenly, a man appeared from the blizzard, holding out his hand to Erith. "Come," he said. Erith was too cold and weary to disagree. The man led him to a small cabin and emptied out a sack on the table, full of cold red gems that gleamed even in the torchlight.*
>
> *"What are these?" Erith asked.*
>
> *"Xucite stones," the man replied. "Straight from Mialyn. Once you set them alight, they can ward off any creature that lives upon this land."*
>
> *Erith's mind leaped at the prospect. There had been famines because wild animals had been*

ravaging the crops. Farmers would pay greatly for these. "Why are you telling me this?"

"I need money. My children have been struck with fever, and my wife is long since gone. I need to go to Astlar and buy some medicine, but I cannot leave my children on their own. Please sell these stones for me and buy me some medicine for my children. That is all I ask."

It seemed reasonable, and Erith agreed. The man told him how to activate the stones. When the storm subsided, he packed up and left to sell the stones. They made him rich, richer than he had ever imagined. But greed hardened his heart, and medicine was expensive. He ignored his promise to the man.

One day he was travelling through the Firdes once more, delivering stones to a rich customer, when he bumped into a man looking haggard and sorrowful. They recognized each other at once.

"You," the man sneered. "I see from your clothes that you are well off, while you leave me here to rot with the knowledge that my dear children are no longer with me."

"I am sorry," Erith pleaded, trying to excuse himself. "I could not procure the medicine . . ."

"How can you stand here and lie to me even in the knowledge that you killed my children? I thought I could trust you; now I see I can trust no one. Greed has consumed you. I can see it in your eyes. Give me those stones. No one else will reap the benefits from them any longer. That is retribution for letting my children die."

He killed Erith, took the remaining stones, and left, never to be seen again. Some say he went back to Mialyn; some insist he killed himself and took the remaining stones to the grave. However, the stones Erith sold still remain, passed down through generations, but since the trader's demise and the disappearance of the man, they soon forgot how to use them. Only a few remember now, and they are unwilling to share these secrets with others...

"This seems pretty feasible," Kai said, returning the paper. "What's it doing in a mythology book?"

"The Xucite stones are rare. They're said to come from Mialyn, but since nobody can agree if it actually exists or not..."

Beside him, Becky gave a little gasp of revelation. "Xucite stones," she said, her voice edged with frustration. "Of *course*."

Kai looked confused, so Felix explained: "Mialyn is an island which is supposedly somewhere in the Deep Sky, but since nobody seems to know where exactly it is—or has ever seen it, for that matter—nobody is really sure if it exists. Most say it's just a myth. Xucite stones are meant to come from Mialyn, like the story says, and the Dracaens are meant to live there too. That's why they're so common in the Deep Sky. People who don't believe in Mialyn's existence don't support this theory either, but then there's the question of the stones. They're not from Keturah; at least, they've never been found there. Well, except the deposits very deep within the islands, but they're too far down to retrieve."

"So you're saying...?"

"Well, the stones have the power to ward off animals when they're lit, like that Dracaen that ran away after you were attacked."

Kai nodded thoughtfully, remembering the bright flash of red from behind him. "Raf said the Talites were pretty freaked out as well. You think there's one of those stones in the staff?"

Felix nodded. "It's the only thing that explains this so far."

"Well, surely we can just light this stone then and scare the Dracaens off?"

"If you can remember how to light the stone again, sure."

Kai blinked. Now that Felix had mentioned it, he *wasn't* really that sure of how he'd lit the stone in the first place.

"Remember the meeting on Teklah?" Becky said. "There're Xucite stones there too. Because the place is overrun with animals now, they light them when we have region-wide meetings. Those stones are huge, and they've only got a range of about the size of the crowd there. If it was small enough to fit into your staff, we're only talking really close range, like less than a metre away. To ward off all the Dracaens on Keturah, that's probably more stones than have actually been discovered."

"I don't even know how to light it," Kai added.

"So who lights the stones on Teklah?" Felix asked.

Becky shut the book she'd been reading and coiled a strand of hair around her finger. "The last few people who know how to light them live on Astlar," she said slowly. "They call themselves the Erithites, after the guy who sold them in the first place. Meridian calls them down to light the stones for the meetings on Teklah."

"So do you reckon they could tell us how to light them?" Kai chipped in.

She shook her head. "They don't go divulging these secrets to just *anyone*. Their aim is to preserve the Xucite stones and prevent people from using them for personal gain, such as Erith did in the legend. They make you take a test to prove you will be responsible with them."

"But I never took a test," Kai said, "and I still managed it."

"That's the part I don't get. You activated yours by accident. I'm not even sure if you can *do* that."

"Well, I don't know about you guys, but I think I've done enough research for today," Felix said, getting to his feet. "I'm getting a headache from all this reading."

As if to advocate this point, the bell for dinner rang suddenly, so they quickly cleared away all their books and went to the dining hall to eat. The food was a blessed release from an entire day spent tirelessly researching, translating, and reading.

"I really think we're on to something here," Becky said earnestly over dinner. "I think if we went to Astlar . . ."

"I'm not sure I want to go out again," Kai said. "I was lucky to escape with my life last time."

"But think about it," Becky said. "We could potentially save hundreds of lives here. If we leave this, the problem will only get worse, and who knows what could happen . . ."

As her voice trailed off, he knew that she was silently imploring him to trust her. Finally, he let out a quick sigh and nodded.

"How about you, Felix?" he asked.

Felix shrugged. "Yeah, I suppose."

"You're not scared of heights anymore?" Becky asked him.

"I . . . I don't know. If I don't really think about it, I can just about get by, but . . . it still freaks me out sometimes. It's improving, though."

Becky smiled. "I guess it's a good thing we climbed that mountain after all."

The next morning after breakfast, they gathered a few supplies and headed out to reception. Meg looked more harassed than usual, her usually neat mousy brown hair uncoiling, falling in scraggly strands down her face, giving the impression that all she really wanted to do was drop down and sleep.

That didn't stop her from intercepting them as they tried to leave the room.

"Hold on *just* a minute," Meg said tautly, her voice tight with stress. "Where do you think *you're* going?"

Becky told her. Meg didn't seem particularly keen on the idea.

"You're going *where?*" she asked incredulously, almost shouting. "With all those Dracaens out there? The sky's not safe nowadays, and that's a long journey. Besides, wasn't Meridian bad enough for you, Kai?"

"Please let us go," Becky begged. "This is important."

"How so?" Meg said suspiciously.

Becky explained without going into too much detail, and Meg still looked unconvinced. "Let me speak to somebody about this," she said finally. "I don't want any more dead students on my hands."

There was an uncomfortable silence as she got up and left. Becky looked awkwardly at her hands, wringing them together tightly, her nails leaving red marks across them. Without looking up, she said quietly, "What did she mean, *dead students?*"

There was no easy way to answer that question, but it was evident they'd all been thinking the same thing. Kai felt the atmosphere crash, darkening heavily. Meg returned a while later with John in tow. Kai wondered what he was still doing at school. He'd seen most of the teachers leave with the pupils; only the caretakers and a few others were left.

"What's this I hear?" he asked in a half-amused, half-serious tone. "You're planning on going to Astlar? Why?"

Becky explained the story. John listened intently as she recounted the events of yesterday afternoon.

"And we figured we should go to Astlar today," she concluded. "Perhaps if they'd tell us how to light the stone . . . I mean, at least that'd be a step in the right direction."

John rubbed the side of his chin thoughtfully and sat down. "Xucite stones," he murmured. "Yes, that *does* make sense . . . now that you mention it . . ."

For a moment, he was silent. Then he abruptly got to his feet. "Astlar it is," he said, clapping his hands. "I'll come with you, though. I don't want any more . . . ahem . . . *accidents* happening on the way." He shot a sideways glance at Kai. "Forwards and onwards, then. Let's move."

A while later, as they were cruising high over Meridian, Becky spoke suddenly, shattering the gathered silence.

"John."

Kai tried to focus on riding his Talite while listening to her. The events of the past few weeks still prominent on his mind, Kai instinctively found himself looking around constantly for that ominous dark shape looming in the distance.

"Yes, Becky?"

"I . . . I was wondering. You know Renee . . . when she got hurt by that Dracaen . . . I was thinking, like, is she okay? Is she getting better . . . ? I mean, we haven't heard much about her since she was taken in, and . . ."

John was silent for a while. Finally, he gave a slow, heavy sigh. "She didn't make it, Becky," he replied quietly, and Kai saw a brief flicker of pain cross his expression. Kai felt his heart wrench for a second, even though he'd never spoken to her or anything. Felix looked troubled. Becky flinched, her eyes quickly brimming with tears.

"I used to share a room with her," she whispered, tears running down her face. "She was . . ."

Kai knew that she was too upset to continue. Kai felt awkward and refocused his attention on his Talite, not wanting to see her cry.

"I'm sorry, Becky," Felix murmured sympathetically. She wiped her eyes and, after a moment, seemed to shake herself slightly.

"It's okay," she replied with a smile, though it didn't quite reach her eyes. "I can't get distracted now . . . The sooner we stop this, the better."

The island appeared on the horizon sometime later. Kai didn't know how long; it was all too easy to lose track of time while flying. Even at a distance, Astlar didn't fail to impress. Kai could hear the faint growl of the steep waterfall plunging over the side of the island, droplets of water fluttering in the wind. The island was robed in green except for a peak of grey where a small mountain protruded from beneath the emerald blanket that lapped the surface.

Leaving their Talites where they landed, the four of them made their way into the main city on Astlar. There were a few people dotted round the marketplace in the early morning air, but generally the place was quiet, a peaceful calm draped over it like a soft mist.

"Where do we find them?" Felix asked. "The people who can activate the stones?"

"Good question," John said. "I'm not sure, but this is a small town. Ask around; somebody's bound to know."

They asked the closest person to them, a small girl of around seven, who sucked on her finger and smiled shyly as she pointed in a northerly direction. "Lorn's Tower," she said, pulling her finger out of her mouth. "It's near the back of the town; just follow that road."

Lorn's Tower was the only surviving building from the fire of Astlar centuries ago; it was a crumbling black tower, stricken with age, blackened sections of charred wood telling grim tales of the past. Even with these afflictions, it still stood proud, governing the island with a silent, majestic unseen eye.

There were several people in a short queue outside the building, even this early in the morning. Astlar had clearly hoped to make the most out of the tower, turning it into a sort of historical tourist paradise. They offered cultural tours around the building, depicting life in the old Astlar city before it was burned to the ground. A woman who claimed to tell the future was in an obscure back room on the ground floor, and the Erithites had taken up residence on the top floor.

"What are you here for?" the bored young guy at the front of the tower said.

"We're here to see the Erithites," Becky said.

"Who's taking the test?"

"Actually, we just want to ask them—"

"Could you just answer the question, please?"

Becky looked about ready to retaliate, but then she merely sighed. "That'd be you, Kai," she said.

"Thank you. First door on your left and then follow the stairs to the top. The rest of you can accompany him, but you'll have to wait outside. Next, please. Come on, keep it moving."

The ground beneath them creaked dangerously underneath their footsteps as they ascended the many steps to the top floor. Finally they came to an elaborate-looking door just beneath the roof of the tower.

"Off you go, Kai," John said. "We'll be waiting here."

Three women sat in the centre of the room, watching him come in with sharp, dark eyes. They introduced themselves, and he guessed that Tura was the oldest of them; she sat cross-legged in the middle with a strict expression tight on her creased face. Setah sat to her right, one eye milky white, the other dark and intense. To her left was clearly the youngest, Kayah. Her face was expressionless, which contrasted slightly from the superior disapproval that radiated from the other two.

"Please sit down," Tura said, gesturing to a couple of mats opposite them. She waited until he was comfortably seated before continuing. "You have come to learn how to wield the power of the Xucite stones, yes?"

Kai paused for a second and then nodded.

"First you must be tested," Setah continued, fixing her one good eye on him rigidly. Kai couldn't meet the intense gaze. "Then we will determine if you are worthy of such an undertaking. Many are willing, but few are able to pass the test. Shall we begin?"

She didn't wait for an answer but instead extended a shallow tray filled with a thin layer of an odd orange-coloured gelatinous liquid. "Place your hand here."

Kai obeyed, feeling the brightly coloured liquid ooze between his fingers. It had an acrid, bitter tang to it that stung his eyes.

"Thank you." She withdrew the tray, and the three of them examined it closely, murmuring in muted tones that reached him as an indecipherable layer of sound. Kai couldn't read their expressions, but he sensed an air of disapproval which made him feel uneasy.

After what seemed like ages, they stopped conferring. "It seems we will not need to continue this test any further," Tura said sombrely.

Kai felt his heart sink, a pang of disappointment flaring. What could they possibly have uncovered about him from just his handprint? "Could I—"

"Don't interrupt me," Tura snapped. Kai flinched, taken by surprise. He hadn't expected more to come. An abrupt dismissal, perhaps?

"I recognize this imprint," the woman continued. "You've taken this test before."

Shocked, Kai took a few seconds before replying. "I haven't been here before. I couldn't have."

"Don't lie to me," Tura snapped, getting to her feet, her thin robe swirling around her. "You may leave."

The youngest woman got up too, to escort him out. His companions outside the door looked up eagerly as he came out.

"That was quick," Felix remarked, frowning. "How'd it go?"

"They said I've taken it before," Kai replied.

"But you haven't . . . ," Felix began, his voice trailing off as he caught sight of John nodding as if he'd been expecting this.

"Aha," he said. "*Aha.*"

The other three kids looked at him blankly. "What do you mean?" Becky asked.

"Excuse me. I don't suppose I could ask you a quick question?" John asked Kayah, who was just leaving the room.

She hesitated and then gave a brief nod. "I suppose so. Please be quick, though. We may have more applicants waiting."

"I don't know if you can remember—but around twenty years ago, were you by any chance visited by a young woman? Around, ah . . . this height." He gestured with his hand. "With curly red hair? With a staff that looks like this one?" John pointed to the staff Kai was holding.

Kai looked at John in surprise. "You mean . . . ?"

Kayah nodded. "Yes. Yes, I do recall her. Faye . . . ?"

John smiled and pointed at Kai. "This is her son."

"Ah, yes, that makes sense now," she said gently, returning the smile.

"Could we speak with the other two Erithites for a moment?" John asked. "It's rather urgent."

She entered the room again, Becky, Felix, John, and Kai piling into the room behind her.

"What is this?" Tura said sharply. "I thought I told you to leave?"

"I'm afraid there's been a little misunderstanding," John explained apologetically.

The woman they'd spoken to earlier explained quickly what had happened. "They want to talk to you for a moment. I'll go tell any people who might be waiting downstairs that we'll be a minute." She left, and the remaining two women turned to John.

"Well, make it quick."

"A while ago, Kai was flying outside when he was attacked by a Dracaen. Fortunately, the Xucite stone on his staff intervened and managed to scare it away, but Kai had never used the stone or, to my knowledge, drunk any of the Xucitus sap before. We were hoping you could shed a bit of light on the situation."

"There is an explanation," Setah said with a curt nod. "What happened was a case of pure luck. Faye passed the test, and to control the stones, we do indeed give them a sample of the Xucitus sap. Xucitus sap is not easily digestible, however, and molecules tend to stick to blood vessels occasionally. I expect, after taking it for a while, traces of the sap were passed down into *your* bloodline."

Tura nodded and continued: "The stones respond to the presence of the Xucitus sap. If it reaches the vessels close to the surface of your skin while you are in contact with or close to the stone, it will activate. Because you were scared, you were pumping blood faster, and the sap managed to activate the stone."

The rest of them nodded in understanding.

"So if Kai were to be able to use the stones," John prompted, "would he need to take the test again?"

The two women paused for a moment before leaning together and conferring. Finally, Tura spoke.

"Usually we would say yes, but times are hard these days. Dracaens are everywhere; one of us got killed by an attack many months ago. And you look like you possess the qualities of your mother which enabled her to pass the test, so . . . here. Take this."

She produced a small bottle, apparently out of thin air, and handed it over to Kai. "Use this wisely," she said, a hint of her usual severity back in her voice. "Once you ingest the Xucitus sap, the stone should light within two minutes or so, provided its close enough to you. The effects will fade after a while."

"How long?" Kai asked.

"It depends on how much of the sap you drink," Setah said. "Larger doses will make the stone's power stronger and make it last longer. Now, kindly leave, if you will, as we may have people clamouring for our services."

They said goodbye to Kayah at the door, and she gave them a brief smile before sweeping upstairs to join her companions.

The first part of the journey to the edge of the island proceeded without a word, the others apparently preoccupied with their own thoughts.

"What else has my mum done, then?" Kai asked suddenly, startling the others, who had settled into a thoughtful silence.

"What do you mean?" John asked, bewildered by the suddenness of the question.

"What else has she done that I don't know about? For all I know, she could have bungee jumped off that waterfall. It just feels like . . . she's done all this stuff that you guys know about and I don't, and she *was* my mother. It's like I don't know . . . who she is anymore."

"Well," John said, plainly struggling to construct a suitable answer. "She, uh… she was… Well, not much else interesting apart from the stuff you've heard at school. That is, until around a year before she left school, in her final year. Then she started acting a little strange."

"What happened?"

"She became very interested in Mialyn. She was always in the library, poring over mythology books and trying to discover something or other. After a while, she must've found something she wanted, because she suddenly decided to take the Erithite's test. She passed it easily—that wasn't a problem—and went out one morning soon after, coming back late in the evening with a shard of the Xucite stone. I've no idea where she got it from. She made your staff in one of our later tech lessons. Then she came and asked for permission to go exploring in the Deep Sky, to look for Mialyn. We were a bit sceptical at first, but she was a talented rider, and the Dracaens weren't as common back then, so we let her go. In fact, I'd never seen a Dracaen in Keturah until then. There *was* an attack about a year or so after she left. Pretty violent. A few people died, and a couple more were injured."

"So did she find it?"

John shrugged. "She never told me. She came back awhile later and refused to talk about the subject. Within a few weeks, she told Mr Shorren that she wanted to go to Earth, and she gave him her staff. She left soon afterwards, and . . . that's it, really."

Felix looked a bit confused. "That seems kind of strange, doesn't it?"

"I thought so too. Whatever she found, or didn't find, clearly had some sort of profound impact on her. I often wonder what happened."

"Did you ever try?" Becky asked. "To find out what happened?"

"I did everything short of flying out to Mialyn myself," John said. "I doubt I'd even find it anyway. So many people have tried to find the island, and I don't think anyone ever has." His words were followed by a short, pensive silence.

"So," he continued brightly, "are we heading back to the school now, or do you guys have other plans here?"

Kai shook the bottle he'd been given, watching the odd yellowish liquid slosh around. "I want to see whether this works," he said decisively, prising the cork off the top of the bottle.

"She said to use it wisely," Becky reminded him.

Kai nodded. "Just a small bit. It's no use to me if it doesn't work, is it?"

He took a sip of the drink. It was thick and sweet, almost like honey. There was a long, expectant pause while nothing happened at all, despite Kai waving his hand in front of the staff, poking it several times, and clutching it in his hands for a few seconds.

"Well, that was a waste of time," he said finally, disappointed. "Looks like I'll just have to—Whoa!"

The stone in the staff suddenly started glowing, a fierce red light emitting from its surface and filling the space around it with its radiance. Kai felt a rush of triumph run through him, but it quickly turned to a wave of dizziness. A flare of pain burst into his mind, and he took a step backwards.

"Are you all right?" Felix asked him.

"It hurts," he murmured. "Is it meant to do that?"

"You're standing too close," John observed, a safe distance away. "The stone generates a strong field of energy around it. If you stand inside the field, then it's dangerous."

"Dangerous?" Kai asked, alarmed. "As in . . . ?"

"It's been known to cause dizzying effects, sharp pains similar to that of a migraine. Sometimes, if the exposure is long enough, it can knock you out."

"Like what happened to Kai earlier, right?" Felix asked. John nodded.

"Could it kill him, though?" Becky put in tentatively.

"I can't say I've ever heard of that happening, but if the stone's power was large enough, I see no reason why it couldn't."

Kai nodded, but even holding the staff out at arm's length did nothing to dull the pain. He was relieved when the stone's light dimmed and finally faded altogether.

"Well, it works," he said, in case that fact had somehow eluded the others. "Shall we go back now?"

Once they returned, Kai found himself back in the library. They hadn't found much that they didn't already know after spending most of the holiday in the library, but it provided them with something to do, and every now and then, they stumbled on something interesting that pushed them further in the direction of complete enlightenment. *It's like doing sudoku*, Kai thought wryly. All they needed was that one crucial number in the right place to set off a chain reaction of discovery.

Despite many days of searching, Kai could only find one book about the Xucite stones. Looking up Mialyn, on the other hand, uncovered a trove of undiscovered information—most of it proving by some means that Mialyn did or did not exist, depending on the author and his views. There were myths, urban legends, and old newspaper articles about people setting off to find the island and returning fruitless.

The book on the Xucite stones was huge, as if to make up for the lack of alternative information. Kai had been reading it intently for a few days now, and most of it covered what they'd found out already. But there were interesting morsels of information hidden in the book as well, which only provided him with more incentive to read further. Skimming through the text, Kai's attention was quickly drawn to a small paragraph near the bottom of a page:

Chapter 18a: The Xucite Phenomenon

While the Xucite stones were readily available and cheap, by means of pure chance, an enterprising jeweller discovered the Xucite phenomenon, that is, when surrounding an object completely with Xucite stones so their energy fields overlap, they can in effect render the object and surrounding stones invisible to the naked eye (see fig. 1.) Unlit stones, however, can penetrate this field if brought close to them, 'creating an effect that seems to make the air around it tremble in its wake', in the words of one witness. An activated stone will disrupt this entirely, making the object visible once more. Incidentally, this effect is also permanent until the fields are disrupted, as the energy from the overlapping fields supports the reaction indefinitely...

"That sounds pretty cool," Felix said, after Kai had shown him what he'd found.

"It sounds pretty useful. Why don't we use this kind of thing more often?"

"The fields aren't that big, though," Felix said. "For small objects you'd only need a couple of stones, I guess, but big things would need loads. And because the Xucite stones are so rare, they're ridiculously expensive; most people can't afford to have enough to keep an object invisible for any length of time. The only way it is used in day-to-day life is the barrier around Keturah. That's linked to the Xucite phenomenon."

"I see," Kai said, turning to the next page, which showed a couple of pictures, but he wasn't really looking at them. His mind was preoccupied, elsewhere, too busy to trouble itself over semi-important issues like pictures. He was thinking about what John had told him about his mother awhile ago.

He'd never thought she had been hiding anything from him, but *this* . . . this was huge. It felt odd when he looked back on his life and realised how little he really knew about his mother. When he'd asked her about her backstory she'd told him readily enough, but her story included her growing up and living out her life entirely on Earth. And her mysterious behaviour leaving up to her sudden departure bothered him as well. It made so little sense that he couldn't even begin to come up with an idea.

He was still thinking about it all through dinner and as he dragged himself up the three flights of stairs to his room just before lights out. Why did she leave? Why didn't she tell him about this place?

He lay on his back, staring into the curtain of darkness that obscured his view of the ceiling, thoughts running through his mind, things he'd heard, read, or seen in the past two weeks scrolling through his mind in one continuous loop, moving so fast that they started to merge together. Even as he faded into an uncertain sleep, words overlapped and thoughts spilled into each other until everything was an incomprehensible mush of disjointed ideas.

And then one thought suddenly got up and announced itself, and everything else paled into insignificance. Even though Kai was asleep, he still felt a rush of satisfaction, victory even. It was as if he'd been trying to work something out all his life—and everything suddenly came together as if it had never been broken apart at all.

FIFTEEN

The next morning, Kai arrived at the table brimming with excitement at his revelation. "Guys, I've just had an idea," he said shortly, sitting down.

"Does this mean we don't have to do more research today?" Felix said. "Because I'm not sure if I can stand another day looking up stuff."

"Depends. You guys know more about this than I do; chances are I'll have missed something."

"Well, fire away," Becky said.

"I was thinking about what John said the other day about my mum being all strange and whatever. You guys know about the Xucite phenomenon, right?"

Becky nodded. "Yeah, it can make objects disappear, can't it?"

"That's the one. So I wondered . . . what if there's a ring of stones around *Mialyn*, enough to cause a reaction like that one? That way, it would be invisible unless you went there with a Xucite stone, and judging by the newspaper articles I've read, I don't think anyone has had that idea yet."

Becky nodded slowly. "It's a theory," she said thoughtfully. "But it's still a long shot. Why would there be overlapping fields of stones on Mialyn, anyway? You'd have to have Xucite stones mounted all around the island for that to work. Under it too."

"Actually . . . that legend, that one about Erith, said that the stones were from Mialyn, didn't it?" Felix put in. "So in theory, if there were, say, deposits of stone at intervals in the rock, as long as the fields overlapped, it would produce the same effect."

Feeling more confident, Kai continued: "And remember when John said that my mum was researching about Mialyn, and *then* she went and took the test before she left to look for it? I think she worked that out too, that you could use the lighted stones to make it visible."

There was a long, thoughtful pause.

"Well, it all makes sense," Becky said. "But it's so much to base on a myth. It just seems like such a leap. I mean, there's every chance you could be right, but then again, it could just be that . . ."

"Mialyn doesn't exist and everything else was just coincidence," Kai finished with a sigh. "I know."

"And what about why she left so suddenly?" Becky asked.

Kai shrugged. "I don't know about that one. Only she can tell us what she saw there, and she's . . . I don't know. Do you think she found Mialyn in the end?"

"She must have found *something*," Felix said. "I mean, that's a pretty drastic reaction she had." He paused. "So . . . no researching today?"

Kai grinned. "We'll leave it for now if you're so desperate."

"Thank *goodness*," Felix said, obviously relieved. "All that thinking was doing my head in."

The rest of the school arrived early the next day in a flurry of activity and noise that lifted the forlorn atmosphere that had settled like mist over the school, replacing it with a livelier mindset that only served to remind Kai how much he'd missed it.

Valcor spent most of the morning in the room, and while Kai watched him unpack, he talked about what he'd done in the holidays which, while in reality was remarkably little and not that interesting, with his powers of conversation, he somehow managed to stretch into a whole hour of avid description.

"Where's Raf?" Kai asked quickly while his friend was pausing for breath.

"Oh, he's gone out on some intrepid expedition with his dad," Valcor said. "They said he was gonna be a few days late for school. Lucky. So what did *you* get up to while we were out?"

"Just researching mainly, following up on what happened earlier."

"You find anything?"

"We've come up with a theory, but it's still a bit . . ." He paused, struggling to conjure up some adjectives to fill in the gap.

"Let's hear it, then," Valcor said.

Kai explained it to him. "Well, what do you think?"

"It is a bit far-fetched," Valcor agreed. "But that doesn't mean to say that it doesn't work," he continued approvingly. "I like it. Makes sense and everything. Does this mean you know how to control the stones?"

Kai nodded. "We went to visit the Erithites on Astlar. They figured out what happened to me earlier, and they gave me the stuff to light them."

"You passed the test?"

"Sort of. Not . . . not exactly."

"Maybe next time I'll stay here too," Valcor said wryly. "You seem to have had more to do than I did."

Now that school was back in session, Kai had little extra time on his hands, but he borrowed a couple of more books on Mialyn and the book on the Xucite stones he'd been reading, resuming his search in the evenings before lights out. For a brief moment, he wondered how he'd view the last three weeks when he was much older and more content to sit and reminisce about the past than do anything else. Would he view it as a pointless waste of time chasing a bunch of children's tales or as a completely relevant and possibly life-changing transitional phase? Kai had no idea.

"Hey, watch it!" someone snarled angrily, and Kai quickly realised where he was, just managing to duck out of the way before colliding with a certain blue-haired individual who was now somewhat irritated.

"Sorry," he muttered quickly.

"I'll say. Would it trouble you to look in front of you next time before you go knocking people over like that?" She flicked a derisive look down at the book he'd just borrowed. "And aren't you a bit old for kids' tales?" she smirked.

"I was just looking . . ." Kai said, somehow feeling the need to convince Wave that he was not what current events had led her to believe. Luckily, the queue shifted then and Kai was able to leave quickly while she was returning her books, escaping back to the safety of his room.

He was coming to the end of the book, currently finishing off a chapter on the stones and their uses in the world today. Valcor was working through his physics and motion homework on the floor, occasionally quizzing Kai on a question he was confused about.

Finally, Kai finished the last page. With a sigh, he closed the book and slid it in his bedside drawer, reminding himself to return it tomorrow, and catching sight of one of his sudoku books, he pulled it out. As he did, something slipped out of it—a small tattered piece of folded-up paper. It bounced off Valcor's head.

"Hey, Kai," Valcor said indignantly. "Why're you throwing paper at me?"

"It was an accident," Kai said hastily, bending down to pick it up. "Sorry about that."

"What is it?"

Kai unfurled the old piece of paper. It was ripped at the edges, the printed lines fading with age. It appeared to be a clipping of a newspaper article. The headline had been cut off, but the article was still perfectly legible:

> *Iren Sinter, an Erithite who set off on a voyage into the Deep Sky two weeks ago, has been found dead on one of the islands close to Ilyas just this morning, apparently killed in a storm. Amongst his possessions were a group of Xucite stones and sap and some navigation equipment. In a recent interview with the Erithites, they claimed he went to banish the Dracaens from Keturah, although they were reluctant to disclose exactly how. Many villagers believe the claims to be false, despite the marked decrease in Dracaen attacks recently . . .*

"What?" Valcor said, after Kai read it out to him. "How come I never heard of this?"

"I don't know. Becky said the Erithites don't want anyone to know where Mialyn is, so they wouldn't have made a big deal of it. Perhaps his mission was meant to be a secret but it leaked out when they found him on the island. I don't get how they were planning to prevent the Dracaens from getting in, though. Wait a second . . . Hey, Valcor. Check the date on this. Isn't it the same year as the fall of Teklah?"

Valcor checked it and nodded. "Yeah, probably. So if the Dracaens' nest really *is* on Mialyn, and if your theory was right, that there was a ring of stones outside it, then it would be easy to just get the Dracaens onto the island and then shut them in by lighting the stones, right?"

"Right," Kai nodded, flipping the piece of paper over. "Oh. That's odd."

"What?"

There was a diagram scribbled hastily on the back. At first glance, it appeared to be a random assortment of scribbles, arrows pointing into the middle distance and an odd-looking drawing of an island fringing the side of the page. He recognized the smooth cursive almost immediately.

"It's my mum's."

"Really?" Valcor raised himself up on his elbows to get a better look. "You sure?"

Kai nodded. "I recognize her handwriting. I used to forge letters from her to get out of games sometimes."

"Tsk, tsk," Valcor tutted in mock admonishment. "I'm ashamed of you, Kai. What is it? Looks like some sort of map, but it's not of any island I know . . ."

A metaphorical light bulb suddenly flicked on in Kai's mind. "This could be important," he said. "John said she got interested in Mialyn a bit before she left. This is probably her workings or something. Let's see if I can read this..."

After spending a couple of minutes deciphering obscure abbreviations and some of the scrawl that she often resorted to while taking notes, Kai got to work and was soon rewarded with a clear understanding of his mother's work.

"So we just follow these instructions and it'll lead us straight to Mialyn?" Valcor asked. "This is good, then, isn't it?"

Kai nodded in response, his head whirling with the enormity of what he'd just found. Maybe he still wouldn't be able to know what had caused his mother to act so strangely after she'd gone searching for the island, but in his hands was the next best thing: the ability to go and find out for himself.

"Hey, John, can I ask you something?"

John looked up from the workstation he was at, clearly startled. "Oh, Kai. I didn't see you there. Go on."

He had practical technology first thing in the morning, so he'd finished his breakfast quickly, hoping to catch him before people started coming in and the lesson began. Kai quickly explained all that he had discovered since they'd been to Astlar.

"That's certainly an interesting theory you've got there," John said evenly, once he'd finished. "Actually, it could help explain our Dracaen problem too."

"It could?"

"The Dracaens' nest is meant to be on Mialyn . . . or somewhere within the Deep Sky," John explained. "If there were Xucite stones on the island and somebody lit them, then the energy field generated would surely terrify them. There's no way they'd go near it, in fact, and all the other islands in the Deep Sky are too small to inhabit. So eventually, I suppose their next option would be . . . here."

"I-I was wondering . . . Would you let me go to Mialyn?" Kai asked hesitantly.

"What about the Dracaens?"

"I've got the stone, and I know how to use it now, so I shouldn't be in *that* much danger or anything. It'll scare them away like it did last time, right?"

John smiled. "Well, you're certainly following in your mother's footsteps," he said. "Stalking her almost. But I don't think Mr Shorren would let you go, definitely not alone. Especially now that it's term time, we can't go with you either, as we're teaching."

"But you let my mum go," Kai protested.

"She was an elite then, much older than you as well."

Some people walked in then, and realizing he had little time to pursue the matter, Kai turned quickly to John. "If I could get some people to come with me, would you consider?"

John paused for a second. "Yes. If you got some experienced riders to accompany you, that would make for a more convincing argument. But it's not me you have to persuade; it's the man at the top." He gestured theatrically to the ceiling, as if Mr Shorren were hovering right above their heads like some sort of omnipresent deity.

A bunch of kids walked in then, a particularly loud conversation scouring out any hopes of continuing their current talk. Kai gave a brief nod of thanks to John before ambling off to the workstation he usually shared with Rafael, deep in thought.

"All right, guys," John said, clapping his hands and distracting Kai. "Today we're going to be looking at a couple of traditional design styles from the second cycle . . ."

As soon as he had free time, Kai set about talking to his friends about his proposed trip to Mialyn. Valcor agreed almost as soon as Kai brought the topic up, presumably as an excuse to get out of school. Becky and Yoko agreed to go, as did Rafael once he returned. Sacha, however, decided against it, claiming she had a huge geography project, and Felix didn't want to go either, but Kai hadn't really been expecting him to anyway and had only asked him because he was running out of people.

He counted five people in total, which seemed fine to him, but after a brief meeting with the headmaster, Mr Shorren told him otherwise, saying he'd consider it if he got one more person to sign up. That was where he hit a roadblock. Kai didn't think he knew enough people to persuade them to go on such a perilous journey, which left him pretty much at a dead end. The only solution was to make friends quickly or persuade his current friends to suddenly change their minds, neither of which were particularly strong character points of his.

Luckily for him, the school's highly efficient rumour system was still up and running at full and generally unfeasible speed, and word soon spread, leeching into and out of conversations like a virus, until finally, at the end of one of his regular morning training sessions, Yoko suddenly stopped and asked him rather abruptly, "Is this plan of yours still on?"

"Yeah . . . ," Kai said, faltering slightly. "I mean, Mr Shorren said if I got one more person to go along with it . . ."

"Have you asked Wave?"

Kai shook his head. The thought had never occurred to him, considering the fact that he'd only spoken to her about three times and she didn't seem to be expressing any sort of favour towards him.

"Not really . . . I mean, I don't think she thinks highly of me."

Yoko smiled. "I don't think she thinks highly of anyone, so you're not alone in that regard."

"She asked you to tell me?"

"She mentioned it. I used to teach her too."

"You teach a lot of people, huh?" Kai observed. "How come you stopped teaching her?"

Yoko shrugged. "She stopped when she dropped out of her elite training, which is a shame because she almost definitely would have passed."

This was news. "So she's not an elite?"

"Not quite."

"But she can do elite theory stuff. I *saw* her."

"Yeah. I think I taught her a bit of elite theory when she was still in training."

"So . . . *you're* an elite?" Kai asked, totally dumbfounded.

Yoko pulled her hat back over her face, the traces of a grin visible on her face. "You've been training with me for three months and you didn't know?" She returned her staff to the racks on the side of the room.

"Ask her, okay? She's definitely interested."

Kai spent the rest of the day hunting for Wave, finally managing to find her on the way to his last lesson of the day that evening, and half-relieved and half-apprehensive, he struck up a conversation. On the plus side, she didn't sound like she wanted to take a bite out of him and mock his extracurricular reading this time, which made him slightly less worried.

"I heard you're going to Mialyn," she said. "So that's what the books were for, right?"

"Yeah."

"So is this open to everyone or only to those invited?"

Kai said warily, "I don't know. I thought you didn't believe in Mialyn."

"I don't. What makes you think differently?"

"I . . . It's just a hunch, really, but it . . . I don't know. Why're you asking?"

"I want in," she said, meeting his eyes with some difficulty. "If that's okay with you."

Stunned at how she'd somehow twisted it so he could completely reject her if he wanted to, Kai paused for a second. Of course, he desperately needed another person to make the trip viable, but the gesture flattered him nonetheless, and she didn't need to know that.

"Sure," he said.

She flashed a quick grin. "Cool. When're we going?"

Realizing how late he was going to be if he kept this up much longer, Kai quickly ushered the conversation to a close. "I don't know. I'll, uh . . . talk to you later."

"Yeah. Catch you later."

SIXTEEN

Mr Shorren had given them ten days of leave. During the period that led up to their proposed date, Kai spent most of his time collecting and mentally filing away any kind of information that seemed relevant. Because he was also navigating for the trip, he took the time to study the few maps there were on the Deep Sky, cross-referencing with the scrap of paper he'd found and diligently copying the route onto a clean sheet of paper.

As the week drew nearer, Kai started to feel a mounting apprehension, and the day before they were due to leave, he actually felt ill. Kai's expression must have somehow relayed this, for that same night, Rafael asked him what was wrong.

"I'm starting to wonder whether this was a good idea after all," Kai admitted.

"Well, it's too late to back out now," Valcor said cheerfully, which didn't really help much.

"It'll be fine," Rafael said. "You've got your staff, so we shouldn't be in any kind of real danger. All you have to worry about is falling off or getting lost or something, but your riding's improved a lot lately. And you're one of the best navigators I've ever seen."

"But what if I'm wrong about this?" Kai asked. "What if it's all just a wild goose chase? I'd have let everybody down. It'll be so awkward."

"This seems a big thing for you," Rafael remarked. "You know, your overwhelming fear of letting people down."

Kai realised that he was right. He murmured something non-committal, and luckily Rafael got the hint and continued. "Besides, I thought you were worried about somewhat more life-threatening things."

Valcor shrugged. "You're getting me a week off school, so I'm not complaining," he said enthusiastically. "And at least you tried. That's definitely commendable."

Kai smiled. "Thanks," he said, the words doing little to ease the growing agitation but still making him feel better. "Someone get the lights, would you?"

He dreamed that night, an odd dream of swirling colours and soundless music that flooded his mind. He didn't remember any of it in the morning, but the feelings remained with him as he opened his eyes early in the morning—a calm, quiet aura of confidence that reassured him and quelled most of his fears.

They met the others outside reception before the morning bell. The air was warm and heavy, with an atmosphere of lingering excitement passing through it like quick jolts of electricity. Kai was too excited to be nervous now as they all trooped over to the stables to pick up their Talites.

They had agreed previously that it would be more convenient to double up on their Talites so they could switch riders, which meant they could cover more distance without stopping to rest. Valcor and Rafael paired up because they'd ridden together before. Yoko and Becky were put together as well; being elites meant they could use more advanced techniques that were already natural to them without confusing the Talites.

Kai ended up riding with Wave, in part because he was the only one who had experience riding with her, but mainly because he didn't have much choice in the matter. She'd quickly insisted they use her Talite; although Kai was sad about leaving Farrell behind on the trip, he was secretly glad he was out of harm's way.

Wave's Talite chirped excitedly as she crouched next to it and rubbed its head vigorously. It nuzzled its furry head into her shoulder, tail flicking eagerly. They seemed really attached to each other. Kai watched in surprise. Especially after what she'd said about it earlier, the open display of affection stunned him.

"Here, come on," she said to Kai, catching sight of him staring. "Get your things so we can go."

Farrell looked a bit disappointed as Kai quickly gathered up some necessary belongings, so he gave him the massive purple stuffed Talite that he'd won at the spring festival, which cheered him up slightly, before stepping out into the brilliant sunlight to join the others.

The first part of the journey took about half of the first day, journeying from Tissarel to Ilyas, the island farthest east in Keturah and therefore the closest to the Deep Sky. The island was a small one, only a small cluster of villages here and there infringing on the flat plains.

In the centre of the island stood the beacon, a huge lighthouse-shaped structure that towered over it. A complex series of mirrors and fire allowed it to shine huge rays of light out into the Deep Sky at night, guiding travellers to safety.

"So what's so interesting about the Deep Sky?" Kai asked absent-mindedly, stirring the drink he'd brought at a small restaurant during their brief rest.

"Not much," Becky said. "It's got loads of space, so it's good for practising complex manoeuvres without things like buildings and other riders getting in the way. But it's still quite dangerous. Storms are common once you get deeper into there, and it's all too easy to get lost. And the Dracaens used to live there before they started moving inland . . ." She watched the others getting up. "Come on, Kai. We're going."

Kai finished off his drink and hurriedly rushed outside to catch up with the others. From the edge of Ilyas, there was nothing but pure, unwavering sky that stretched out for miles like a long blanket. Plumes of clouds billowed into obscure shapes, a river of sky streaming lazily along just beneath them.

Kai took a deep breath as he quickly scrambled onto the Talite behind Wave. This was it. From here on out, it was nothing but him, the other five with him, a sparse dappling of uninhabited islands, and a pure expanse of sky.

Wave twisted round to look at him, a fierce, excited grin on her face. "You ready?"

He nodded. "Ready as I'll ever be."

She took off in a flickering flurry of white wings and exhilaration, and the others quickly followed suit. Kai forced himself to breathe deeply to soothe his already agitated nerves; he was navigating for the group, and he needed to be vigilant and look around to keep them from getting lost.

Besides, he wanted to remember this for the rest of his life, and the nervousness was ruining the moment.

Skyriders

They swapped riders later in the evening, which meant Kai had a turn at flying Wave's Talite. He'd been worried about working with a Talite that wasn't his, especially while navigating. He realised that Becky had been right about the Talites having different personalities. He could tell the difference immediately. While Farrell was generally inquisitive, absent-minded, and playful, Wave's Talite was more staid and adept, and it was clearly more docile than its rider was. Kai quickly got used to riding it, secretly relieved that it wasn't going to spontaneously chase after bugs at inappropriate moments.

The sky darkened rapidly as the tawny evening set into night, the air sharp with cold and a mounting apprehension. The moon hid itself behind a cloud somewhere, and the very air around them seemed to be holding its breath, waiting.

As they continued farther, the clouds whipped themselves up into ominous dark looming towers. The wind started to pick up, and the air growled with tense, nervous trembles. Kai had been too busy focusing on navigating to pay attention to the warning signs, but luckily Wave had been slightly more attentive.

"There's a storm coming," she said, her voice low. "We'd better get out of the way."

Becky nodded. "We should probably find some other islands, wait out the storm. How close is it?"

"Pretty close. A couple of minutes away, I should think."

She was right—it was close. She'd hardly finished speaking when a tremulous roar split the air. The sky exploded with a blistering crack of light, and it abruptly started to rain. It was a marvel to watch from above the first layer of clouds, which would have obscured most of it to those on the ground. A crackling rumble and streaks of lighting danced between the clouds, flickering dangerously close to the Talites as they nervously weaved through the storm.

Kai slowed to let the others catch up.

"This is *bad*," Becky said. "Stuck in the middle of a storm with no islands in sight."

"Well, this is a spot of bad luck, isn't it?" Valcor remarked.

"You seem pretty enthusiastic about getting blasted out of the sky," Wave said. "I think we should go down. It's mostly sheet lightning; it won't touch us if we're underneath it."

"Down? Wave, that's *suicide*," Becky said. "At the rate the storm's heading, it won't stick to sheet lightning for much longer, and the weather's too violent to be able to dodge it."

"Wind and rain's fine, but lightning's a killer, Wave," Yoko added. "I know you'd rather not stay up here, but it's better if we avoid it."

"I know how to do this," Wave said obstinately. "I've done it before—"

"And what about the rest of us?" Becky said, her voice rising against the thunder. "What about Kai? He's riding; he's never done this."

Wave looked at him, a slight smirk playing on her face. "He'll pick it up."

Rafael shook his head. "No. Besides, the wind and rain will be stronger, and it's an absolute nightmare to ride in as it is. We'd be safer on an island. And we can't try to ride it out; the storm could last all night."

A bolt of lightning crackled as he spoke, singeing the tip of the wing of Valcor's Talite.

"Look, anything's better than sitting out here waiting to get fried," Valcor stated, his Talite whining in pain. "We either go down or find an island, but we get moving now."

"I'm staying here," Rafael said finally.

Wave scowled at him. "Kai, let's go," she said, her tone inviting no argument. "If these guys want to get killed, so be it."

"We'll come for you if we find something," Valcor added helpfully.

Yoko nodded. "It's better if we go down with Wave, then. Make it quick."

They ducked under the clouds, emerging high over the earth below, with Becky and Yoko just in front of them. As Rafael had said, the weather was worse there. The wind was ridiculously strong, and it was an effort to push against its howling, furious gusting. The rain lashed down mercilessly, and there was the occasional thunderous crack and flare of light above them.

"You *know* it's safer up there, Wave," Yoko said to her. "Why are you doing this?"

"I'm not taking any chances in this weather," Wave muttered, the rain plastering her hair to her face. There was another flash, and fingers of light flicked across the sheet of clouds, illuminating her face for the briefest of seconds before snapping back into darkness. She seemed more angry than usual, but Kai could feel her shifting around behind him, and her voice had an edge to it—a wary, nervous hardness that was unlike her. "I know people who have and didn't live to tell the tale. You can see the lightning forming when you're underneath; it's easier to avoid."

Becky looked at Kai. "Watch for light forming above you, like over there—that's where the lightning strikes next," she told him. "And stay close. We don't want to lose each other."

She gave him a brief, hesitant smile, and then the two of them put on a burst of speed, swerving fluently into the rain.

"All right, Kai, you're riding so *concentrate*," Wave said sharply, clearly noticing his attention wavering. "Watch out for—" She stopped quickly and suddenly shouted, "Kai, *move!*"

Startled, Kai obeyed, a split second before a streak of lightning plunged downwards in front of them. Wave swore loudly, her words masked by the thunder around them. Kai paused, dumbstruck with shock. If he'd been just a second slower, or if Wave weren't so alert . . .

"Concentrate, I said," Wave hissed. "Otherwise, we both die, and I'm blaming you."

It was like a video game: ducking and weaving away split seconds before lightning struck. Sometimes it was just inches away from them, and Kai could feel the blistering heat on his face for the split second it took for the lightning to flash by them. Kai's heart was racing, and he wasn't really thinking properly. His mind was just on autopilot: *Watch for light. Keep on moving . . . faster. Look out—there's one there, left, left. Whew, that was close. Quick. Keep watching; keep up with the other ones. Look out!*

Kai slanted away from an upcoming bolt, barely missing it. It flashed right by him, so close to his face that he was blinded by the light as it struck past. Kai flinched instinctively, but this made the Talite, who'd already been on edge with the lightning, totally out of control.

"Aw, come on—" Kai said, automatically tightening his grip on the band as the Talite lurched forwards in terror, dashing around with no regard for anyone's safety. "What's it doing?" Kai yelled over the raging thunder.

"I don't know!" Wave shouted back. "Let's swap places so I can calm it down. Quickly or we're screwed."

With an immense amount of difficulty, Kai managed to swap with Wave without falling off and plunging to his death below. The others were well ahead of them now, but Wave soon managed to gain control of her Talite, and nearly being an elite worked wonders for her riding. She was skilfully dipping away from the lightning as if she'd been riding in storms all her life.

They'd nearly caught up with Yoko's Talite ahead of them when Valcor and Rafael appeared from somewhere above them, nearly crashing into them as they swooped downwards.

"What are you doing?" Wave asked, startled.

"We found an island," Valcor said breathlessly. "Get the others quickly."

Finally, after a perilous half hour, the six of them landed on the island that they had found. The ground was wet from the rain, flashes of rippling light reflecting in the glistening surface. In the deep darkness, it was difficult to see much else.

"We should be safer here," Rafael said. "Although it'll be hard to sleep while the storm's still going."

Between the six of them, they'd packed enough supplies to last them a week, plus a few extra days' worth of emergency rations in case anything went wrong. Kai was exhausted after the terrifying flight, but there were still things to be done before he could relax.

Ideally, they'd have put up shelters and got everything ready for the night while the sun was up, but the storm had quickly put an end to *that* notion. Lighting a fire was out of the question as well; one look at the sky clarified that. Working by the intermittent flashes of light behind them, a few of them draped a sheet of waterproof tarp over a couple of sticks, fashioning a crude shelter—but enough to keep off the rain. Once they'd secured it off with rope and formed a makeshift carpet out of a tarp and a few blankets, it was surprisingly dry inside. But it was still pretty cold, and their drenched clothes did nothing to aid the situation. It was dark inside as well, and all they could do was sit tight and listen to the slightly muffled sounds of the storm raging outside.

"If the storm lets up a bit, we might be able to get a second shelter up." Becky said thoughtfully, passing round a few bags of food for everyone. Kai realised that he hadn't eaten since midday, and as soon as he received his dinner, he ate it eagerly. It was a small meal, but it was satisfying enough, and the prospect of being fed and having a light conversation kept their minds off everything else. Kai didn't know how much time passed. His clothes were damp with the rain, and it only got colder as the night progressed, but the presence of six people in a small space made it cosy in their shelter, save for the sudden draughts of bitter air that intermittently flooded through holes at the bottom of the tarp. After a long day's flying, he could hardly keep his eyes open, and it was all too tempting to drift off to sleep . . .

He woke up with a start sometime later, with the oddly comfortable weight of Becky leaning on his shoulder, her face soft with sleep. He couldn't remember falling asleep, having nestled into a sleeping position leaning against one of the supporting poles. The shelter was eerily quiet, and not just because he was the only one awake; after a minute of groggy speculation, Kai realised that the storm had finally abated. He could see faint tendrils of light creeping underneath the shelter, but other than that, he couldn't determine what time it was. Early morning probably, too early to get up, at any rate, and right now it was probably easier to catch up on his sleep while he could.

Valcor shook him awake a short while later. "C'mon, Kai," he said. "We've got to pack up soon, and we're cooking breakfast outside."

Kai yawned sleepily, trying to make sense of his surroundings, and mumbled something incomprehensible before staggering to his feet and taking a few tentative steps out of the shelter. It was much brighter and warmer, and even though the ground was wet beneath his feet, reminding him of the night before, the morning air still sang with the promise of a new day.

Luckily, someone had thought to pack some dry firewood, and a hearty fire bristled over a wire cooking mesh that they'd brought with them, the enticing smell of barbecued meat clouding in the air.

"Kai's up," Valcor announced, emerging from the shelter behind him. Becky handed Kai a plate.

"This looks good," Kai remarked, relishing the warm heat of the meal rising into his face.

"Usually I wouldn't cook so openly; it might attract unwanted attention," Becky said. "But we had a rough night, so I reckoned we could use the warmth. Eat it quickly; we'd better go soon."

"So," Wave said coolly, "where exactly are we?"

Kai opened his mouth to answer, but realizing with a sudden dread that he'd lost track of where he was in the storm, he filled it with a piece of meat instead.

"Uh . . . I'm not exactly sure," Kai said sheepishly, once he'd finished his mouthful.

"Well, that's just great. Now we're lost, to top everything else off. Nice going."

Kai had the makings of a headache forming, and he wasn't at his best in the mornings. "Why did you ask to come if all you're going to do is yell at me all the time?" he replied irritably. "I've said one sentence to you, and you're already complaining."

She scowled at him. "*You're* meant to be navigating. Once you're this far in, you can't afford to get lost."

"I'd like to see *you* navigate when you can't even see three metres in front of you," Kai retorted.

"Guys, we don't need to start fighting now," Yoko advised, helping Valcor and Rafael untangle Valcor's Talite from the tarp it had unwittingly gotten wrapped up in. "Get it together, *both* of you."

Realizing there was no point in arguing with someone he was meant to be riding with for the foreseeable future, Kai looked away. "Sorry. I'm just tired, okay?"

Wave shrugged but didn't reply. He quickly finished off the rest of his breakfast and pulled out a large map he'd drawn earlier, a neater, more legible version of his mother's map.

"We were around here when the storm hit," he said. "And given the winds were sort of to the . . . uh . . . left of us, so that's westwards, and we were flying forwards . . . I'd say we are around . . . here-ish."

"It's still a bit vague," Becky said. "How close are we going to have to be for this to work?"

"Pretty close," Kai said. "But Mialyn is in the northeast, so as long as we keep flying in that direction, we shouldn't be too far off. I'll look out for landmarks. Sorry about screwing this up," he added, feeling guilty.

"As long as you know where we're going," Becky said. "I totally trust you on this."

"It's not like you have a choice," Wave said derisively, before stalking off to help pack up their things.

The respite period was brief, and they were soon off again. The sky was milder, and as they journeyed into the day, it got warmer as well. Kai navigated as best as he could during the journey. Wave kept up a frosty silence all day, even when they paused briefly to swap riders and have a quick snack around noon.

Days and nights blurred into each other. Kai checked the map, rechecked it, and cross-checked it until the picture of it was almost etched into his mind. Watching the skies, watching the clouds, trying to get an idea of where he was . . .

The wind speed started to pick up again a few evenings later. Kai had braced himself mentally for another storm, so he was both surprised and relieved when they finally stumbled into a large clearing of open sky towering upwards. Surrounding it were swirls of voluminous clouds that wrapped around the clearing, so when you looked up, all you could see were walls of clouds on the sides. It felt a bit like being inside the eye of a completely stationary tornado. Strong wind currents propelled upwards and outwards in high-speed streams like flume rides, threatening to suck anything that came close enough into an express ride across the wind.

"Sky tunnels," he murmured, consulting his map. He'd done his research on them during his many days in the library, and it was finally starting to pay off. "So we're back on track."

They were back on track, but the setback had cost them a few precious days. Kai was painfully aware of their dwindling time left. He had to pick up the pace a little if he had any hopes of completing this on time.

The others slowed to a halt behind him.

"Whoa," Valcor breathed admiringly, staring up at the towering pillar around them. "This beats school by *miles*."

"This is part of the plan, right?" Rafael said.

Wave still wasn't talking to him, which was fine by Kai. She'd probably only have something negative to say, anyway.

"'Course," Kai said, feeling more confident now that he knew where he was. He showed Rafael the map, making sure he kept his grip tight. The map flapped wildly in the air but stayed in his hands. If he lost it, it'd be a disaster. "See here? Sky tunnels right there. So we're getting close."

"I've heard about these," Becky said. The wind was driving her hair into flippant strands that streamed behind her. "The tunnels are just high-speed wind currents. Jet streams."

"What are we meant to do with this?" Rafael asked.

"We've just got to find the right one," Kai said. "See how the currents flow out of the clouds on the side? They'll take you to different places all around the Deep Sky. One will put you straight on course for Mialyn, and . . . I'm not too sure about the others."

"Well, that sounds suspiciously simple," Valcor said. "So . . . which one?"

"Yeah . . . I've uh, gotta get this right. It'll take a day at most to backtrack back here if we get this wrong, and I've only got star charts on this map."

"But it's, like, mid-afternoon," Valcor protested. "It's not even dark yet."

"Exactly," Kai replied.

"So . . . we're just gonna sit here and wait till night then?"

Kai shrugged. "Better than getting it wrong, I guess."

They doubled back to the last island they'd seen, a few minutes from the clearing. Wave's Talite was getting a bit tired, and with a chirruping sigh of contentment, it collapsed onto the ground almost the moment they landed. The island was pretty small, and apart from occasional patches of grass and the odd tree, there really wasn't much worth doing. To pass the time, Kai busied himself drawing pictures in the ground with a stick he'd found, but it wasn't much of a distraction, and he soon found his interest wandering.

He unhooked the staff from the thin strap wrapped around his back and examined it idly, gazing within the Xucite stone. He remembered how he'd felt when he'd only taken a sip of the Xucitus sap—an odd hot, lancing agony, even at arm's length—and he was sure he would need to take a lot more than a sip if he ever got to Mialyn. It'd probably benefit him a lot more if he could keep the stone as far away as possible from him next time, he decided.

He detached the spearhead from the top of the staff and, using it as a sort of craft knife, started carving away the beautifully polished wood around the stone. He felt guilty doing it but reasoned that he'd rather not knock himself out again while using it.

It was a pastime of sorts, and he quickly got into a rhythm of scraping away the wood around it until finally it popped into his hand: a crude gem with uneven slanting edges. He packed the wood shavings into the hole the stone had once occupied, securing them by tying a piece of fabric around the staff's length; using the spearhead, he then set about drilling a small hole in the top of the stone. He'd made a veritable indent in the gem by the time dusk started falling, and as soon as they could see enough stars to navigate by, Valcor, who was getting a bit impatient, dragged them off to resume their journey.

But by the time they reached the sky tunnels again, it was a deep, impenetrable blue around them, and Kai realised with a start that he'd screwed up again: it was pitch-black outside, and there was no way he could see his hand a metre in front of him, let alone read and study a star chart.

He explained the situation to the others, who were not best pleased.

"So... what now? We're gonna have to wait till it gets light again?" Valcor asked. "Can't we just light a fire or something? We brought lanterns."

"Wind's too strong," Rafael reminded him. "And it's blowing towards us, so it'd probably torch the map."

"Well, this is great," Yoko remarked unhelpfully. "Just look at all the time we're wasting."

Becky nudged him. "The stone," she said to him. "Do you have it?"

Comprehension dawned upon Kai as he realised what she was getting at. "Oh, yeah. That'd work, wouldn't it?"

He took out the bottle of the Xucitus sap the Erithites had given him, the yellow liquid glowing eerily in the half-light of the night, and took a quick swig. It was more than he'd intended, but it was too late to worry about that because the stone suddenly flared with a bright red light, washing everyone in a smooth glow.

Kai had forgotten about the energy fields. He could only hold the stone in his hand because he hadn't finished hollowing out a hole, which left him straight in the wake of the field. The first wave hit him like a gentle brand of fire, making him feel sick and dizzy. His mind reeled for a second, but he forced himself to look at the map.

"Kai, what is this?" Wave snapped. He could tell she'd felt it too.

"Hold the . . . map for me," he said to her, struggling with the pain.

Becky understood, her realization showing in the gasp he could hear from her. "The fields," she said softly. "Kai . . ."

"What fields?" Valcor asked.

"The stone generates an energy field around it when it's lit," Becky explained. "It knocked him out last time . . ."

Kai could hear Becky talking to them, but he forced his attention on the map, reading the star charts.

"Start with the North Star," he murmured to himself, transferring his gaze to the sky. He found the star easily and quickly started tracing the routes across the sky, flicking between the map and the sky above him.

He could have done it in less than a minute if it weren't for the blinding pain generated by the stone. After the first minute, he couldn't find the energy to keep looking down at the map. Wave caught on and started reading out the stars for him, which lessened the effort.

"Kai, you should stop now," Becky said. "You look terrible."

"I'm . . . nearly finished . . ." His hand was wavering now, the light flickering. His vision swam until he could hardly see the stars anymore, just smears of silver against the dark velvet sky. Unable to fight the pain anymore, he slumped forward, against the Talite, the starlit clouds around him swirling until they faded into darkness . . .

The pain suddenly lifted; it was still there, at the corner of his mind, but not nearly as strong. Managing to conjure up some last reserves of energy from somewhere, Kai quickly sat up again.

Where is the stone . . . ? he thought wildly. Had he dropped it? But no, he could still see the light flickering behind him. He twisted round.

Wave had the stone. She offered him the map, wincing with the pain. "Do it quickly," she said through gritted teeth.

Hurriedly, Kai focused his attention on the map once more. Just the last step was left, the most crucial one. "Connect to Rigel . . . and trace," he said to himself, following the path down from the bright star above him to the tunnel directly below it.

"It's done!" he said to Wave. "Give it here."

The stone was still alight, and Kai had no idea how long it'd last, so he stuffed it in his bag and covered it with all the equipment until he could no longer see the light. Once it was covered, he let out a gasp of relief, a pounding headache and a lingering nausea all that remained.

Skyriders

Wave rounded on him. "What were you *thinking*?" she said. "Reading it like that? What use are you to us if you're not even *conscious*? Who'd read the map then?"

"I got it, though," Kai replied.

"Are you all right?" Rafael asked him, concern edging his voice.

Kai shook his head. "I think you'd better ride," he said weakly to Wave.

"So, uh, how are you planning to make this work if the stone knocks you out?" Yoko asked as Kai and Wave changed places.

"I'm working on it," Kai said. "We've got to keep moving."

"Oh yeah," Valcor said. "Which one?"

Kai pointed up to one of the currents further up, swirling up in a tight corkscrew. "There. Don't get too close to the others or they'll suck you in."

They followed Wave up to the tunnel. By the time they reached it, the current was so strong that it was impossible to resist the pull.

"Hold on tight!" Wave called to him as they were pulled into the wind stream. From there, it was just one teetering, jolting roller coaster, hurtling from one side to the next, swooping round in tight circles until the world blurred. It was all Kai could do to hold on. The wind rushed in his ears, his face, his hair, flailing behind him as they swerved sharply up, down, this way and that.

The ride ended abruptly as they were flung out of the wind stream and into a comparatively calm spot a few minutes later. Wave turned round, her eyes alight with excitement.

"You're still there? Was that awesome or what?"

She seems in a better mood than she was this morning, Kai thought, which he couldn't say about himself. The lurching ride had done nothing better for his headache, and he felt ready to throw up. He nodded weakly, trying not to aggravate the pain.

The other two Talites appeared beside them a couple of seconds later.

"That was *epic*!" Valcor grinned. "Please tell me you got it wrong so we can go back and do it again."

Rafael, on the other hand, looked considerably shaken. Becky shook her head firmly.

"No, thanks. That was an absolute nightmare from start to finish. There's an island over there, and I think it's getting late. How far from here, Kai?"

He shrugged. "If we got the right one . . . we should reach it by tomorrow."

Owing to the lack of rain and a good supply of dry wood, they soon managed to set up shelter for the night and consume a satisfying dinner. Kai felt better after food, a long drink of water, and the prospect of undisturbed sleep ahead of him, and he resumed work on hollowing out a hole into the stone, loosely threading a piece of string through it once he'd finished. Finally, he pulled out the map again, staring at the familiar slanted handwriting as he studied it. Had his mother come through the same way, looking at the same map, sitting on the same island? He'd never know for sure, but he felt an odd sense of closeness as he traced their route ahead of them with a finger. It felt as if she were sitting right next to him. Feeling reassured, he closed the map and headed back to get some sleep.

They set off again early the next morning, Kai feeling slightly wary of the day ahead. From here on, there was no room for mistakes; because the stone had such a pathetic range, an error of just a few metres meant they'd fly right by and never notice it. And they didn't have much time either. He buried himself in navigation, vigilantly checking the map and his surroundings, trying to keep them exactly on track.

"Kai," Wave said suddenly, snapping him out of his concentration.

"What?" he responded, slightly irritated at the distraction.

"I thought I saw something."

"Like what?"

She said, "I don't know. It was like a . . . It's difficult to explain."

"That's not really helping," Kai said shortly, but then he stopped suddenly, something catching his attention.

"There!" Wave said jubilantly. "You saw it too?"

Kai nodded. The others slowed to a halt behind him and crowded round.

"Why'd we stop?" Valcor asked.

Without replying, Kai took out the stone by the loop of string he'd attached it to and swung it in front of him in a broad arc. The air seemed to flicker slightly, rippling like it was water. Something soft and glittery danced in and out of view. There one second. Gone the next. He couldn't have seen it if he weren't looking for it. But it was definite.

"Is that . . . is that it?" Becky asked.

"One way to find out," Kai said, fishing for the bottle of Xucitus sap. There wasn't much left of it, he realised, taking a cautious sip. He waited until the stone started glowing, then hooked it on the edge of his staff and thrust it out in front of him.

The glow intensified, much brighter than it had ever been. The air around him seemed to shimmer, flickering, exploding in odd, hot flares. The sky was charged with a kind of invisible electricity that crackled around them, sending shivers of adrenaline up Kai's spine.

This is it, he thought, but he couldn't get much further than that, because there was a sound similar to an explosion, and Kai felt blown backwards even though he didn't move. The noise around them dropped into silence, and the stone's glare flared outwards, as if it had caught fire. There was a flash of light so bright that Kai had to look away, red and white and all the different hues and shades of the spectrum exploding in his mind even though his eyes were closed, and above it all, a high, lilting, fleeting melody of colour that caught in with everything, mixing it up, rising with the wind . . .

Suddenly, it all faded away, like a dream evaporating. Stunned, Kai blinked a couple of times, everything around him slowly regaining its familiar shape as the last of what he'd seen dissolved from his mind. He felt a rush of elation, and as he turned back to where the stone had been and caught sight of the island floating below them, it was quickly combined with a thrill of excitement, of triumph.

They'd made it.

SEVENTEEN

There was a moment of stunned silence, as if none of them quite believed what they were seeing. Then they simultaneously decided that it was in fact Mialyn they were staring at, and they suddenly broke into a spate of wild cheers and applause that lasted for a few minutes. Finally, taking in the wild, untamed scenery, flanked by a deep, pure sky that suddenly seemed much brighter, they descended upon the island and started to look around.

It was mostly layered with enormous thick plants that criss-crossed precariously around each other, save for a path that had been cut down to the dusty, stony ground of the island, creating a rudimentary trail to the middle of the island. There stood a huge jagged cave jutting spontaneously out of the ground, the yawning mouth of the cavern looking somewhat ominous even in the fierce glare of the afternoon.

Mialyn was somewhat smaller and less impressive than Kai had originally imagined it, but luckily the disappointment was minimized by a much greater feeling of achievement. They'd found Mialyn. He was standing on ground that few others had ever stood on before. He felt as if he'd conquered the world, or got to the end of a particularly difficult sudoku puzzle.

Kai realised immediately what was keeping Mialyn from sight: deposits of Xucite stones at the edges of the island, some shards of deep red stones sticking up in bunches out of the rock, others buried within it. They'd deactivated as soon as he'd stepped onto the island, for the lit stone he was carrying disrupted the energy fields and extinguished the light.

"So the Dracaens will stop attacking Keturah now?" Kai said once they'd established the layout of the island, the words coming out more question-like than he'd hoped.

"Hopefully," Yoko said.

"I wonder what's in the cave," Wave said.

"The Dracaens' nest, so I've heard," Rafael replied, taking packs of food out of his bag. "Anyone hungry?"

The reappearance of the island had taken the edge off Kai's hunger, but now that he'd settled down, he realised he was indeed ravenous.

"I think we should check it out," Valcor said, taking a bite out of his sandwich. "There's probably something interesting inside."

"There're probably *Dracaens* inside," Rafael countered.

"But if there *were* any inside, they'd probably have come out by now," Kai said thoughtfully. "Now that these stones are all deactivated, anyway," he added, slipping his now dull stone back into his bag.

There was a pensive silence while they all finished off their sandwiches, just in case there were any Dracaens inside that were perhaps otherwise occupied and a bit late coming out. Finally, they reasoned that there couldn't be much going on in the cave, and, curiosity getting the better of them, they ventured inside, Valcor and Wave leading the way with flickering lanterns casting shadows on the wall. Their footsteps echoed eerily off the huge walls around them, bouncing off them until they cumulated in a huge rippling, inescapable crunching sound. High up near the top of the cave was a long ledge that ran like a huge stone shelf along the sides, padded neatly with large leaves and bunches of dead grass collected from the island and been entwined to form flat bedding. And more eerily, the occasional skeleton of a Dracaen here and there. But despite the long rows of the beds stretching out on either side of the cave walls, there was no sign of any actual Dracaen presence.

Or so they thought, until suddenly Valcor gave a little yelp of surprise a while later, taking a couple of steps backwards and colliding with Yoko behind him. The lantern he was holding dropped out of his hand, flickering into darkness as it smashed against the floor.

"What the . . . ?" Wave murmured, holding up her lantern to see better, her voice a mixture of shock and fear.

Kai froze as he looked up and saw what they were talking about. It *was* a Dracaen after all, but everything about it that was deadly in the slightest seemed to be magnified to epic proportions; for a start, it was unbelievably huge, three or four times the size of the normal Dracaens, and they were big enough. Its wings crumpled against the roof of the cave to make room for its oversized body, razor-sharp spikes lining the edges, running down its back and along its huge dark tail, which tapered off into a spiked ball that held a terrifying resemblance to a medieval flail. It had clearly been asleep in the cave until Valcor's shout awoke it.

Cold yellow eyes stared unflinchingly at the group of them. Then it opened its huge mouth, showing rows of slanting, jagged teeth, and let out a shattering, slicing shriek, awkwardly getting to its feet and lashing out with its tail. The ball at the end crashed into the wall, making the cave shake, stones crashing down onto the floor.

"I think we should probably leave," Valcor said, but the others had already decided it wasn't worth sticking around. They turned round, dashing headlong away from the Dracaen, which was now lumbering along behind them, the spikes on its wings and tail grating loudly against the floor.

For a few lurching, terrifying moments, they dashed back through the cavern, the Dracaen's loud shrieks fading into the distance as their frenzied running put more distance between them. Kai couldn't hear himself panting for breath anymore, and the ground shuddered whenever the spiked tail slammed into the wall. Their only advantage was that the Dracaen was too big and too clumsy on land with only two legs to be able to catch up with them like this, but once it got into the air . . .

Kai was completely shattered as they reached the mouth of the cavern and emerged into the sunlight, but he could hear the Dracaen screeching behind them, slowly gaining on them with each passing heartbeat, and he was too frightened to stop and catch his breath.

"What . . . what was that thing?" Kai panted.

"I don't know," Wave replied, also breathless. "But we don't stand a chance against it once it gets into the air. Light the stones again!" she commanded, gesturing wildly to the groups of stones that encircled the island. "That should keep it out."

Kai fumbled for the bottle of the viscous yellow sap, desperately juggling trying to prise open his backpack and trying not to trip over, but a thought suddenly struck him, and he paused in mid-action.

"What are you doing?" Wave snapped, noticing him stop.

"It we light the stones now, then the Dracaens won't be able to come back," Kai said. "All those people'll still be in danger."

"If we don't, then we're screwed," Wave replied. They'd reached their Talites by now; having heard the Dracaen, even from outside the cave, they were noticeably agitated. Wave stroked hers behind its shoulder blade to calm it down a bit before jumping neatly onto it, with Kai scrambling on hastily behind.

"Guys, guys," Valcor panted, coming up behind them. "What are we doing? We can't run away; it'll catch us in, like, ten seconds."

"We can't light the stones here, either," Becky said, clearly distressed. "Otherwise, they'll keep attacking Keturah. They'll kill more people . . ."

Kai wondered for a brief moment if she was still thinking about Renee.

"Then . . . uh, what *are* we doing?" Rafael asked, getting onto his Talite anyway.

Kai loosened his mother's staff from the holder on his back, the familiar weight in his hands filling him with a moment of confidence.

"We're fighting it."

There was a moment of stunned silence as everyone stared blankly at him.

"Hang on a second. When did I agree to *this?*" Wave questioned.

"Kai, we can't fight this," Rafael said. "We'll *die.*"

"Unless there's an easier way to do this, this is the only way we have a chance of getting out alive. If we can take it down, then we have a chance."

"You've missed the bit where we all get killed and eaten," Yoko said, but her voice was light and resolute. She'd brought her staff along with her too, and she had already fitted a spearhead on the end of the shaft.

"You're crazy, Kai," Valcor said with a sideways grin. "Completely stark raving mad. But you've got a point. I'll fight."

There was an ear-splitting screech as the Dracaen finally emerged from the cave, shaking itself, loosening its crumpled wings and grinding the ground beneath it to powder as it prepared to take off.

Wave gave an exasperated sigh. "You'll kill us all," she said, but she didn't seem to be opposing anything.

Becky stared at him, her expression unreadable for a short while before settling into a quiet fierceness that surprised him. "Let's do this."

The six of them launched into the air with the Dracaen in hot pursuit, twisting its huge body as it rose so its tail flailed wildly around it. Kai gripped his staff, waiting for an opening to strike. Wave was riding, and she skilfully ducked under the strike, spinning upwards a second later, smashing into its side.

But it retaliated quickly, much faster than Kai had expected it to. Wave had only just managed to pull them out of the way when it lashed out with a front leg, a hooked claw grazing Kai's shoulder. He winced, but the cut wasn't too deep, and he quickly jabbed forwards, burying the spear point in its leg.

Becky and Yoko were keeping up a skilful offence, expertly dodging the Dracaen's attacks, Yoko slashing at it at every opening, while Valcor's Talite was riding with a somewhat reckless streak, launching wild, unexpected attacks at the most bizarre moments—which, given that Valcor was riding it, was not entirely surprising. It was an impressive performance, but the Dracaen didn't seem to be weakening in the slightest, and already they seemed to be fighting a losing battle.

I wonder if my mum saw this Dracaen while she was here, Kai thought spontaneously, and suddenly an idea flashed into his mind, so quickly it was like a spark of lightning, a breath of wind. What she'd seen at the island, why she'd left so suddenly . . .

It all made sense.

"No," he whispered to himself, shaking the notion out of his mind, but he'd allowed his concentration to wander for too long. With a start, he realised where he was, but before he could even react, the Dracaen's tail slammed into him, knocking him clean off Wave's Talite in one smooth, hard motion.

Kai gave a yelp of surprise as he found himself plummeting through the sky, desperately waving his arms around in some sort of inane hope that he could convince himself to fly before anything untoward happened.

"Kai!" Wave shouted at him, noticing the sudden loss of her partner. She flipped round in mid-air, descending rapidly, but the Dracaen, sensing an easy kill, swung round to face him as he fell. The tail hit him across his body, spikes ripping bloody cuts across his skin. Pain exploded across his chest, and he heard some other people shout his name but was too petrified to identify them. The Dracaen gave a jubilant screech before swooping underneath him, jaws wide open.

The prospect of dropping into the stale, rank breath its mouth produced scared Kai much more than the idea of actually being eaten. He slashed blindly at it with his staff, pain lancing across his body with each movement, hoping to somehow scare it out of eating him, and suddenly felt the spearhead at the end of the staff cut into something.

He opened his eyes. The Dracaen recoiled backwards, shrieking in agony, a line of bright blood slicing across its nose. Seconds later, Wave reached him, cutting underneath the Dracaen and slamming it in its face, neatly catching Kai on her Talite's back.

"You all right?"

Kai, convinced he was going to die, was still somewhat stunned by the whole thing. "I'm fine. Thanks for catching me."

"Let's focus on *not* dying, please," Wave responded tightly, slanting across to avoid a tail smashing into them. "You got a plan?"

"Couple of minutes, perhaps?" Kai said.

"It's fine," Wave replied thinly. "Take as long as you like. I'll get us some coffee and a pack of biscuits."

Kai turned to the other two just in time to see Yoko throw her own spearhead at the Dracaen. It struck with alarming precision, sticking out of its eye, blood pouring out from the socket. Half-blind but no less infuriated, the Dracaen turned, swiping at the Talite, who leaped backwards before launching into a flurry of wild counter-attacks that left no room for even the briefest of openings.

It was getting harder, Kai realised grimly, ducking as the tail slashed past where his face had been a moment ago. John's words flashed into his mind: *Fall designed all his species to be able to pick up an opponent's style quickly. That's why the longer you battle with any of the Fallite species, the harder it'll be...*

"We've got to finish this quickly if we want any chance of surviving," Becky called from above him, evidently thinking the same thing.

Wave grinned at Yoko. "Nice trick you pulled back with the spearhead."

"Yeah, but it's still stuck in its eye," Yoko responded. "Not much use there."

The spearhead, Kai thought with a start. *That could work.*

"Wave," he said urgently. "Can you get close to its face? I need the spearhead."

Wave shrugged. "I'll try."

She swooped downwards before curving across towards its sightless eye. Kai knew the Dracaen couldn't see her from that angle, but it could evidently hear them approaching, for it twisted away, snarling, snapping at the Talite. It jumped backwards just as gnashing teeth closed shut against the air in front of them.

"It'll hear us if we go for it on the Talite," she panted. "Got any other ideas?"

Kai thought fast, crazy, half-formed ideas spinning through his head, clearly devoid of logic.

"How about you... jump onto it?" he murmured, not realizing what he'd said aloud.

Wave shook her head fiercely. "No. *No.* That's just mad, even for you and your crazy ideas."

"Yeah. No, I was just thinking..."

"I'll have a go," Valcor said unexpectedly, appearing next to them for a second. Rafael stared at him.

"You'll die," he said bluntly.

"We haven't got much time left," Valcor replied pointedly, and before anyone could reply, he'd swivelled across and swung gingerly onto the Dracaen's neck just as it shot between them, spikes on its tail tearing bloody gashes across the three of them.

"Valcor, what the . . . ?" Kai yelped in surprise, the pain across his arms overshadowed as he watched Valcor move quickly into a crouching walk on the Dracaen's back.

"Oh, that's just great—leave your Talite in the middle of the air without a rider," Rafael said, scrambling forwards for the band which Valcor had left unattended. He'd come off lightly; all he had was a shallow cut across his face to worry about. Wave's Talite had taken the brunt of the attack: a huge slash across its side, blood quickly soaking into its fur. Wave looked concerned.

"What do we do?" Kai was panicking.

"Stay close to it; catch him if he falls off or something," Rafael said, trying to grab at the band but missing. The Talite was also panicking without a rider, jerking about, wild clicking sounding from it. "Stop *moving!*"

Wave stuck close to the Dracaen's writhing body as Valcor climbed cautiously up onto its head, clinging on tightly to it as it thrashed about wildly, unable to see him, trying to shake him off. He reached down for the gleaming spearhead sticking out of its eye . . .

The Dracaen's huge tail rose up high above its body, preparing to smash downwards, just as Valcor grasped the hilt of the spearhead and pulled it out of the eye socket. "Valcor, *watch out!*" Rafael warned, grabbing on to the band at last, calming down the Talite.

Kai looked away, and the next thing he knew Valcor was landing painfully between him and Wave and the spiked ball sticking into the back of the Dracaen's neck.

"Here's your spearhead," Valcor said, wincing slightly. Wave's Talite couldn't cope with three riders and a rapidly worsening injury, and it gave an anxious whine as it struggled to keep airborne, rapidly losing altitude.

"A bit more warning would have been nice," Rafael said, drawing up alongside them. "Get on quick, before it pulls that thing out of its head."

Valcor quickly scrambled back over to his Talite. "Eeesh. That looks painful."

"Hey, you got my spearhead back," Yoko said, dropping next to them.

Kai smiled in spite of everything and handed it back to her. "Here. You'll need it."

"You've got a plan, I take it?" Becky asked.

"Might not work," Kai stated.

Becky shrugged. "Anything's worth a shot."

"Val and Raf, you distract it for a bit. Yoko, do you think you could take out its other eye?"

"Not easily," she said. "It'll probably expect something like that to happen. Did you have something in mind?"

Kai hesitated. "It'll work better if it's blind . . ."

The Dracaen finally managed to pull its tail out the back of its neck, its skin lacerated with the injuries it had caused itself. It gave another terrifying roar and lunged forwards at them, and they quickly scattered. A curved claw slashed at Wave's Talite, and this time it managed to connect, slicing deep into its wing. The Talite jolted awkwardly to the left as it sprang away, whining with the pain, clearly favouring the injury.

"It's not gonna be able to fly much longer," Wave said anxiously. "Whatever you're planning, do it *quickly*."

"Kai!" Becky called from somewhere behind him, the Talite dodging underneath a wild blow from the Dracaen. "Kai, the stone!"

"What?"

"Light the stone," she said urgently. "Then you can control its movement—"

She broke off abruptly as the Dracaen lunged at them again, driving them backwards with a series of wild swipes at the Talite.

"What did she mean?" Kai asked Wave. "Surely the stone's too weak to scare it off."

"She didn't say *scare it*," Wave said.

She'd said to control its movement, Kai thought desperately. And if they could control its movements, then surely they could—

"Of course!" Kai said, hurriedly fumbling for the stone and the bottle of sap in his bag. He pulled the cork out of the bottle.

"Wave, get it to chase us," he said, passing her his staff. "We need it to be facing us when this lights."

Wave nodded and dived forwards, driving the staff deep into the Dracaen's body as Kai drank the sap and pushed the rest of it back into his bag. The Dracaen spun round with a shriek, clawing wildly at them, and Wave's Talite turned and fled, the wing injury making movement painfully slow, the Dracaen closing in on them. Becky must've told Yoko what they were up to, because the two of them closed in just behind the Dracaen, Yoko readying her spear.

"Turn around now!" Kai commanded, and Wave quickly pivoted round the left wing of her Talite, exactly as Kai had seen John do in the first lesson he'd watched, seemingly a long time ago. Kai held up the Xucite stone in the Dracaen's face as it nearly crashed into them, the red glare making him feel weak and dizzy. The Dracaen gave a shriek of pain and terror and flinched backwards, turning round as if to escape the glare, straight into Yoko's Talite. Yoko drove the spear into its good eye with a quick thrust, and the Dracaen screamed again, lashing out blindly.

Completely blind and rapidly weakening, the Dracaen was a lot easier to defend against, its wild attacks missing their targets completely. However, it wasn't running away as Kai had hoped, which only left one more option.

"Wave, get underneath it," Kai instructed. "When I say so, get out of the way *quickly*."

"What are you going to do?" Rafael asked.

Kai smiled. "I'm letting it do some of the work this time."

The two of them flew underneath the Dracaen. Gripping his staff tightly in his hand, Kai thrust it upwards into the underside of the Dracaen's tail. Blood splattered onto them like a shower of gruesome rain as Kai twisted the shaft, causing another howl of pain. The Dracaen shook its tail hard in an attempt to shake them off, but it couldn't dislodge them. Finally, it spun round with an infuriated snarl, looping underneath them, locating their position solely by the feel of the staff embedded into its tail. It raised its huge dark foreleg, hooked claw poised to strike.

"Get ready," Kai murmured, watching the Dracaen carefully. Everything, so it seemed, rested solely on this moment. Do or die.

"Now!"

Wave dived out of the way as the Dracaen sped past where they'd been a moment ago, its huge talon cutting a broad slice clean through its tail. There was on odd squelching crunch as the claw emerged cloaked in glistening blood, soon followed by an almighty scream of pain and fury as the tail—which the Dracaen had inadvertently cut through—was detached from the rest of its body.

Kai reached out and grabbed it, grazing his hand on one of the spikes as he caught it. It was much heavier than he thought it would be, and already he felt his grip straining. He handed the tail gingerly over to Wave's Talite, who took it between its teeth with a hesitant whine. Wave grinned at him.

"*This* I like." Then she said to her Talite, "Let's go!"

The Talite gave a weak answering chirrup and shot high into the air, vertically powering upwards until it was high over the Dracaen. Then it twisted, plummeting straight downwards like a bullet. Wind rushed madly in Kai's ears as they approached the dark figure of the Dracaen, his heart hammering with exhilaration and fear.

The Dracaen must have heard them coming, for it suddenly swung upwards, a claw arcing through the air, slashing deep across the Talite's neck. The Talite gave a yelp of pain, but gritting its teeth in determination, it raised its head, moving the tail in a wide arc before swinging it back down with force, hitting the Dracaen on the back of its head with the spiked ball at the end, sending it crashing down towards the island. It hit the ground with a sharp, hard thud and slumped motionless in front of the cave.

There was a shaky, stunned silence.

"Is it . . . is it dead?" Becky asked tentatively.

"I don't know," Kai replied. "Are you guys okay?"

Yoko, Rafael, and Becky had come off the attack surprisingly unscathed, a few shallow cuts all to show. Valcor had a few deeper cuts and was limping slightly; Wave had a couple of serious-looking wounds. Kai had taken several injuries, bleeding from cuts on his chest and most of his right arm. Perhaps "okay" wasn't exactly the word he was looking for, but they weren't dead, which was always a bonus.

"You look pretty bad, Kai," Becky said. "And the Talite does too. We'd better get you sorted out."

Wave's Talite was losing altitude fast. Unable to bear the load of two riders and the pain of the injuries any longer, it sank to the ground, collapsing in a tired heap just beside the Dracaen, the other two Talites following shakily after. Luckily, Rafael had brought along some medical supplies, and he and Becky set about cleaning up and bandaging wounds and cuts. The Talites curled up near them, their furry bodies tucked up into fluffy balls. Becky was quietly attending to Kai's injuries, while Yoko had started up a small fire in the centre of their loose circle, filling the air with the stale smell of smoke. Valcor had wandered off to get some more firewood.

Rafael and Wave were sitting beside her Talite. Rafael washed his hands and looked the Talite over, lightly touching its forehead and checking the heartbeat. He then examined the deep gashes across its body and wing, blood trailing from the wounds and mingling with its cream fur and the dirt on the ground.

"Where'd you learn how to do this?" Kai asked, watching him attend to the Talite.

"My parents breed and look after Talites when they're very young," Rafael explained, without looking round. "Too young to support the weight of a rider, at any rate. I used to help them when I was younger."

Eventually, he gently turned the Talite onto its side and sat back with a sigh, not meeting anyone's gaze.

"Look, I'm not gonna lie to you, Wave," he said finally. "It's not looking good right now. It's lost a lot of blood, and I'm not sure how well it's going to take it. I can only do so much with the supplies we have. I'm very worried about the neck wound . . ."

Wave's expression was set in a hard, quiet mask, but there was a flicker of uncertainty in her face. She nodded but didn't say anything.

Becky neatly tied the last knot in the bandage across Kai's arm, securing it tightly. "There you go," she said brightly. "Take it easy for a bit, okay? C'mon, Wave, let's have a look at you."

Wave poked the fire. "I'm fine."

She had blood dripping from her arm, soaking into the sleeve of her shirt even as she spoke, but seemed unconcerned.

"You sure?" Becky asked.

Wave didn't respond, so Becky murmured, "Suit yourself." She began packing up.

The night was sneaking in on them; by the time Kai was aware of it, the sky had settled into dusky shadows that made everything around them look ominous and terrifying. The atmosphere had a cold bite to it, and the air flickered with growing insecurity.

Rafael spent the best part of the next two hours attending to the Talite's injuries, washing and suturing the wounds, but it only grew weaker and weaker as the night drew on. Finally, he checked the heartbeat one last time, then stood up and backed away.

"Sorry," he mumbled quietly to Wave, who scrambled over to the Talite, pressing her head against its bloodstained body. It was lying on its side, breathing rapidly, its eyes glazing over. The crimson slash across its neck gleamed in the flickering dance of the fire behind them.

"No," she said breathlessly. "Please, *no*. Don't die on me, not now. Please..."

She fell silent as her Talite whined softly and nudged her forehead with its nose. Then it gave a last, fluttering breath and closed its eyes, motionless.

Nobody spoke, and the silence hung in the air for a long time, the atmosphere, laced with mourning, making it impossible not to feel upset. Kai looked away, wondering how he'd feel if it was Farrell who'd died. The thought of it made his heart clench inside him, and he'd only known Farrell for less than a year...

"Wave, I'm sorry," Becky said, looking rather miserable herself.

"Are you okay?" Kai asked her hesitantly.

"Do you *think* I'm okay?" she said bitterly. "This is all your fault! I told you we should have just lit the stones; if you hadn't made us fight that Dracaen, this wouldn't have happened."

Kai raised his hands defensively. "But if we lit the stones, then the Dracaens would keep on attacking. And if we ran, then we'd be killed. There was nothing else, I swear. It's not like I wanted this to happen, okay, and I'm really, really sorry it happened like this... but it was a better scenario than the other two options. At least now the Dracaen's dead..."

Wave turned on him. "*You'll* look pretty dead in a minute," she snarled angrily, her eyes dark with grief and anger, the blood streaking her face making her expression look almost savage.

"It wasn't his fault!" Valcor protested.

"Cool it, Wave," Rafael said warningly.

Ignoring them, she lunged forwards and struck Kai hard across the side of his face. He stumbled backwards, reeling from the unexpected assault, pain exploding across his face. The second blow sent him sprawling onto the ground.

"Wave . . ." he said, desperately, raising his hands to deflect the third attack, but Yoko quickly stepped in and pulled her back.

"Stop," she said coldly. "Stop taking your anger out on Kai; he hasn't done anything. Without him, it'd be more than just your Talite dead, okay? It'd probably be you—and the rest of us too. I'm sorry this happened, truly, and I'm sure everyone else is too. But if anything, you should be thanking him, not trying to punch his lights out."

Wave shook herself out of Yoko's grasp and took a couple of steps backwards. "Stick up for him, why don't you?" she said frostily, gesturing to Kai, who flinched involuntarily. Then she turned around and stalked off into the undergrowth surrounding them, mingling with the gathered shadows.

Valcor helped him to his feet. "You okay, Kai?"

Apart from the shock and an incessant throbbing at the side of his face and blood trailing from his nose, Kai was mostly fine.

"I don't understand," he said, wiping the blood off his face. "Does she hate me or something?"

"She doesn't hate you, Kai," Yoko said, watching her leave. "I think she just wanted someone to blame, and I guess you were the easiest target."

"But that doesn't justify her attacking you like that," Valcor said indignantly. "That was *way* out of order."

He shrugged. "People take anger out in different ways."

"It must be hard for her," Becky said sadly. "I'd feel terrible if my Talite died,"

"Yeah, guys, we've got a problem . . ." Rafael said, staring at Wave's Talite.

The four of them looked at him. "What?"

"How are we getting those two home if her Talite's dead?"

The realization hit home with a shock. Talites couldn't carry three people for more than a couple of seconds, and with no other means of transport, they were literally stuck there, unless a miracle descended from heaven itself to aid them.

"Oh, *man,* this sucks," Valcor said. "What are we gonna do?"

Becky looked anxiously at Kai and said miserably, "I don't know."

There was an awkward silence that hung around for much longer than it really needed to. Finally Yoko spoke.

"We can worry about it later," she said. "All I want to do now is get some rest."

EIGHTEEN

Kai should have felt happy.

He'd discovered Mialyn, hopefully put an end to the rising Dracaen problem, and to top it off, managed to defeat a Dracaen thirty times his size and emerge almost unharmed, but after watching Wave's Talite die, he couldn't seem to summon any sort of happiness of any kind. In fact, he just felt depressed and had a mounting feeling of uncertainty. Despite all the good they'd done, there were still enough problems to keep him occupied. Wave hadn't returned from wherever she went, and Kai was starting to wonder what she was up to, and to make matters worse, he seemed to be the only one who felt like this.

The air was still as the others slept, but Kai couldn't coax himself into resting. He didn't see the point of sitting around when he clearly wasn't tired, so he got to his feet and softly padded out of the cave and into the cool night air.

His original idea had been to go look for Wave, but any encounter between them was bound to be either unbearably awkward or just a repeat of what had happened last time and, if anything, only reinforce his feelings of depression. So, he mentally talked himself out of it and sat down on an overturned log a short distance from the cavern, deep in the surrounding undergrowth, alone with his thoughts. It was one of those rare nights when the clouds drew back and the stars gave the air above him so much depth it seemed he could drop into it and never hit the bottom, continuing listlessly up into eternity.

"You okay?"

Kai jumped, startled, and then relaxed when he recognized the voice.

"Yeah. Why're you up? Couldn't you sleep?"

Becky looked a little embarrassed. "I saw you get up so . . . I sort of followed you. You looked kinda down. I just wanted to make sure you were all right—not planning on throwing yourself off the edge of the island or anything."

Kai looked at the floor. "I was thinking . . . ," he began, somewhat reluctantly, trying to figure out how best to phrase this. "You know that huge Dracaen in the cave?"

Becky nodded.

"Well, I thought the map—*her* map—led here, to Mialyn, so she must have come here at one point . . . and if the Dracaens hadn't been on Keturah when she came, they'd have probably been here as well. And if that huge Dracaen attacked her too, then she'd have probably lit the stones herself to keep it away."

"Yeah?"

"So . . . it was *her*," Kai said. "She caused all this, the Dracaens and everything. It was her fault this whole time that all those people died . . . She killed Renee . . ."

"The Dracaens killed Renee," Becky said firmly, fiercely. "Don't say that *ever*, Kai. People make mistakes all the time. Even if that *was* what really happened, she's not to blame for any of this. She was on her own, and she did the most logical thing she could do defend herself. Anyone else would have done that in the same situation."

"You really think that?"

"Of course."

Kai didn't reply for a moment, mulling over her words thoughtfully.

"Thank you, Becky," he responded finally, placated but not entirely convinced, a small smile working its way onto his face.

Becky grinned back. "Now there's a smile. Don't worry, everything's gonna turn out fine. At least you got us all this far."

Kai woke up with a start from a dream that comprised of the events of the previous night torn up and stuck together in the wrong order. He found himself leaning against a small tree, with Becky nestled comfortably against his shoulder, a warm patch of sunlight streaming onto his face through a gap in the leafy canopy above him. He had a vague headache and dim memories of the night before, but above it all, an odd feeling of reassurance made him feel more than content to watch the world pass by without him.

It was only when he heard Valcor's cheerful voice rising above the plants that he remembered the others he'd left last night.

Beside him, Becky stirred. "Wha...?" she murmured, sitting up. "I heard something. What's going on?"

Kai shrugged. "Nothing. Let's get back to the others."

Valcor and Yoko were up, and Wave had returned as well. The three of them were sitting beside a small fire, something cooking over it. Valcor grinned at the two of them as they returned.

"Hey, there you are. We've got breakfast."

"Where's Raf?"

"Sleeping still. Said he wasn't hungry."

Kai accepted a dish of whatever was cooking and took a bite. It tasted delicious, but it definitely wasn't anything he'd tasted before.

"What is this, exactly?"

"Dracaen meat," Yoko responded with a mischievous grin. "What do you think?"

Kai blinked. "Dracaen meat?"

Valcor said, "Well, it wasn't doing much lying around over there."

"So . . . do we have a plan yet?" Becky asked. "For how we're getting them back?"

Kai suddenly noticed a change in atmosphere.

"The only way I can see is if we . . . leave a couple of people here and come and pick them up later," Yoko explained uncomfortably.

Kai had been hoping it wouldn't have to come to this.

"There's nothing else?" Becky asked.

"Nothing that I've thought of," Yoko replied. "The journey out here took, what, six, seven days? And that was with the storms and everything. So, it'll be less than two weeks here, maximum. Unless someone else has something?"

There was a desolate silence. Kai sighed heavily.

"Who's staying behind, then?"

"I don't know. We'll have to flip a coin or something. It's not like anyone's gonna get up and offer to stay here."

"I'll stay," Wave said.

"There goes *that* hypothesis," Yoko muttered.

"I'll have to stay as well; she's my partner," Kai said reluctantly.

"But we need you to navigate," Valcor said.

"Raf's good at navigating too," Kai replied. "I'll give you the map and everything. Besides, I'll be missing two more weeks of school," he added, with a weak attempt at humour.

"You two, then," Yoko said, a brief nod in their direction. "Have fun."

Yeah, because nearly two weeks stuck alone on an island with nobody but Wave for company is going to be so much fun, Kai thought.

NINETEEN

Kai had known it was going to be hard, but he hadn't realised just how difficult until the other four had packed up and left, leaving behind about a week's worth of emergency rations, plus whatever nourishment the dead Dracaen had to offer, a first-aid kit, and promises to return and collect them as soon as possible.

Now that they'd left, the island suddenly felt so much larger, quieter, and ridiculously empty. Wave was either still angry, or upset, or both, or just refusing to talk to for reasons only she was aware of. It would have been okay if there were someone around to talk to, but with the gaping metaphorical chasm that had spontaneously seemed to open up between him and Wave, he realised that there was little to nothing he could do to pass the time.

The day dragged on like an everlasting prison sentence, and Kai was only too glad when the sky darkened and he began to feel tired again. At least sleep would give him a form of escape.

The next day continued along similar lines, and Kai was beginning to feel boredom setting in, threatening to drag him down into a deep void of insanity. Wave must have taken some sort of lessons in holding grudges; Kai wasn't sure anymore how she could possibly be dragging this out so long. He just couldn't take it.

"All right, you know what, Wave?" he snapped at her over breakfast on the third day, the irritation finally getting the better of him. "I'm sorry. I'm sorry for whatever it was I did to make you mad. I'm sorry that your Talite died and you punched me in the face. I'm sorry that even *three freaking days* after that, you still can't bring yourself to talk to me. I'm sorry that you're so cold and heartless, and right now I really wish you'd just go home and shoot yourself in the head."

For a brief moment, there was a long pause, and Kai wondered if she was going to get up and punch him again. But instead, Wave made an odd sound, as if she were trying not to laugh, which wasn't really the effect he'd intended.

"I forgive you," she responded, with a wry grin. "I wasn't expecting something like that." Then, finally, with what appeared to be great reluctance, she continued: "Sorry for taking it out on you earlier. I just . . . wasn't thinking straight. You really think I'm heartless?"

"Ah . . . did I say that?" He was flustered. "I was . . . people do stupid things when they're angry, I guess . . ."

Wave laughed at his obvious embarrassment, but not unkindly. It was the first time he'd ever heard her laugh.

"Still stuck here, though," Kai said dully, reality announcing itself with a harsh knock.

"Yeah, that's a bummer."

There was a Dracaen gliding overhead, its sleek body casting a swooping shadow over the ground below. Kai looked up, startled, and quickly made himself scarce, diving into a pile of bushes next to him.

"Kai, what're you . . . ?" Wave said, bemused by his sudden odd behaviour. Kai pointed skywards; Wave quickly followed suit.

The Dracaen circled the island a couple of times, occasionally coming close to the edges, but mainly keeping its distance. Finally, it landed gently, cautiously, and began a careful inspection of the area, sniffing inquisitively at the mounds of deactivated Xucite stones that penetrated the surface, pawing mournfully at the dead body of the giant Dracaen that they still hadn't figured out how to get rid of, and finally bounding into the cave, its excited shrieks rippling off the cave walls.

"At least someone's in a good mood," Wave said, watching the Dracaen explore the cave's interior.

"Do you reckon it's safe to come out?" he asked Wave.

She shrugged in reply. "I don't know. Probably."

Another sweeping shadow signalled the arrival of a second Dracaen, so Kai kept to the bushes. It went through similar motions, but instead of heading eagerly for the cave like the first Dracaen, it inquisitively approached the bushes where they were crouched, sniffing the ground, then the trees around it, before poking its head into the undergrowth so the three of them were literally a couple of inches apart.

Kai yelped in shock and scrambled into a stumbling run as the Dracaen lunged forwards, snapping at the two of them, launching off a nearby tree and giving chase. Kai dove forwards and grabbed his pack, rummaging desperately inside for the Xucite stone while trying not to trip over. The Dracaen hurried forwards, jaws closing just behind him, the sound of its heavy breathing loud and incessant behind him.

Wave was faster than he was, and she flung herself at the nearest tree, hurriedly scaling the boughs, pulling herself onto a branch reasonably high up. Fumbling with the cork of the bottle of sap and with the Dracaen right on his heels, Kai was slower in climbing and only just managed to get out of reach as the Dracaen's claws raked against the bark of the tree.

The Dracaen snarled and dropped into a crouch, preparing to spring at him, but as it jumped, Kai waved the lit stone in its direction, and it snapped its wings out wide to prevent it from coming any closer, hovering uncertainly in mid-air before dropping back onto the ground with a low growl.

Kai watched it leave, his breath coming in panicked gulps. This proved that the Dracaens were definitely returning, spelling trouble for the two of them. Once his breathing had calmed a little, he leaned across and slung the lit stone on a branch a little higher up to keep the Dracaens at bay, and then he turned to Wave.

"We can't stay here if the Dracaens are coming back," Kai said. "We'll be killed before the others reach us, and I'm *really* not in the mood to get eaten today."

Wave gestured to the rest of the island. "We've got nothing, Kai. Unless you're planning on sprouting wings and flying out of here—and I seriously doubt you are—there's no way we're getting off here."

"So we're going to live in a tree for the next ten days?" Kai asked incredulously.

"I'll go for it if it means we don't die." Then, after a pause: "Can I have a sandwich? I'm kinda starving right now."

They ate in silence, Kai deliberating on what they were going to do next. Wave *was* right; there was nothing. There was no way they could get back to Keturah without flying there. He was typically tolerant about most things, but he drew the line at spending the next ten days living in a tree. And if the number of Dracaens was set to increase, then their life expectancy was at an all-time low. The presence of two was bearable, as long as they were vigilant all the time; twenty was a completely different story.

Making sure the Dracaen didn't appear to be coming back, Kai retrieved the stone from the branch above him and dropped back to the ground, moving quietly and making as little noise as possible, thinking hard.

He went over to the dead Talite, gently slipping the leather band off its head. He deftly wove and knotted it so it formed a figure-of-eight shape with two loops, one much bigger than the other.

Wave looked at him. "What're you up to now?"

"We're getting out of here," he said, with much more resolution than he felt.

"How, exactly?" she asked, part cynically, part curiously.

He didn't want to tell Wave what he was up to, because he wasn't sure he could trust her not to openly mock his idea, and he was already rather doubtful of it himself, so he kept silent.

But this wasn't the sort of thing he could rush into. He spent the rest of the afternoon waiting, watching a couple of more Dracaens arrive, watching a few of them leave later on, hiding out in the bushes whenever they got too close, clocking their return as they turned in for the night, trying to determine some sort of flight pattern. But they were too random, too unpredictable, and he needed to know exactly which direction they were heading in; otherwise, the plan would most definitely fail.

"I'm intrigued, Kai. What's with all the staring?"

"I'm just . . ." He opted to change the subject. "What's that?"

"What's what?"

"In your hand."

She outstretched her hand to show him a crudely cut blunt red stone. "Seeing as they're so ridiculously expensive back in Keturah," she explained with a wry grin, "and there's nothing better to do with my life . . ."

Kai felt an idea forming. "The stones," he said elatedly, getting to his feet. "That's it! Thanks!"

"You're welcome," Wave replied in a bemused tone, tucking the red stone into her pack. "Call me when you're ready to explain."

Kai rooted around in his pack until he found the bottle of the Xucitus sap and his own Xucite stone. The bottle only had a sliver of iridescent sap left, probably only good for one more use. He quickly drained the bottle, hooked the stone onto the end of his spear, and set about lighting all the stone deposits except for the ones directly in front of him, until the island was alight with evenly spaced red auras that glowed faintly in the approaching darkness. Now that the Dracaens only had one entrance, their flight pattern would be much more predictable.

He approached the edge of the island apprehensively, until his feet were just over the edge, standing on the perfect border between land and sky, the wind streaming though his hair and the ground solid beneath his feet. A Dracaen appeared on the horizon, heading towards the island, but it stopped several metres shy of it and circled it warily, prevented from landing by the fields generated by the stones. Finally it found the gap and started flying forwards, straight towards Kai.

This is it, Kai, he thought to himself, subconsciously tightening his grip on Wave's band. Everything else faded into insignificance until it was just him, the Dracaen, the edge of the island, and a handful of doubts.

This is stupid, his inner logic told him. The Dracaen's figure in the distance increased in size with each passing moment, with each heartbeat.

For some strange reason, that didn't seem to bother him, even though he knew it *was* stupid. Far too risky. Completely, utterly insane. There was a greater chance that he'd miss and plummet to his doom than actually pull it off.

Oh well, he thought, feeling a kind of reckless abandon he'd never felt before. *Anything's possible.*

He stepped off the edge.

TWENTY

The world spun madly around him as Kai fell, plummeting through the sky with a yell that resembled a cross between some sort of insane battle cry and pure, unadulterated terror.

Above him, Wave rushed to the edge of the island. "Kai! It's not that bad! We've only got nine days left!"

The Dracaen looked up, startled, as it heard Kai descend rather unexpectedly in front of it. The leather loop slid over its head, Kai jerking to a painfully abrupt halt as he hung from the Dracaen's neck, clutching onto the band for dear life. It twisted in mid-air, trying to shake Kai off, but the loop held firm and Kai managed to swing himself onto its back, his heart racing with exhilaration.

Not used to having anything on its back, the Dracaen started to panic, thrashing about madly. Kai realised he'd overlooked quite a crucial part in his plan: he had no idea what he was planning to do when he had got onto the Dracaen.

To be honest, he hadn't even been sure he'd even get this far.

Positions wouldn't work, that much he knew, but the only experience he'd had riding was on a Talite, and he found himself automatically switching into different stances in the hope that some sort of miracle would occur. But the Dracaen only thrashed more, struggling against every movement, and Kai realised that this clearly wasn't working. With a loud screech, it snapped into movement, twisting, jolting, and writhing. He held tightly to the band, trying to quell the rising panic as it zoomed in wild circles in the air, even going so far as to deliberately crash into the side of the island. The soft light of the sunset merged into his terrified shouts as he desperately tried to maintain his hold on the band, the world spinning round him in a vortex of colour and panic.

Spontaneously, the Dracaen dived back towards the islands, slamming into the ground, crashing through the thick layer of trees around it. It hit the ground with the smattering of breaking branches sounding around them like applause, and before Kai realised what it was up to, rolled onto its back. Kai tried to scramble out of the way but was squashed underneath its weight, trying hopelessly to extricate himself from under it. He was starting to feel light-headed, spots of light clouding his vision as he took in a few desperate breaths, quickly running out of energy.

The Dracaen flipped back over suddenly, back on its feet in a flurry of movement. Kai let out a gasp of relief, shakily getting to his feet. His chest felt tight, and as he coughed violently, it came out sounding hoarse and high-pitched. His head spun from the lack of oxygen, and the dull throb of the wounds he'd received earlier only compounded the effect. The Dracaen let out another cry, about to take off again. Not wanting to let his only chance of escape get away, he flung himself at the band as it launched again into the air. Breathing heavily, the pain thumping continuously in his head like an incessant drum beat, he levered himself back onto its back and braced himself for another session of mad dashing across the sky.

Instead, it stopped moving altogether, its breath now coming in ragged, deep pants. It was tiring, and Kai felt very much relieved. But that fact alone wasn't making it any more co-operative, and he had no idea what to do. It was an improvement of sorts, but he still couldn't control it. All he'd achieved was making it stop moving. Kai's mind frantically flicked backwards through all the stuff he'd read and heard in his life that could possibly help him with this. He knew that riding was about the bond between the two of them, but he'd never seen the Dracaen before, and he was pretty sure it was probably more concerned with eating him than anything else. He had to make it trust him.

But how . . . ?

"Hi," Kai said awkwardly, feeling insanely self-conscious. The Dracaen tensed, as if preparing to bolt again, and Kai nearly panicked. "Wait, don't . . . Just, uh, j-just listen to me for a bit, okay?"

The Dracaen didn't let its guard down—it was still tensed and on edge—but it appeared to be listening. Kai floundered hopelessly, wondering what to say to it. He could hear its ragged breaths, feel its body quivering with . . .

Was that some kind of fear or just exhaustion?

"I . . . I-I'm not trying to hurt you . . . ," he said, trying a different tack. "We just need to get back home, that's all." Still talking in a placating voice, he slowly reached forwards and rested his hand on the top of the Dracaen's head, stroking it gently. The Dracaen flinched but quickly relaxed again.

Now they were getting somewhere. Kai continued talking to it in a low, calm voice, rubbing his hand in gentle circles underneath its neck like he'd seen Farrell do to her cats when he lived with her. Then he slipped his hand into his pack and quickly took out the sandwich he was going to have for dinner, split it in two because he suddenly realised how hungry he was, and offered half to the Dracaen.

It sniffed curiously at the offering before grabbing it from his hand, tossing its head back and gulping the sandwich down. Then it looked back at Kai, eyeing the other half of the sandwich.

"This is mine," Kai told it. "You've had your half."

The Dracaen gave a low growl at that, so Kai consoled it by giving it the remaining two days' worth of emergency rations, quickly unwrapping the packages in a bid to feed the food to it at the same speed it was gulping it down. It gave a contented hiss as it swallowed the meal and after a while made an odd gentle whirring in the back of its throat that was strangely reminiscent of the sounds Talites made when they were feeling contented.

Kai sat up a little straighter, feeling bruised and battered but realizing that he'd definitely made some sort of breakthrough.

"Okay, let's try this again," he murmured to himself, and just like that, the Dracaen started moving forwards, haltingly at first, but picking up speed as the two of them gained confidence. Kai couldn't tell how he was doing it; it was all instinctive, in the back of his mind, almost sensing every move it made before it made it, like the two were inextricably connected by an invisible thread.

The first few minutes were shaky as Kai got his bearings, but as he started to get the hang of it, trusting his subconscious and the Dracaen to perform together in unison, it got much easier. Spiralling in wild loops through the sky, Kai gave a nervous shout of elation, the air rushing free and clear around him like applause and the rippling shrieks of the Dracaen echoing in his ears.

Finally, coming back to his senses, he hovered beside the island, grinning at Wave's stunned expression.

"What'd I tell you? Come on, let's get out of here."

Dracaens could fly much faster than Talites and were evidently much stronger as well, which meant they didn't need to stop for much during their flight. Adrenaline kept Kai awake from the start of their journey at dusk, through the night, flanked by the starlit sky and the rushing darkness, as the sky faded into dawn, across the broad light of the morning, until deep into the afternoon. Kai had been navigating by what he could remember of the map, and if he was right, they were only a day and a half away from reaching Keturah when they stopped to rest.

If he was wrong, then they were probably hopelessly lost, but he quickly pushed the thought out of his mind.

"Do you think we could catch up with the others?" Wave asked thoughtfully.

Kai calculated the distances in his mind. It had taken them around six days to get there, but that was because of the storm and the difficulty with the sky tunnels, and hopefully the others would have been trying to get back as quickly as possible. That meant their journey would take around four days, and with a three-day head start, it meant they were only about a day away. The Dracaen had been flying for the whole day, and with the added speed and stamina, if they kept up the pace, perhaps they could just about make it back in time to meet the others.

"At this rate, probably. We'd better find them soon, or they'll come back for us and find us missing. We could've passed them for all we know; the Deep Sky's so big." He paused and let out an exaggerated yawn. "Watch the Dracaen for me; I'm gonna go try get some sleep."

Half an hour later, they were back in the sky again. Kai realised just how shattered he was going to be after missing out on so much sleep. To keep himself awake, he busied himself by talking to Wave and to the Dracaen while she rested, leaning against his back.

"Wave?"

"Yeah?"

Kai hesitated slightly. "You don't have to answer, like if you don't want to, but . . . why'd you drop out of elite training?"

"Who told you that?" she asked, her voice a bit sharp.

Kai shrugged, not wanting to drag any names into it. "Uh . . . I just heard, you know. People say stuff."

Wave was silent for a while, and Kai wondered if he'd offended her. It seemed like a personal question at any rate, so he was surprised when she answered.

"I'd been riding all my life, since I could walk, when I got my first Talite . . . the same one I've had since. My dad taught me when I was a kid, so I qualified for rider at eight years old. It seemed the most obvious thing I should do next was qualify for elite. They let me take the test when I was eleven, but he wanted to make sure I was solid before I qualified; he was like that. He wasn't strict or anything, but he was so organized, wanted everything done to the last tiny detail. He told me if I could master free riding, he'd let me go for training."

"But that doesn't make any sense. Free riding is much harder than elite theory."

Wave said, "I guess his theory was that if he could free ride, then it couldn't have been *that* difficult. He could ride like that; but then again, he was crazy about riding. Then one night he went out on some sort of voyage into the Deep Sky to practise something, got caught in a storm, and was struck by lightning. He died before I mastered free riding. At first, I thought, *I'll take the test now, seeing as he's not here to stop me.* But I couldn't bring myself to complete the training. Every time I went for class, there was this annoying little voice in my head telling me my dad wouldn't approve of what I was doing. It was like I was letting him down by disobeying him, even if he was dead and gone."

Kai nodded. He knew the feeling.

"So I dropped out and made the same promise to myself. If I could master free riding, I'd let myself take the test. So I tried, and I never got the hang of it. He was the only one around to teach me, and I kept forgetting what he'd already told me."

She paused, sighing. "And yet . . . *you* can do it, and you've been here for, what, a year or something?"

"I haven't been here long," he said. "I guess it's easier for me to forget what I've learned, positions and everything."

She shook her head. "It's not that; it's just that they'd get every freaking newcomer free riding like there was no tomorrow, that spineless friend of yours included."

"Who?" Kai asked, mystified.

"Don't remember his name. Came with us to Summit Peak."

"Felix isn't... He's just a little afraid of heights, that's all," Kai said defensively. "So what is it then, if it's not me being here long enough?" he added quickly, not wanting to risk another argument.

"It's about the bond between the two of you—that's what you told me, remember? You've got a way with them; they just warm up to you ridiculously easily. Even with my Talite, he settled down quickly enough the first time you rode him." She sat up a little straighter behind him.

"What?" Kai asked her.

"See that?" she said, pointing up ahead. It was getting deep into the night by now, and Kai wondered how she could expect him to see anything at all, but he looked anyway. A sweeping beam of light flickered faintly in the distance, pivoting round in a broad circle.

"Is that...?"

Wave nodded. "The beacon," she said, finishing his sentence for him. "We're nearly there."

The sky started to take on a suspicious countenance as they progressed, so they stopped off on one of the nearby islands and took shelter for the night in a small cave. Kai was glad they did; almost as soon as they'd settled down, another storm whipped up. The Dracaen, after watching the lightning storm for a few minutes, lost interest and curled up to sleep, its tail flicking back and forth as it dozed off. After sharing the last of Wave's rations for dinner, he too managed to get some sleep that night, albeit with difficulty; his dreams were punctuated with the booming roars and slashing cracks of the raging storm. By the time Wave shook him awake, there was a faint light creeping into the cave's shadow, and the storm had tapered off into a pattering of rain, soft against the ground. The air was light, swirling with the scent of fresh rain and damp soil.

"We'd better get a move on," she said. "The quicker we get back, the better."

The rain didn't let up during the journey, and Kai was starting to feel damp and cold, but that didn't do much to dampen his mood because he could see the island of Ilyas hovering in the horizon, signalling the end of the meaningful part of the journey. And after all the time they'd spent out in the Deep Sky, Kai couldn't wait to get back to Keturah, even if it *did* mean school.

"Do you want to have a go at riding?" Kai asked Wave.

"No. I suck at free riding. You know that."

"At least try it. I mean, what if I fall off or something? Who'd ride it then?"

"Why would you fall off?"

"Who knows? Expect the unexpected. You never know . . ."

The sound of someone talking loudly drifted over to them, distracting Kai. The sentence forgotten, he looked around, trying to determine the source of the noise, and ultimately wasn't surprised to see two Talites behind them, their images marred in the distance by the slanting rain but easy to make out.

"Is it them?"

"Who else?" Wave grinned. "You can hear them from a mile away."

"That'd be Val, I suspect." Then to the Dracaen: "Don't eat anyone, okay?"

It responded with a low growl. Kai turned the Dracaen round, wondering how he could get their attention without scaring them. That ruled out charging straight at them, he supposed.

"Guys!" he yelled, waving. "*Guys!*"

The two Talites paused some way off, their riders evidently trying to piece two and two together and coming up with a lot more than they'd expected. Finally, someone yelled back, "*Kai?*"

The disbelief was evident in the voice, and as Kai approached them, he could see it was clear on their faces as well. Kai grinned.

"Hey."

TWENTY-ONE

Valcor was the first one to get over the shock. "I thought we left you on the island," he said, the surprise clear in his voice. "Are you seriously riding a Dracaen? Why aren't you dead? How'd you manage to do that? I thought it was impossible to ride a Dracaen. Everyone else says so. Sacha said so, I mean..."

Becky stared at him in shock. "Wow," she whispered, unable to say much else. "That's just... *wow*..."

"I thought you were crazy before," Rafael said, clearly impressed. "But this is, like, *insane*."

"What on earth possessed you to ride a Dracaen?" Yoko asked, sounding mildly amused.

"The other Dracaens started returning," Kai explained, "so we figured we should get out quickly, and this was... the only available option."

"You know, everyone's gonna freak out when they see you," Rafael said seriously.

The thought hadn't occurred to Kai. "Oh. Yeah..."

"Never mind," Valcor put in cheerfully. "We'll paint it cream and stick white fluff on its wings. Nobody will know the difference."

They reached Ilyas in the early evening. The sight of the familiar orange street lamps lining the streets below them filled Kai with a sort of nostalgia, despite the fact that he'd only been to Ilyas once. Luckily, the approaching darkness gave the Dracaen an excellent cover, and Ilyas had a small population, so nobody seemed to notice the large creature land in a field far from the main village.

They hid the Dracaen out of sight, where random passers-by would be unlikely to stumble upon it, and secured it firmly so it wouldn't run away. They then began the quick trek up to the main village. It was dark by then, the street aglow with the soft orange hues from the lanterns and shop windows. They chose a quiet-looking café overlooking the main street that ran straight through the village, ordering some hot drinks and a plate of warm, sweet cakes; they'd had their dinner of sandwiches earlier in the evening.

"Are we riding back tonight?" Becky asked. "Or are you guys tired?"

"I'm exhausted," Valcor said, lacking none of his usual enthusiasm. "And I'm pretty tired of sleeping on the ground. I'd kill to be back in a bed."

Rafael shrugged. "I don't think we have enough money to stay here anyway," he said pointedly. "We barely had enough to cover the food."

Kai stirred his hot chocolate, pouring in too much sugar and staring absent-mindedly out of the window. There was a middle-aged man outside, his hair greying and large spectacles in front of his eyes, waving his hands and talking rapidly to someone in a breathless voice, his face pale. The message must have been an alarming one, for the recipient of said message immediately went as pale as the first person, who was now shouting something at the rest of the people in the street. Kai had just taken his first taste of the hot chocolate, letting the sweet flavour linger on his tongue, when a woman burst through the front door with a bawling child in her arms, the bell jingling merrily.

"There's a Dracaen running wild in the field!" she gasped, to the obvious horror of the few people in the café. Outside, Kai could hear people shouting and general noises of panic.

"Oh, for *crying* out loud," he muttered, thumping his head gently against the table.

"Isn't that *your* Dracaen?" Yoko asked.

"Probably," he said. "Timing's too perfect."

Abandoning his hot chocolate on the table, he battled against the surging crowd, trying to get to the field where they'd left the Dracaen, the others close behind him, aware of the strange looks he was getting from the people running in the opposite direction. They reached the field, panting heavily.

The Dracaen was heavily camouflaged against the darkness of the night, so the only way Kai could locate it was using its rippling shadow, the sound of the rope they'd used to tie it up dragging against the ground, and the gleam of its eyes, soft against the moonlight. It wasn't quite on the rampage, but it was jumping about in the field in a way that he suspected would be somewhat alarming to an innocent passer-by.

"Told you we should have tied it up more securely," Wave grumbled.

"All we had was rope," Rafael said.

Kai took a couple of tentative steps towards it, murmuring something under his breath. The Dracaen stopped moving as soon as it heard his voice, and as Kai got near, he quickly rubbed it under its chin. A rippling, contented growl echoed across its throat.

"There you go," Kai said. "I thought I told you not to terrorize the villagers..."

"Right, *now* I've seen everything."

Kai didn't recognize the voice at first, but he could hear a kind of light amusement in the words. He looked round.

"John?"

The night was calm, soft like a breath of wind, quiet as a whisper. It was the kind of night Felix would have liked to have been out in, but he'd somehow managed to accumulate a lot of homework over the past week or so, and he had no time to spare. He'd spent most of the night working steadily through the pile of homework on his desk, and while it was certainly diminishing in size, it still looked as if it would take him a couple of days to get through it.

He'd hardly started on his natural science assignment when there was a deafening crash from somewhere within the building. It shook the ground, and his books slid off the table and clattered onto the floor. Startled, Felix scrambled to his feet and pulled open the door. There were no obvious signs of damage from where he was standing, but the people who had rooms on this corridor had already gravitated into a loose group in the middle of the hallway, discussing what could have happened. Felix drew closer in an effort to see what was going on.

"What was that?"

"Do you think it's safe to stay here?"

"We should tell someone about this. Someone might be trying to break in or something, like..."

There was another loud crash, and the ground shook again, more violently this time. The lights around them flickered, flashed once, and then went out with a quiet *click*, plunging them into a confused darkness.

"What the heck?"

"This is crazy. I'm getting out of here."

Felix had come to a similar conclusion himself and started to retreat back down the corridor. He'd been living in the building for enough time for him to be able to locate the nearest door in the eerie darkness, but as he pushed against the door, it wouldn't open. The handle turned fine, but there appeared to be something blocking it from the outside. He could hear the sounds of other residents pouring out from their rooms, their confused, worried shouts mingling into an indecipherable blur of voices in the distance. Feeling slightly uneasy, he turned away and thought about his options.

Something had definitely happened, and he felt rather apprehensive about returning to his room. He knew the layout of the building enough to know there was another door somewhere, which hopefully wouldn't be obstructed, and if push came to shove, there were windows farther down that he could break open. It seemed like an ideal strategy, but before he could act on the idea, he heard a loud, grating screech from the corridor behind him that he recognized all too well...

Valcor looked at John suspiciously. "What are you doing here?"

"Looking for you guys," he replied.

"Why?" Becky asked. "Has something happened?"

"Not that I'm aware of," John said. "However, Mr Shorren only gave you ten days, Kai."

Kai looked sheepish. "I know. We're a bit late..."

"Four days late, to be precise."

"Have you really been here for four days?"

"Not exactly. I think Mr Shorren was ready to give you the benefit of the doubt for a couple of days—it's all too easy to lose track of time in the Deep Sky—but yesterday he told me to go out and have a look for you guys. So it's been just under two days, I'd say."

"How'd you find us here, though?" Rafael asked. "I mean, it'd have been easier to find us when we were back in the village, instead of out here in the field."

"I saw you in the café," John said. "As I was about to pop in, someone started talking about a Dracaen on Ilyas, and the whole street was suddenly full of people rushing to their homes and protecting their loved ones. And then I saw you six running urgently *towards* the place where the Dracaen was seen."

"People were giving us funny looks," Valcor said, sounding a bit put out.

John smiled. "I can imagine why. I was wondering whether you six had a death wish, so I followed you here..."

He looked over pointedly at Kai, the Dracaen poking inquisitively at his hair with its nose.

"... and I think I must've missed quite a lot," he concluded. "So how'd it go? Did you find Mialyn?"

Valcor quickly filled him in on the details, sparing next to nothing.

"Well now," John said, once the story had finished. "That sounds like quite a journey. At least you're all in one piece, which is a miracle in itself, given what you've been through. And this Dracaen here... simply amazing, Kai. How did you manage it?"

He shrugged. "I wasn't thinking properly," he admitted. "I just wanted to leave, really."

"You seem to have acquired your mother's gift for dealing with animals," he said. "The Talites always seemed to be fond of her."

They heard shouts and the flickering glare of flaming torches in the distance, and a ragged group of people soon emerged onto the field, carrying an assortment of weapons: from rudimentary things they'd grabbed out of their homes, like broomsticks and mops, to serious weapons such as crossbows and pitchforks.

"There it is!" someone yelled, pointing his scythe at the Dracaen, which crouched into a battle stance with a low, threatening growl.

"Kai, Wave, get out of here," John instructed, swiftly sizing up the situation. "We'll catch up with you on the south side."

Kai didn't need telling twice. He scrambled onto the Dracaen's back with Wave close behind him and murmured something at it, keeping a wary eye on the villagers. The Dracaen launched itself into the air with a shriek.

The guy with the crossbow in front and a couple of others behind him fired at the Dracaen, unable to see its riders owing to the darkness and its wings, beating powerfully beside them and obscuring any image of the two of them. Small, hard bolts whizzed past, with flashes of air trailing behind them. One grazed its shoulder, drawing a thin bloody gash and a wail of pain. Without warning, the Dracaen spun round in mid-air and charged back at the villagers.

"Kai!" Wave shouted at him.

"It's not listening!" Kai yelled back frantically as the Dracaen dived forwards, snarling viciously. The villagers jabbed at it with their weapons as it swooped low over the ground, slashing at them with its tail, knocking a few people over.

"Get to the Talites," John said to the other four kids, who quickly obliged. He turned to the villagers.

"Stop attacking it!" he said to them.

"Are you crazy?" someone yelled back at him, hurling his pitchfork at the black creature. "It'll kill us all!"

John attempted to pacify the villagers while Kai struggled to control the Dracaen as it readied for another attack, but it seemed intent on avenging its injuries, which had now stretched to several body wounds and a pitchfork sticking out of its side.

The Dracaen lunged forwards at a young-looking guy who'd been slashing at it with a small knife. He managed to duck under the first attack, but he stumbled backwards and fell to the ground, his knife dropping harmlessly to the ground. The guy backed away as the Dracaen advanced on it. Kai watched helplessly as the Dracaen raised its tail high above it, ready to end the young man's life with a single crushing blow.

Wave lunged forwards and in a swift, savage movement jabbed two fingers into the gash on its shoulder. The Dracaen flinched, the tail thumping irately against the ground. The guy quickly scrambled to safety as the Dracaen twisted round to snap at them.

Kai held his hands up in surrender. "Sorry," he said. "You were going to kill that guy. Perhaps you could consider—"

The Dracaen clearly was in no mood for considering, for it launched itself back into the sky again, apparently readying for another attack. The onslaught from below had tapered out into a vague shouting; John appeared to be winning them over.

Kai looked at Wave. "Do you still have the first-aid kit?"

"Yeah," Wave rummaged around in her pack and handed it over. Kai quickly flipped it open and finally took out a small dark bottle which he thought said DISINFECTANT but wasn't entirely sure because the darkness made it impossible to see much.

"This might sting a little," Kai murmured, dabbing a little of the sharp-smelling substance onto the wound. The Dracaen jerked away as he applied the disinfectant but started to calm down again as Kai attempted to dress the injury, using *The Complete Guide to Herbal Remedies* and what he'd seen Becky do earlier as his guide. He pressed a wad of cotton against the wound before winding a bandage around the shoulder and the top of its front leg.

The Dracaen poked inquisitively at the bandage wrapped hastily around its shoulder, staunching the flow of blood, before looking back up at Kai. Kai wasn't sure what the effectiveness of the crude remedy would turn out to be, but the message was clear.

"Okay, let's get out of here," Kai murmured, and this time the Dracaen seemed to take notice. They fled the scene.

They met John and the others on the south side of the island and quickly proceeded with their journey home. By now, Kai was exhausted, and all he really wanted to do was dive into bed and fall asleep. The thought of rest was tantalizingly tempting, and he was dangerously close to dropping off when Wave's voice sounded, hard and tense behind him.

"The island's on fire."

Not all of it, perhaps, but enough to cause alarm.

And worse: a collective screeching, shrieking noise that could only belong to an aggravated bunch of Dracaens.

The combination of the deep night and the power cut meant that the Dracaen was practically invisible. Felix didn't know where it was or how it had managed to get in, but he could smell its stale breath, and the shrieks were almost deafening, so he knew it was close. Close enough to kill him.

Something hard crashed into the wall beside him, so close that he could feel the spines on the end of it raking across his arm. He gave an involuntary yelp of fear and pain, and the Dracaen zoomed in on the sound, lunging towards him with a terrifying scream. Felix twisted away just before a set of teeth clamped shut just an inch away from his head. He scrambled away, dashing down the corridor, trying desperately to quell the rising fear, but with a Dracaen on his tail, it was impossible. It was too dark to see where the corridor walls were, let alone a door. He probably could have passed it by now and never noticed . . .

Unexpectedly, his foot hooked into something lying across the floor and he crashed to the floor with a dull thud. He could hear the roaring of the Dracaen behind him, its footsteps pounding against the floor, using its wings to cover great gliding leaps in its pursuit. His pulse racing with fear, he tried to scramble to his feet again, but he felt a hand on his arm pulling him down.

"Stay down and don't make a sound," a voice close to him hissed, and he obeyed, pressing himself against the floor. He could feel the Dracaen's feet just beside him, next to his face, and then they lifted up again as it unsuspectingly continued down the corridor, its screams tapering off into the distance.

Felix let out a trembling breath as he sat up again, aware of how close he'd been to getting eaten. His eyes had grown accustomed to the dark by now, but all he could make out of the person to whom he owed his life was a blurred figure just beside him.

"You okay?" she asked. Felix didn't recognize the voice.

"Yeah, I'm . . . I'm fine . . . ," he replied, his heart still hammering. He could feel blood trickling into his eye from a cut he'd sustained earlier, and he reached up a shaking hand to wipe it away. "Thanks."

"No problem."

"Do you know what's going on?"

"What, me? No idea. I was just walking to my room and heard this crashing sound, and the next thing I knew, the lights were out and Dracaens were running wild through the school. But we'd better get the heck out of here before we run into another one. I think the door's down the way you just came . . ."

"It's blocked," Felix said. "I tried it; it wouldn't open. Perhaps something fell down in front of it or something . . ."

The girl swore softly. "Nothing's ever easy, is it? Well, there must be a way out *somewhere* . . ."

They'd started walking again, feeling their way along the corridors and crouching low against the walls whenever they heard the shrieking sounds of the

Dracaens near them. The cut above Felix's eye persistently leaked blood, and he had to resort to keeping his hand pressed against his forehead to staunch the flow. Finally, after what seemed like hours of walking, Felix noticed the darkness start to take on a vague iridescence, the shadows fading slightly.

"It's getting lighter," he murmured.

"There should be a window soon, or something," the girl agreed.

It *was* a window, but it wasn't quite what they'd expected. As they rounded the corner, they caught sight of the dim light from the half moon streaming in from a skylight above them, faintly illuminating the corridor. It had been broken open, which presumably was how the Dracaen had got in, errant shards of glass littering the floor.

"See?" the girl said, with a grin. "Nothing's easy in this place."

Felix could see her properly now. She was a bit on the short side, with dark skin and long black hair, and after a while, he remembered hearing a teacher calling her Norelle at chess club.

"The ceiling's not too high," Felix said.

She nodded. "I reckon we could reach it." She broke off abruptly as the sound of frenzied screeching filled the corridor.

Felix looked at her disbelievingly. "Again?"

"Quick. You're taller; I'll give you a leg up."

She locked her hands together to make a platform, and after a couple of seconds of adjusting, managed to lift him up towards the skylight. Felix grasped the edge of the window, wincing as the jagged glass edge cut into his skin, and managed to scramble through the hole. He leaned down and stretched out his hand.

"Hurry, it'll be here any second," he said frantically as the shrieks grew louder and louder. She clasped his hand, and he started to hoist her up, but at that second, the Dracaen appeared round the side of the corridor with an almighty roar that almost made Felix let go of her hand. Catching sight of Norelle, it dropped into a snarling crouch, preparing to jump at her.

Felix struggled to pull her through the skylight; he'd never been impressively strong, and her weight was tiring his arm out. He only had her a couple of inches higher when it sprang. Norelle responded instinctively, swinging round and kicking it brutally in the face. It scrambled backwards with a cry of pain, but it wouldn't be long before it was back up and ready to attack again.

Felix hurriedly pulled her through the skylight just as the Dracaen sprang upwards again, scrabbling furiously at the gap through the ceiling with an angry snarl, the glass creating bloody gashes across its legs not seeming to deter it in the slightest. The two of them backed away as it dug into the ceiling with its claws and hauled itself up onto the flat roof of the annexe with an explosive snarl.

It advanced towards them, growling menacingly, its pointed teeth gleaming like jagged daggers in the ashen moonlight, swinging its tail behind it. They took another couple of steps backwards as it pounced forwards, its claws closing on empty air. The next jump pushed them right to the edge of the roof, cutting them off from any escape.

Except down.

Norelle looked round. "We'd better jump," she said urgently. "It's not that high."

"Yeah," Felix responded uncertainly. From where he was standing, the ground suddenly seemed a lot farther away, bringing up a dizzying wave of nausea. The Dracaen was readying for the last strike, but as he looked helplessly down at the ground beneath him, he knew he couldn't convince himself to jump. His hands throbbed with a dull persistent pain where they'd been sliced by the glass, and the drop beneath scared him almost as much as the Dracaen behind him did.

"What's the matter?" Norelle said.

"I . . . can't," he said, stricken.

"Well, we don't have a choice," she replied grimly, and before he knew what she was doing, she'd pushed him with a sudden flash of movement, sending him tumbling over the edge with a yell of startled terror.

He landed awkwardly on a grassy knoll behind the building, twisting his ankle but miraculously still in one piece. The Dracaen looked as if it wanted to follow, but something seemed to persuade it otherwise, and it turned away with a sudden, harsh screech, melting into the gathered darkness.

Norelle dropped gracefully beside him like a cat, flashing him a brief, mischievous grin.

"So you're a rider and you're scared of heights?"

She didn't sound as if she were mocking him, just mildly amused by the whole thing.

Felix looked away. "Can we talk about something else?"

"I must say, that is a pretty impressive combination."

"Yeah," he said, evasively, and then, for the first time since he'd got outside, looked around properly.

Felix had assumed it was just a small Dracaen attack on the building they were in, but as they rounded the corner, the full extent of what was happening hit them like a fist. Faint plumes of fire scarred the sky in the distance, not in the school itself but in the surrounding villages. The sounds of terrified screaming filled the air, and as Felix looked up, he could see why: there was a Dracaen flying over the school, its ragged wings tearing into the tops of the school buildings.

And another one following quickly behind it.

And another two shrieking somewhere in the distance.

And behind them, a writhing, screeching mass that instantly sent a shockwave of fear down his spine.

This wasn't good . . .

Beside him, Norelle gave a faint gasp. "What the . . . ? This is *huge*. Like an apocalypse or something. That crazy old woman was right all along."

Felix didn't reply, thinking hard. The Dracaens were frenzied, attacking blindly and randomly at anything they could find. They tore at buildings, crushing small wooden homes underneath their powerful tails, destroying sections of walls with single aggressive blows.

What the old woman had said earlier at the meeting seemed to have come to pass, but hadn't Kai gone out to Mialyn to solve this very problem? And if the Dracaens were here, then what had happened? Did they not find it . . . or did they simply get lost? Or had something more sinister happened?

The thought hit him like a slap or a sting, a sharp jolt of pain and shock. He shook his head, trying to think more optimistically, but once he started, more things kept flowing in: how Kai and the others were already four days late, and that John had been sent out two days ago to look for them and hadn't reported back since . . .

"We should probably get out of here," he murmured, trying not to let his growing apprehension show.

Norelle looked out across the school grounds. The Dracaen attack had already taken a heavy toll on the school buildings; most of the taller structures had been damaged, and the tower, usually soaring high over the school, had been razed almost to the ground. Piles of rubble, crumbling bricks, and shattered glass lay strewn around the ground in dejected heaps. The Dracaens were flying in unpredictable flight patterns high over the school but not generally attacking anyone unless they saw something move. "I . . . can't believe it. How could this happen?"

"I don't know either. But if we stay out in the open, we won't be around long enough to find out."

They stuck to the shadows, weaving in and out of the dark spots beneath the buildings, trying to evade detection.

"What's happened to all the others?" Norelle asked tentatively. "I haven't seen anyone since the lights went out."

Felix thought about the annexe they'd just escaped from, and the Dracaen running loose in the pitch black darkness, and the locked door, the different ideas synthesizing to form a grim picture.

"I don't know," he replied, and then he abruptly stopped walking.

"What is it?"

He paused, listening intently. "Did you hear something?"

"All I can hear is the Dracaens," Norelle replied. "Why, did *you* hear anything?"

It was hard to catch over the collective sounds of a huge horde of agitated Dracaens, but it was definite: a high-pitched lilting wail that sounded like the mournful sound of someone in serious pain.

"Here," he said quietly, motioning for Norelle to follow him. He darted through a door beside them, which led into a part of the main school building.

The roof had been ripped apart here, the sky gaping at them from a huge hole in the ceiling. A shivering figure lay trapped in a corner of the corridor, a grave-looking leg injury and a snarling Dracaen preparing to strike preventing her from escaping. Instinct kicked in before Felix could think about what he was doing. In one swift, reckless movement, he'd picked up a nearby stone from the collapsed roof and hurled it at the Dracaen.

It glanced off the side of its head, distracting it from its original target but shifting its focus to Felix and Norelle instead. With a fleeting rush of horror, he realised the full extent of what he'd done as the Dracaen turned to them, coiling into a crouch before pouncing at them like a spring.

Felix ducked under the attack and, figuring he might as well finish what he started, dashed forwards and collected the person who'd been cornered, helping her to her feet.

"Quickly," he said, guiding them towards a door that led into a classroom as the Dracaen lunged forwards at them again. "Norelle, the door!"

Luckily, Norelle had anticipated this and flung open the door, grabbing hold of the two of them and pulling them into the deserted classroom rather sharply as the

Dracaen threw itself forwards once more, crashing into the door just as Norelle slammed it shut.

"That won't keep it for long," she said breathlessly. Already a hammering sounded behind them, the door buckling inwards under the pressure. Norelle hastily jammed a couple of desks in front of it, buying them a few more precious minutes, before turning her attention to the girl they'd rescued.

Felix recognized her almost immediately, despite the fact that he'd only seen her once before, briefly.

"You . . . ," he said, groping wildly for a name and coming up short. "I know you . . . You were with us at the festival."

She levered herself up onto her elbows. "Yeah," she replied shortly, brushing her ginger curls out of her face. "It's Sacha. You're Felix, right? Thanks for saving me out there."

Felix nodded, although his heart was still racing with the enormity of what he'd just done. "It's fine. How's your leg?"

Sacha gave it an experimental test, flexing her leg and wincing with a hiss of pain. "Not good."

"What happened?" Norelle asked.

The hammering against the door sounded more persistent than ever, the desks grating and jerking against the floor.

"We were supposed to meet in the hall . . . once the Dracaens started attacking; one crashed through the roof as I was making my way over there . . . and the next thing I knew, I was trapped and my life was flashing before my eyes and everything . . ."

Norelle and Felix exchanged glances. "We're meeting in the hall? So that's where everyone is . . ."

A hooked claw ripped through the door, sending wood splintering into Felix's face. "If we're meeting in the hall, we should get there," he said, aware that the Dracaen was hacking the door to pieces behind him.

"We've got to get out first," Norelle reminded them. "And the door's *very* much out of the question, I think."

That only left one other escape: the window on the other side of the room. Between them, Felix and Norelle managed to lift Sacha outside, and they started to creep back round the school building to the main hall, moving painfully slowly because of Sacha's leg. Felix's heart skipped a beat every time he heard a Dracaen's wild screech in the distance.

The fires were much closer to the school now; he could see the flames burning hot and bright on the other side of the grounds. Sacha looked over at him.

"They're probably gonna call for an evacuation," she said miserably. "The emergency services are on their way from Meridian and everything." She hesitated, and then added, "Have you . . . heard anything from Kai and the others yet?" She asked the question haltingly, as if she were afraid of the answer.

"Nothing," Felix replied, unable to meet her gaze. "But you know, with everything that's going on and stuff . . ." He couldn't bring himself to finish the sentence.

Sacha's eyes brimmed with concern. "I'm really worried about them," she said quietly, and Felix couldn't help but agree.

The six of them looked in horror at John. "What happened?"

John looked justifiably alarmed. "The Dracaens are attacking," he said slowly, as if he couldn't quite believe what he was seeing.

Becky gave a gasp. "Like . . . like on *Teklah*? That's . . ." Her words trailed off, but the rest was painfully evident.

As they drew closer, they could see the full extent of the damage: the fires were mainly in the small villages to the northeast, near where the school was situated. The school had suffered a few damages so far: the top two floors of the tower had been demolished, and a couple of taller buildings had also been destroyed, but most of the main school building was still intact, although Kai wondered how long it would stay that way. The villages that weren't in flames had suffered major damage: houses had been destroyed, ripped into, knocked down, roads cracked, trees felled. People were screaming, shouting, wailing, and crying. The Dracaens, flanked by the darkness, flashed in and out of vision, briefly lit by the soft, destructive light of the fires, before disappearing into the shadows.

"How could this happen?" Wave demanded. "We've already fixed this, back on Mialyn. They shouldn't be attacking like this."

"Yes, but they don't know that right now," John said. "It'd take a while for them to realize. And I suppose, in the meantime . . ."

So close, Kai thought desperately. Just when he'd thought everything had smoothed out, something crazy like this happened to ruin it. It was as if the past two weeks were just a futile endeavour, a massive waste of time.

Valcor looked unusually troubled. "What are we going to do?" he asked.

"You? Nothing," John said firmly. "Keep out of the way for now. It's far too dangerous to go back there. The council should be ordering the evacuation of the island soon."

"But our Talites are still down there," Kai protested. Farrell would probably be terrified. "If they're evacuating, then they'll be left behind."

John paused. "I need to find out what happened," he said finally. "Whoever needs to get their Talites can come with me to the stables. Under any circumstances, don't stay any longer than you need to. The nearest evacuation point is on Meridian; I expect the rest of the school will join you there shortly, if they haven't already. Go there and wait for the others. I'll be there soon."

They landed just inside the school grounds. Kai could see the carnage up close now, hear people's terrified shouting in the distance. The Dracaen seemed agitated.

"Remember what I told you," John said to them, quickly disappearing into the main building. Kai looked over at the Dracaen.

"What should I do with it?" he asked.

Wave shrugged. "Release it probably. I can't ride it, and it's not doing much good here. I don't want to be attacked again by angry villagers."

"Then what's to stop it from attacking us?" Rafael asked.

"One more Dracaen probably won't make much difference. Anyway, hopefully, it's too fond of Kai to pay us any thought by now," Yoko said.

Kai slipped the band back over the Dracaen's head and murmured a quiet farewell as it took off skywards, melting into the shadows. Valcor left soon after, with

Wave sharing Yoko's Talite, leaving Kai, Rafael, and Becky to make their way to the stables.

The fire was much closer to this side of the island, dangerously close to the wooden structure of the stables. The heat seemed to suffocate him, the thick smoke prickling at his eyes and making him cough. The stables were empty by now; most people had picked up their Talites when the Dracaens started attacking.

Kai found Farrell clawing at the ground like he did when he was nervous, anxious whining rising in his throat. He gave a happy yelp when he saw Kai, bounding up to him and nuzzling his face.

"Hey," Kai said, relieved Farrell was all right. "Come on, quickly. Let's get out of here."

He turned to leave, but behind them, the wall closest to the fire suddenly flared with bright hot flames, and Farrell gave a terrified whine as sparks leaped ecstatically onto the grass in front of him, setting it alight. A line of fire leaped up in front of them, cutting off any access to the exit, already spreading to the walls around them. Farrell sprang backwards, the glare of the flames reflected in his fearful eyes.

Kai backed away from the flames, the air thick and heavy with the heat and the smoke billowing from the grass in front of him, making his eyes water, coughing frantically. He couldn't breathe; the acrid smoke clung to his face and hair, scratching his lungs.

"Farrell," he said brokenly, calling to his Talite. Farrell gave a low whine in response and pressed against the ground, shaking. There was a crackle above them as the ceiling caught on fire, burning wooden logs raining down in front of them as the fire burned away the ceiling. Kai grabbed Farrell's band and swung himself onto his back, feeling him instinctively relax as he climbed on.

The flames were all around them now, a sea of fire that darted backwards and forwards in an eerie flickering dance. The heat pounded at him mercilessly, making him feel hot and dizzy.

"Farrell . . . listen to me, okay? We're going to get out of here in just a second; I just need to . . ." He looked up, the gap in the wooden roof catching his attention.

Farrell gave a hesitant whine, already sensing what he was planning and quick to voice his concerns.

"Trust me," Kai said pleadingly. "It'll be fine . . ."

Another shower of glowing red-hot wood came raining down from the ceiling just in front of them. Farrell jumped away, startled, and this seemed to persuade him. He launched into the air, the ceiling zooming closer with a rush of blistering heat until they burst out of it with an explosive *crash* and a shower of sparks that whizzed around them, and suddenly there was nothing except the cool night air and the deep indigo sky sweeping in a broad curve above him. Kai took a deep breath of fresh air, and Farrell gave an excited clicking sound as they bounded over the top of the stables, landing in a breathless, slightly singed heap beside Rafael and Becky.

"Thank goodness you're here," she said, very much relieved. "We'd better get out of here."

As they lifted into the air to make their way to Meridian, they could see the makings of what looked to be a long and bloody battle stretched out in front of them. The emergency response team had been dispatched already, and they were spread around Tissarel in well-defended groups of six, some helping people escape from the island where the Dracaen attacks were the worst, others slashing at them with swords that glinted silver in the vague moonlight. In the background, groups were struggling with a huge device that looked like a cannon, manoeuvring the barrel so it faced the sky and shooting large, heavy cannonballs at the retaliating Dracaens with loud, dull bangs.

Riding at night with Dracaens swarming around the island was a precarious matter, but Kai was depressed, and he sensed that the others felt the same. He was so deep in thought that he missed all the warning signs: the Talites' increasing anxiety and the sound of something streaming in a quick blur past them. In fact, he didn't even notice the Dracaen until it slammed straight through the three of them, sending Kai reeling away. The impact jerked him hard to the side, but he managed to steady himself before he fell off.

Becky, however, wasn't so lucky. The attack flung her off her Talite, sending her plummeting to the ground. They hadn't been flying for more than five minutes at most, so they were away from the town centre, where the Dracaens weren't so frequent, and while the drop was small enough to survive, it was still a rather long way down.

"Becky!" Kai called, quickly sending Farrell into a sweeping dive and landing a couple of seconds after she'd hit the ground, with Rafael following up just behind. He jumped off Farrell's back and crouched next to her unconscious figure, grabbing her wrist to feel for a pulse.

"She's alive," Rafael said. "But that fall must've been pretty painful. We should probably get her to a doctor or something..." He got to his feet with more caution than

Kai thought necessary—until he turned round and saw what he was looking at.

The Dracaen had already landed and was advancing towards the three of them, a deep, hard snarl rising in its throat. Kai realised with a sense of dread that the distance was too short for them to be able to get back to the Talites and get away before it attacked, and they couldn't leave Becky like this even if they could.

The sword seemed to appear out of nowhere. One second Kai had been staring straight at a hungry Dracaen, and the next it was stumbling back, the hilt of a blade sticking out from its chest as it recoiled away. An impressively armoured Talite landed beside them, dropping into a battle stance and baring its teeth, while its rider, donned in a tight-fitting brass helmet and a steel breastplate, complete with shoulder guards and a patterned scabbard secured to a belt around his waist to hold his sword and a pair of heavy boots, jumped off it, pulling a curved knife from a concealed pocket in his trouser leg and facing off the Dracaen, shouting a brief command to his Talite.

While the Talite sprung at the Dracaen's neck, the man charged forwards towards its feet. The Dracaen ducked to avoid the Talite's attack, and with a sharp, deft movement, he slashed the blade upwards, cutting deep into its shoulder, while he retrieved his sword with his free hand. The Dracaen shrank back, whining with the pain, and the Talite sprang at its shoulders, knocking it to the floor and holding it there. The man raised his sword high above his head and brought it down with a swift, savage thrust. The Dracaen screamed in pain, its eyes fading shut.

The rider slipped off his helmet and advanced towards them.

"Shouldn't be flying over this way, kids," he said disapprovingly, pulling the sword back out of the dying Dracaen's chest, the blade glistening with its dark blood. "It's too dangerous. What happened to her?"

"We were trying to get to Meridian," Kai said, not entirely sure to whom they owed their lives. The impressive get-up certainly meant he was important, though. "It attacked us, and she fell . . . Do you think she'll be all right?"

The man shrugged. "I don't know, son. I'm not a doctor. If you're going to Meridian, you'd be better off going via the Firdes. It's longer, but the Dracaens aren't around that side of the island."

"Thanks," Rafael said. "For taking care of that Dracaen."

The man smiled and pulled his helmet back on with a jaunty two-fingered salute. "That's what we're here for. Keep safe till you get to Meridian, okay? There're some doctors there; they'll help your friend."

Kai suddenly understood; the man must've been one of the emergency response team members who'd been dispatched to help fight off the Dracaens on Tissarel.

With Rafael's help, he managed to get Becky safely onto the Talite in front of him, with Rafael trailing behind, coaxing Becky's Talite to follow them. They didn't talk much on the way to Meridian. The events of the night had carelessly, effortlessly undone any kind of satisfaction he'd managed to weave for himself. And one thought sailed loud and undisturbed above the indecipherable mass of all the others.

She did this. Your mother.

The atmosphere on Meridian was tense. Every so often, they'd pass stunned groups of injured, burnt, weeping people making for the evacuation point, or squads of well-protected emergency response teams, armed with a variety of weapons, which only served to remind them of what they'd left behind on Tissarel. They found the evacuation point already filling up with people. Tired-looking volunteers handed out flasks of warm drinks and sleeping bags, and a couple of medics went round giving treatment to the mildly injured. One looked the three of them over and, before attending to Becky, deftly cleaned and bandaged some of Kai's older wounds he'd sustained during the Dracaen attack a couple of days ago.

"Is she going to be all right?" Kai asked. He was worried about Becky, and he realised with a start that he had no idea what had happened to Felix and Sacha since he'd left them. He looked around; there were a couple of people from the school, but the majority seemed not to have arrived.

The medic smiled. "A few broken bones, but they ought to heal fine. Seeing as she's still unconscious, I'll have to take her to the emergency centre farther up, all right?"

Kai was too dejected to sleep. He joined Wave, Yoko, and Valcor on the far side of the room. Valcor was asleep, leaning against the wall, limp strands of hair falling into his face. Wave looked angry.

"Hey," Yoko said as the three of them sat down. For a while, nothing was said, all of them immersed in their own private thoughts.

Suddenly, Wave punched the wall irately, her eyes hard. "This *sucks*," she said fiercely, accurately summing up the situation.

Kai stared blankly at her. The feeling of apprehension pressed against him, his mind hot and heavy. He couldn't face anyone like this; he needed to be alone. Without a word, he got up and slumped in a corner elsewhere, burying his face in his arms and refusing to speak to anyone—until someone dropped down next to him and said his name gently.

Kai pretended not to hear. He didn't want to talk, and he did his best to ignore whoever it was.

"Kai?"

He recognized the voice; it was Felix.

"If you don't want to talk, that's okay. I can go if you want..."

Something in his voice made Kai look up. Felix looked almost as depressed as he felt, with a couple of scratches above his eye and a deep gash cutting across his palm, which had been hastily bandaged.

"You okay?"

The night was still thick and black and dark, filled with the haunting shrieks of Dracaens ravaging the area. The room was pressed for space now, and people were still arriving. Kai recognized people from the school now, clumped together in miserable groups.

"Been better," Kai replied desolately. "You?"

News was arriving thick and fast as the room filled with people, especially when the rest of the school finally arrived. The noise never rose much higher than a grim whisper, but he could hear fragments of conversation round the room. Everyone had a different tale to tell, and no two stories seemed to be the same. Some said the emergency forces were driving back the Dracaens; others insisted they'd been scattered. Some said the fires were still raging out of control; others claimed they'd been put out.

"We were kinda worried about you," Felix replied honestly. "I thought you'd . . . something had happened, or . . ." He looked away and quickly changed the subject. "How'd the journey go?"

Kai related the events of the past two weeks to him.

"You rode a Dracaen?" Felix asked in a low, awed tone. "*Wow*. That's crazy. It all sounds crazy. I'm sort of glad I didn't go." He paused for a second. "You say you deactivated the stones?"

"Yeah."

"So it . . . didn't work?"

"It worked," Kai said. "I mean, the stones are deactivated and everything. I think if the Dracaens lived on Mialyn, then they wouldn't know everything's back to normal . . ."

"Ah. If only there were a way for someone to tell them."

"Like a signal or something?"

"I don't know. As long as they know, they won't be attacking us, will they?"

Kai shrugged and looked away, and Felix didn't say anything else.

The night progressed. People were still arriving sporadically, their injuries worsening as the night drew on. It seemed to last forever. Kai's efforts to sleep were clouded with half-formed nightmares, and as he struggled awake from his latest attempt, he could see the first rays of dawn framing the sky.

The world was light, calm, and quiet in the soft morning glow. Most people had managed to get to sleep. The few who were awake looked grim and depressed, reflecting Kai's mood perfectly.

The sound of people talking loudly in the street outside bristled through the silence of the room. Kai couldn't hear what they were saying, so he navigated his way gingerly across slumped heaps of sound asleep people. A few other people who were awake also had similar ideas, and they slipped outside in a ragged, curious group.

The emergency squad who had been fighting off the Dracaens had returned in somewhat lesser, more worn-out, and tattered numbers. But their faces were flushed with the pride of a successful night, and they'd clearly lived to tell the tale, which could only mean good news.

Most had quickly gone back to their stations on Meridian, but their presence had drawn a small crowd of curious individuals, and the ones who'd been lagging behind paused to answer the questions fired at them.

"What happened? Did you take them down?"

One of the guys, his uniform tattered and his vaguely ginger hair matted and singed from a night's hard work, nodded proudly. The badge on his lapel said MERIDIAN SQUAD C-6, and underneath was a small brooch in the shape of a pair of wings. "I doubt you'll see many Dracaens on Tissarel after tonight. Or anywhere else, I hope."

The crowd let out a jubilant, ragged cheer that lasted for several minutes.

"Tell us what happened!" someone else shouted out, and he seemed happy to oblige, launching into an epic tale of last night's proceedings.

"The Dracaens were everywhere. It was an absolute nightmare from start to finish. Personally, I wasn't sure we'd be able to do it. They could take down five of us in one go if we weren't careful. Every time we killed one, it was as if three more appeared in their place. I thought we were done for when they managed to destroy the cannons early this morning; they were our best defence against the blights."

"But you showed them what's what, didn't you?" a person in the crowd crowed. "Showed 'em who's boss!"

The guy looked slightly sheepish. "Well . . . not exactly. It was the darndest thing. A battle like that could've gone on for days, really. But they all just upped and flew away early this mornin' in a big crowd."

One of the women who'd just joined the crowd gave an elated sob and hugged her young child tightly, rapidly murmuring her thanks under her breath.

"They simply left?" someone in the crowd asked.

"But why would they do that? Dracaens wouldn't *all* flee together, not when they're that many of them."

The ERT member at the front of the crowd raised his hands. "I don't know either. All I know . . . I mean, it was just the strangest thing. The Dracaen at the head of the group seemed to be leadin' them on, I guess. And . . . and he had a little bandage wrapped around its shoulder, just like that." He gestured to his left shoulder, and the crowd noise dropped into awed whispers. "I can't imagine where the little blight got it from . . ."

TWENTY-TWO

Recovery work on Tissarel began and stretched on for a long time. The school had suffered a fair bit of damage. Most of the taller buildings had been knocked down, which meant that for a few months, the library was temporarily relocated to the gym, resulting in piles of books generally interfering with the Guild sessions, and Mr Shorren's office had moved to a storeroom in the apprentice block.

Once Kai had got used to the sounds of people working outside on restoring the tower all through the day and seeing charred holes in the ground where villages once stood, life started to take on its usual countenance. It would take a while to rebuild, to smooth over the incident and carry on as usual, but they could get by fine until it happened.

A couple of weeks later, once everything had dwindled down and Kai had done his best to forget about most of it, John caught him during one of his tech lessons. Kai was just finishing up his most recent project: a new staff to replace the old one he'd lost in the fight with the Dracaen, including a convenient slot for the Xucite stone that he could open and close with a quick twist of the staff, in case he needed to shut out the dizzying glare of the stone. John was occupied with fixing the clock that had dropped rather unexpectedly off the wall in the middle of their last lesson, so Kai hadn't really been expecting him to say anything, but he looked up and smiled briefly. "It looks a lot like the old one," he said.

"Well, it's a replacement," Kai said ruefully. "I guess I didn't want to lose her. It probably sounds strange... but I feel closer to my mum when I'm using it."

"No, not at all," John assured him. "That's perfectly understandable."

There was a short pause.

"I don't suppose on your travels you ever found out what she saw?" he said finally, sounding slightly tentative about approaching the question. "To make her leave?"

"I... I think so."

There was an expectant pause. Kai realised John was waiting for him to continue, so he dropped into the chair in front of the desk and plunged on.

"When she got to the island, the Dracaens were all inside the nest on the island, but they couldn't leave because of the fields surrounding them. When she deactivated them, they probably would've flown out because they were tired of being stuck there all along. The big Dracaen would've taken its time getting out. It's too big to move very fast, but once it got out of the nest, it probably would've attacked her, as it did to us. There was no way she'd have fought it at those kinds of odds... The only logical reaction would be to light the stones again. It would have scared the Dracaen away from her, but it would mean the others couldn't return. Once she realised what she'd done, especially after that Dracaen attack shortly after she returned, she must've felt guilty and then... run off to Earth. So she didn't have to face the consequences. Like what happened last month."

John looked at him then, gripping a piece of tape between his teeth. "Hmmm. That makes sense." He quickly wrapped it around two pieces of the second hand, joining them together. Then, casting a concerned look at Kai, he asked, "Are you okay?"

Kai shrugged. "Fine."

John smiled. "You said that to me at your mother's funeral as well. I don't see how *anyone* could possibly feel 'fine' after either event."

"It's just . . . all this time, everyone's been saying, 'Oh, your mother was amazing at this' and 'She was a really great person' and all that stuff, and then you find out . . . she's caused the deaths of all these people, made them lose their homes and stuff . . . I feel kinda betrayed, really."

"That's understandable," John said. "But a small unfortunate accident like that doesn't make her any worse a person, and if she was anything like you are now, I'd still be proud of her. I only wish she were still here so I could tell her that too. And life works in strange ways, Kai. If it weren't for that, you wouldn't be here, and you've done a lot since you arrived. If you'd been here longer, we'd probably have no choice but to promote you to elite."

Kai felt a rush of pride at the praise and mumbled, "Thank you."

"There!" John said brightly, holding up the fixed clock. "We'll probably need a new clock, but this should hold up until we get a replacement. Goodness, is that the time . . . ?"

After his morning lessons, Kai took a quick detour on the way to his bedroom, emerging cautiously into red carpet opulence, framed with gold and the luminescence of the chandelier hanging from the ceiling. The row of portraits at the back of the room seemed to warmly beckon him and fiercely challenge him at the same time. He took a deep breath, shut out all his other thoughts, and once again came face-to-face with the picture of his mother, her radiant smile shielded behind thin glass.

It still haunted him, still stalked him. Maybe she hadn't meant to do it, but she'd lit the stones, hadn't she? Did that make her responsible for the Dracaen attack—injuring and killing so many people, robbing them of their homes?

She was still young when it had happened, barely an adult. It was an accident, unfortunate. Anyone else would have done the same in her place. There was no way he could attribute the entire thing purely on that one action, which even *she* hadn't seen the consequences of . . .

He shook his head. Even her picture looked slightly different now. He tried to think back to the mother he'd known for his first fifteen years of life.

He didn't think he knew her at all now.

Kai, I'm sorry . . .

He looked up sharply at his mother's face, straight into her eyes.

Oh, Kai, look at you. You've come so far, done so much. Why won't you be happy?

I . . . I don't know.

There was a pause.

It took me a while to get over it too . . . once I realised what I'd done. But you have to let the past go sometimes. If only I'd known that before. Let it go and start again.

Start again?

Start afresh. Don't dwell on what's been. Focus on what will be, what you can be. Although you've done quite enough already, I should think. It'll be you they'll be calling the greatest rider who ever lived. I'd better get used to that before they forget about me.

They can't forget about you. You're in the hall of fame. You're a legend.

Perhaps, yes.

She paused again, and the air filled with a hesitant expectation.

Do you still think so? she asked.

This time, Kai answered with perfect conviction. *Of course.*

And you will be too, in time. I know it. It's in your blood. Now, how about a smile? And some ice cream too, perhaps. Can't be unhappy when there's ice cream.

Kai didn't know about the ice cream, but the smile came easily enough.

There you go. That's better. We should do this more often. And who's this . . . ?

Kai looked round and was more than a little surprised to find Becky standing behind him. She'd recovered quickly after her injuries, but there was a subtle but definite limp as she walked.

"Becky?"

"Hey. Uh, are you okay? You've been looking at that photo for five minutes now."

"I'm fine," Kai said. "Were you following me?"

Becky looked embarrassed. "I . . . no," she said, flustered. "I just . . . wanted to make sure you were okay. You've been kinda down since the Dracaens attacked. Are you thinking about . . . ?"

"Yeah," Kai said. "But I think I've got it sorted out now. Put it all behind me."

Becky nodded. "About time too. You seem a lot happier."

"I am," he replied confidently.

"Come on, then. There are much better things to do outside than in here."

She turned to leave. Kai cast a final glance back at his mother's picture and then followed Becky out of the room, into the soft, bright light of the afternoon, for the first time since he'd got here, feeling truly at peace.

It felt good.